UNLIKELY TO TELL

A PARKER LAKE NOVEL
BOOK FOUR

OLIVIA SHERWOOD

LIMITLESS PUBLISHING LLC

Unlikely to Tell

DEDICATION

To Bucky and AsJa: I never knew what being loved and accepted for who you truly are meant until you two became my best friends. Here's to watching reality trash tv and drinking cinnamon whisky until we're old and gray.

CHAPTER 1

$\mathcal{B}$rody Cooper let out a sigh and stared at the house in front of him. Rickety carport that looked like a small Oklahoma gust would send it crashing to the ground. Crooked white shutters in need of a cleaning. Old work boots on the front porch.

About the only thing that had changed in his childhood home was the navy blue porch swing. Instead of hanging from the rafters as it was when Brody was a kid, the old swing was now sitting on the concrete of the porch. His only guess was the chain holding it had finally given up the fight.

When Brody Cooper walked across the graduation stage at Parker High School almost seventeen years ago, he expected to never return to his small hometown unless it was to visit his dad and sister on holidays and special occasions. But here he was. If only his coworkers in New York City could see him now. They'd definitely be having some laughs at his expense. He wanted to bash his head against the steering wheel of his rented Ford Focus at the turn his life had taken. Pun intended.

Brody finally got out of the car, shivering in the frigid

1

Oklahoma wind, and grabbed his bags out of the trunk. Hearing the door of the car slam, his dad walked out onto the porch and squinted his eyes against the setting sun behind Brody's back. Shielding his face with his hands, his dad called out, "Can I help you?"

Brody took a deep breath before letting it out and squaring his shoulders. "Hey, Dad. It's me."

His dad's face broke into a grin, crinkling his eyes in the corners. For the first time ever, his dad's weathered skin from spending years in the sun was starting to hint at his age. "Well, well, well. Of all the people I expected to be in my driveway, it wasn't you, kid. You told me you weren't making it home for Thanksgiving. To what do I owe the pleasure?"

"Change of plans. Haven't been home in a while and I figured it was time to meet my niece," Brody said. There was no way he was going to tell his dad the real reason he was home. He knew his dad would figure it out eventually. He just wanted some peace before the inquisition began.

"Breck's been sending me pictures of little Miss Emma. She's too cute to pass up. I had some time off from work. Thought I might stay home for a little bit. Catch up with everyone and make sure my niece knows who I am."

"It's about time you made it down to see her. I told Breckin I thought for sure you'd be here for the birth of her first baby."

And there it was. The guilt trip Brody knew was going to come. At least his dad got it off his chest now instead of waiting until he had an audience to do so.

"I've been really busy," he said. "With work and everything."

Or lack thereof.

Brody followed his dad up the steps of the porch of the house he had grown up in and walked inside. It hadn't changed one bit. Same bachelor pad with sports memorabilia on every available surface, worn furniture all facing the gigantic flat screen television. The only thing different was all the baby gear in the middle of the shag carpeting. His niece was laying in some sort of fancy baby rocker in the middle of it all sucking on a big, green pacifier, her doe eyes peering up at him.

"Well, aren't you a cutie?" he said softly, rubbing her silken black hair. "Can you talk yet?"

His dad laughed. "Talk? She can barely hold her head up, you knucklehead. Kids don't start talking until they're a year old, and even then they only say one or two words you can understand."

Brant shrugged his shoulders. "How am I supposed to know that? It's not like I've been around babies a whole lot."

"You were around your sister when she was a baby."

"I was also six."

His dad chuckled. "You always had a good memory. Figured you might have remembered something."

"Where did my sister and her husband or whatever he is run off to? I figured they wouldn't let their little girl out of their sight."

"He's not her husband yet," his dad said with a frown. "Said they didn't need a wedding ring to know they love each other. It ain't right, but what am I gonna do about it?"

Since Brody thought it was none of his dad's business *what* Breckin and Griff did or did not do about the whole marriage thing, he didn't reply. His dad was a good guy…he was just old school through and through.

"Griff had to cover at the bar and Breckin had to run up to the school to do something. It's about time the two of them got out. They've been cooped up in their house, only letting people see this little doll if they visited at their house. Said they didn't want their daughter exposed to *germs*. I'm surprised they brought her over here to let me watch her."

"I'm surprised you were their first choice."

"Oh, I wasn't. Annie and Wyatt are having some sort of Christmas thing out at Sophie's Haven, and CC and Brant are in Oklahoma City with his mom."

"Brant?" Brody asked.

"If you came home more often you'd be more familiar with all the new folks in town," his dad muttered.

"Funny. I didn't know Parker, Oklahoma ever got any new people in town."

His dad frowned at him. "Brant's the nurse practitioner who took over running the clinic when Henry Harvey retired. He left for a spell but came back when no one else could put up with the old crazies in this town."

"Why'd CC go with him? Are they an item or something?"

"Oh! Yeah. They got together when he helped her work on her gym."

"What gym?"

His dad scratched his head. "Just how long have you been gone *this* time, son?"

Brant tried not to roll his eyes. "I don't know. I think I was here when Sophie died."

"My god! No wonder you don't know anything! That was three years ago."

"So I haven't been home in a while."

"I'd say three years is more than a while. A lot has happened. Parker is small and all, but time don't stand still."

"I know, Dad. I've just been—"

"Busy," his dad finished for him. "Trust me, I know how busy you are. I just don't really know what exactly *makes* you so busy."

Brant shrugged his shoulders. He wasn't about to tell his dad how *un*-busy his job was currently making him. "So, tell me about everything that's been happening since I've been gone."

"CC opened the gym I was telling you about just down from her beauty shop. The town held an auction for eligible bachelors to raise the money for her to get it up and running. It is really top of the line. I bet it's as fancy as the one you use in New York City."

"How do you know I go to the gym?"

"Those biceps don't make themselves that big," his dad said. "Besides, what else would you do without knowing anyone up there?"

And that was why he avoided talking about his life with his dad. His dad couldn't picture Brody as anything but the nerdy kid with glasses who preferred being on the academic team to playing any sport. The loner who kept to himself, waiting for the day he could leave his hometown. Never mind Brody turned himself into a wealthy, successful businessman living in the big city. A man who frequented parties, had dozens of friends, slept with as many women as he wanted. At least he used to. Funny how things changed when he found himself hitting rock bottom.

"I have a lot of friends in New York, Dad," he said, refraining from rubbing his temples. *Had,* the obnoxious voice in his head said. You *had* a lot of friends. "But yes, I did go to the gym."

"Well, if you want to keep in shape, check out CC's gym. Like I said, it's top of the line. Since you said you might be staying for a while and all. How long exactly *is* a while?"

"I'm not sure yet. Just tell me about the rest of the changes in town, why don't you?" Brant wasn't about to go into detail. Not just yet.

"Well, Annie and Wyatt got hitched."

"I know. I saw the pictures they posted on social media."

"Did you know they turned that farm of hers into a little zoo and sanctuary for abandoned animals?"

"That I *didn't* know."

"Yep. People come from all around to see them. She's got all sorts. Tigers, llamas, emus, kangaroos. Even has a petting zoo with all those Disney animals of hers and a gift shop. It's a big deal. Brings lots of people to town."

"Sounds like it."

"Let's see. I know there's more. Oh! Burt and Kelda are together. So are Marty and Madge. And I—"

His dad's front door opened. "Where's my Little Miss Sunsh—"

The woman standing in the doorway stopped when she saw Brody sitting on the couch. "Hello," she said hesitantly. "How are you, Brody?"

Brody knew it was rude to stare but he couldn't help it. She looked familiar but he couldn't place where he knew her.

"I'm Griff's mom," she said. Brody then recognized her. She was the woman who was in the stands for every one of her son's ballgames. The woman who raised her son as a single mom when she kicked her drunk of a husband out the door. She was also the daughter of crazy Kelda Vanderburgh and Breckin's baby's paternal grandma.

"Of course. Nice to see you again, Ms. Stephens."

Griff's mom waved his way. "Oh, please. Call me Susan."

"Are you the reason Griff and my sister let my dad watch their baby?"

Susan smiled. "It *might* have been one of the reasons. People tend to trust grandmas more than grandpas for whatever reason."

"Don't really understand it myself since I raised two kids on my own," his dad complained.

To Brody's shock, Susan walked over to his dad, leaned up on her tiptoes and placed a kiss on his lips. "Hey, Honey."

Honey? What. The. Hell? Griff's mom and his and Breckin's dad? Wow.

"Don't get that look on your face," his dad said, pointing a finger Brody's way as he wrapped his arm around Susan's waist.

"What look?" Brody asked, trying to act nonchalant. "I don't have a look."

"You have a look that says you can't believe I'm with Griff's mom when Griff and my daughter are an item. It's not like me and Susan are gonna have any babies to confuse Griff and Breckin's babies. So don't say anything."

"Didn't plan on saying a word," Brant replied. He never knew what was going to happen in his small town. *Welcome home, Brody,* he thought. *Welcome home.*

KAREN POSEY ARCHED her back and groaned. She had been sitting at her desk in her classroom for what felt like forever. When she looked at the clock, however, she realized it had only been forty-five minutes since the last bell had rung. Thanksgiving break had officially begun. For most teachers, having the entire week off and then going just three more weeks before having two weeks off for Christmas was one of the perks of being a teacher. For Karen, it just meant time alone in her quiet house, counting the hours until she could go back to work and be around people again.

Karen heard a knock on her door. Breckin, one of her good friends, one of her *only* friends if Karen was being honest, peeked her head around the corner. "What are you doing here so late? Don't you know teachers leave as soon as the bell rings for Thanksgiving break? I don't know why they just don't let us have the entire rest of November and all of December off. December is a total waste for learning anything."

"I just needed to finish up some things," Karen replied. "I'm getting ready to leave right now. The more important question is what are *you* doing here? I thought you were supposed to take off for the year."

Breckin shrugged her shoulders. "I just had to get some things together for next semester."

"What?"

"I told Griff I couldn't take off again. I love my baby more than anything in the world, I do. But I'm just not a stay-at-home mom. I'll go crazy. I'm having a hard enough time staying out until after Christmas but Griff insisted. I need interaction with people who don't puke on my shoulder when I burp them or cry for hours at a time in the middle of the night."

"I'm not going to say I'm not that unhappy about your decision. I've really missed having a buddy to eat lunch with," Karen replied. "I got lonely eating by myself this semester."

"I told you, you need to branch out and talk to more people. I don't know why you're so closed off. If everyone got to know you like *I* do, they'd love you. Promise."

Karen shook her head. She remembered a time when she had many friends. Hosting parties. Girls' nights. Shopping trips. But those days were long gone. It saddened her to think about it so she tried her best not to. Much like she tried not to get close to anyone in her new life. Too bad Breckin had wormed her way into Karen's life with the determination of a bulldog. Still, there were some secrets Karen could never share, no matter how close she became to anyone.

"You know how shy I am," she replied instead. "I would just rather keep to myself."

It was Breckin's turn to shake her head. "Suit yourself. First lunch is on me when we come back, though."

Karen grinned. "I'm holding you to it."

Breckin tapped the doorframe. "Don't stay too late."

"I won't. I'm heading out right after you. Promise."

True to her word, a few minutes after her friend left, Karen donned her coat and headed to her car in the parking lot. Yesterday, it had been seventy degrees and sunny. A cold front had blown in overnight, dropping the temperature to thirty-two with a wind chill of seventeen. No matter how long she lived in the state, Karen didn't think she'd ever get used to Oklahoma's crazy weather that changed as much as its wind blew.

Pushing the door to the school open, Karen bowed her head to the bracing wind and pulled her coat tighter around her. She was really glad she parked right in front of the school this morning.

It only took her a few minutes to get home. One perk of living in a small town was everything in such close proximity. Quickly heading into the small bungalow she rented from Mason, the man who owned the marina at the lake, Karen took a deep breath and shut the door.

Taking her coat off and placing it on the coat rack by the front door, she headed into the kitchen to make herself some peppermint tea. As soon as her Keurig spit out the last drop, Karen headed into the small living room and plopped down on her sofa. Taking a drink, she looked around the space. Same worn, brown sofa and couch that were in the house when she moved in, chipped wooden tables next to them. Not one picture hung on the wall. No trinkets adorned the mantle or end tables. A person walking into her house would never guess she had lived in Parker, Oklahoma, for almost seven years. It was the way Karen wanted it. No past to haunt her. No future to look forward to. Just taking things day by day. It was the way she'd been living for so long she'd forgotten what it meant to look forward to things, to what might become.

Mindlessly, she turned on her television and opened one of the many recordings she had of *House Hunters* on HGTV.

"You're making a mistake if you choose that one, Donald," she said. "The closets are too small."

Apparently, Donald didn't agree. He chose the tan Craftsman against Karen's advice, the ending of the show featuring Donald and all his friends gathered around his granite-topped island in the open living-kitchen area, eating fruit and drinking wine.

"It'll be nice now, Donald. Just waiting until boyfriend Kyle moves in and wants to share that tiny closet."

Draining her teacup's contents, Karen stood up and walked toward the miniature Christmas tree she had centered on the sofa table in front of her picture window two days ago out of sheer boredom. She never put the Christmas tree up until after Thanksgiving before. Before being the operative word. Her life was a far cry from where it used to be and would never be that way again. So it didn't really matter when she decided to take out the Christmas tree.

Taking a red bulb out of the box sitting on the table, she placed one and then another on the tree, finishing quickly. Looking at it, she smiled a sad smile. It wasn't the massive tree from her past, but it still had red bulbs. At least some things of her old life could remain the same. What few were left, anyway.

BRODY HAD BEEN HANGING out at his dad's house for the last couple of hours. Most of his time had been spent holding his niece. No one ever told him babies smelled so good. And did so little. He thought little Emma Kate would do…something. But other than a few grins and some squirming, she wasn't that entertaining. Cute, but not entertaining at all.

Griff's mom told him the fun stage would really begin

when Emma started walking. Brody had smiled politely and shrugged his shoulders when she asked how long he planned to be in town. She might have been trying to find out for his father how long he planned to stay. Since he didn't know himself, her attempts were in vain. When he wasn't holding his niece, the remaining part of Brody's time had been spent studiously avoiding his dad and Susan's blatant PDA. Talk about awkward.

After yet *another* kiss that had Brody's face turning red, he stood to go...well, he didn't really know where he planned to go since he had nowhere to live. But he couldn't take it anymore. Maybe he'd go to his old room and hole up on the top bunk of his bunk bed until Susan left. If she spent the night...lord help him.

"Dad, why is there a Ford Focus sitting in your drive—" Brody's sister, Breckin, walked through the front door of his dad's house as soon as Brody turned to walk down the hall. At the sight of him, she dropped her purse to the ground, ran over to him, and threw her arms around his neck.

"Brody!" she squealed. "What are you *doing* here? I thought you weren't making it for Thanksgiving!"

"Hey, Punky Breckster," he said, smiling into her hair. His sister was one of his favorite people in the whole world. "I had to come meet your kid before she turned one. What kind of uncle would that make me if I didn't?"

"A stupid, crappy one. And really? Punky Breckster? You haven't called me that since we were kids and watched the *real* Punky on TV," she said, poking him in the side. "Now, let me go. I need to make sure Daddy hasn't broken my kid."

"Hey, now!" their dad called from his recliner, where Emma was propped in his lap. "I was just educating my granddaughter on the rules of college football."

"Is there even a game on?" Breckin asked.

"I can always find a game," their dad replied. Brody

shook his head. He knew from growing up in this very house his dad's statement was true. He could *always* find some game or another, no matter what the sport. His dad would sometimes even find a bowling match on ESPN and make fun of the participants, saying how *unsporting* bowling really was.

"Seriously, though, Brode," Breckin said, taking her baby out of her grandfather's lap and planting kisses all over her chubby cheeks, "I thought you had to work over the holiday."

"Well, something came up and they decided to let us have some well-earned time off," he said evasively. No need for them to know it was, for him, probably permanent time off. "Figured I'd use the time to catch up with my family."

"I would write your bosses a thank you letter or email, but since I don't even know one little thing about what you do or who I would send it to, I guess you'll have to relay the message for me," she said with a grin.

"I'll pass along the message."

"Are you going back or staying until after Christmas? You haven't been here in ages. Surely you have some time you can take. You can't be *that* important."

Brody tried to answer but his sister continued speaking.

"So, what do you think of my baby?"

Brody grinned. "She's a really cute baby."

"I sense a *but* following that."

"But she doesn't do much of anything."

"She's only three months old!"

"That's what I told him, Breckin," Susan called from her perch on the arm of his dad's recliner. He'd been looking at her in that exact same spot all night. It would never stop being weird. "I don't think he believed me."

"I know. Weird, isn't it?" Breckin whispered. Brody knew exactly what she was talking about.

"How? When? *How?*" he whispered back.

"A few months ago during the bachelor auction. She bid on him and won. They've been together since."

"Won't this be confusing to Miss Emma when she gets older, having only one set of grandparents?"

Breckin shrugged her shoulders. "After I got over the initial shock, I just figured it would make things easier."

"How do you figure?"

"No rotation of holidays. No Thanksgiving with his family one year, my family the next. We'll just be one big, happy family every year!"

Brody shook his head. "Always the eternal optimist, my kid sister."

"Better than being the brooding bookworm," she responded with a grin.

"Ouch. That hurts."

Breckin rolled her eyes. "No, it doesn't."

"You're right. It doesn't." Brody looked at his sister. "You look really good, sis. Happy."

"I am. So very happy," she said softly. "Happier than I ever thought I'd be."

He kissed her on her forehead. "You deserve it."

"Babe! Is everything okay? I thought you were just going to run in and get—" Griffin Stephens stood in the doorway, looking even larger and formidable than Brody remembered him.

Even though he was a few years older than Griff in school, Brody remembered him towering over everyone when he walked the halls as a freshman. It appeared time had only made Griff more…hairy, muscly, and tattooed. If Brody didn't know from his sister how kind-hearted Griff could be, Brody would probably be scared for her to have a baby with the hulk of a man. But since Griff had put up with his Grandma Kelda's antics his entire life and Breckin told Brody how many times Griff baby-talked and sang to her

13

belly while she was pregnant with Emma, he knew his sister was in safe hands.

"Well, hey, man," Griff said, removing his gloves and holding out his hand for Brody to shake. "Brody, right?"

"Right," Brody responded, taking Griff's hand in his and shaking. Damn. The dude could *shake*. Brody tried not to grimace. "I don't think we've ever officially met. Well, as adults."

"Not since high school, no," Griff said. "It's nice to finally talk to you in person."

"Likewise. Well, I guess I better be…going," Brody said, quickly realizing he had nowhere to go.

"Go where?" Breckin said. "You're not leaving, are you?"

"No, I'm not leaving…um…Parker. I'm just…I don't know…I—"

"Why don't you stay here, son?" his dad said. "I moved your bed out to make room for my inversion table for my back but you can have the couch."

Susan leaned over and whispered in his ear. To Brody's surprise, his dad's ears *and* face turned bright red. "Now isn't the time," he whispered back.

"Now's not the time for what, Dad?" Breckin asked. "Is something going on we should know about?"

"Well, your father and I have been *talking*—" Susan started.

"Now, before you all get too judgy," their dad said, "I want you to hear us out."

"Dad, that's not even a word."

"Still, just listen."

Susan's smile lit up her face. "Well, we sorta did a thing the other day."

Breckin and Griff frowned. "What kind of *thing*, exactly, did you do?" Breckin asked.

"Well…we…um…you see—"

"Just spit it out, Dad!" Breckin yelled. "What. Did. You. Do?"

"We got married!" Susan said, holding up her hand and showcasing a simple gold band. "We went to the courthouse in Lakeview last week and did it."

Brody, Griffin, and Breckin didn't say a word, all their eyes focused on the ring encircling Griffin's mom's left ring finger.

"You got married," Breckin said softly. "Before me."

"Now, Breckin! You can't get mad at me gettin' hitched when you said you didn't want a label on *your* relationship," their dad said. "Me and Susan *do* want a label. We don't wanna live in si—"

Their dad stopped his preaching at Susan's stern look. "We just felt it was the right thing to do," he said. "So we did. And we're happy. So you should be happy for us."

"Of course we are, Daddy," Breckin said. "It's just a surprise, is all. Have you told Kelda?"

Susan let out a breath. "No. I've been avoiding it as much as possible. She'll flip her lid when she realizes I got married before her."

"Isn't Kelda like a hundred?" Brody asked Breckin quietly.

"Ninety-two, but a hundred is close enough," she replied. "But she expected to walk down the aisle before *everyone*, including me and Griff. Once she finds out Susan beat us all, she'll shit a brick."

Brody shook his head. He remembered why he left. The elderly residents of Parker, Oklahoma, were crazy.

"So since we're now legal and all, I'm gonna be moving in with Susan. We were gonna do it after the New Year, but since you're home, I'll just do it now and let you have the house."

"Dad, no—I don't want to kick you out of your own house."

"You're not kicking me out. Susan said under no circumstances was she living in a sports-worshipping bachelor pad. It was just going to be vacant before you came. You might as well live here so it doesn't get all musty. At least until you go back to New York, anyway."

"Well, thanks, Dad. That really means a lot."

"You're welcome, son. It's yours for as long as you need it. We're just happy to have you home."

CHAPTER 2

*K*aren found herself walking the aisles of Swanson's Grocery Store aimlessly. It was the second day of vacation and she was going stir-crazy sitting alone in her house. She hadn't seen Breckin since the day she stopped in Karen's classroom. Since Karen didn't have any other friends, it was just her. Alone with a television folder full of *House Hunters*.

She finally couldn't take it anymore. There was no food in her house except a package of microwavable macaroni and cheese, she ran out of toilet paper that morning, and the lightbulb above her kitchen sink had finally given up the fight. Karen had decided to venture out in public to buy some much needed supplies. As it currently stood, if the zombie apocalypse occurred tomorrow, she'd be the first one eaten.

When she walked through the doors of the grocery store, Karen had gotten the bright idea to fix herself the Thanksgiving meal she had always made back when she had a life and friends and family to share it with. As she filled her basket with more and more items, Karen realized she was making a meal for about thirty people, not a single, lonely lady stuck in a small Oklahoma town. Shaking her head at her stupidity, she started walking back down the aisles, returning the items one by one.

"What are you thinking, Karen?" she said to herself as she placed a box of Jiffy cornbread she used to make homemade stuffing back on the shelf. "What a stupid idea. Like you need a reason to be more depressed."

"Now why would a pretty girl like you have any reason to be depressed?"

Karen turned at the sound of the voice. An extremely handsome man was standing in front of her basket, his arms crossed over his chest and an impish smile on his face. The picture of nonchalance. This was a man who was used to getting what he wanted from the opposite sex. He probably expected Karen to drop her pants right where she stood and hand him her panties. Too bad for him that wasn't going to happen. One, because she hadn't done laundry in about a week and she was currently sporting her most comfortable pair of granny panties. Two, she wasn't that kind of girl... even if he was the definition of the type of man often part of Karen's sex-starved dreams.

Disheveled, dirty blond hair. Amber colored eyes. A body that would turn any woman's head. Something told her he would look delicious in an Armani suit. Even so, the low-riding sweatpants and NYU hoodie were doing uncomfortable things to her libido she thought long-dead. She hadn't ever seen him around town. In a town as small as Parker, she knew everyone. Probably visiting family for the holidays. Not that she cared.

Oh, you care, a voice inside her head whispered. She shushed it with a frown.

"I don't really think that's any of your business," she said tartly. That usually discouraged men from asking any more questions, no matter how attracted to her they were.

"Hmmmm, beauty with a bark," he said, not deterred in the least. "I sense a story."

"Not likely," she said with a roll of her eyes. "Just a girl out shopping for groceries. Too bad I got stopped by an ass with nothing better to do than harass a girl in a grocery store."

He laughed. "I don't think I've ever been called an ass before. Charming, handsome, sexy. Yes. Ass, not that I can recall. Oh, wait...there was that *one* time..."

Handsome Ass smiled.

"Nope. My mistake. I was told I *have* a nice ass," he said with a wink.

"Guess there's a first time for everything," she said with another eye roll. This guy was too much.

Again, he ignored her obvious insult. "Funny, I don't remember you at all. Since you're such a beauty, I *know* I would remember your face. You must be new in town. Since I was born and raised here, I know everyone. Even if I've been gone a while, one thing I know is Parker doesn't get new people."

"That's where you're wrong," she said. Karen didn't even know why she was responding to the ass. She should've just walked away. But the fact he thought one smile would have her begging him for his time rubbed her the wrong way. She wasn't some weak, mindless female. Years of loneliness, heartache, and regret had ripped that away from her. "I am new. And I'm tired of talking to you. So bye-bye now."

He *still* didn't move. Karen had the ridiculous notion to stomp as hard as she could on his foot. Finally, after what felt like an eternity, he moved out of the way and held out his arm as if he was giving her permission to pass.

"Until we meet again, Raven."

"Raven?"

The guy had the audacity to take a strand of Karen's hair and twirl it around his finger. "The only black I've seen this dark is on the wings of a raven," he said with an evil grin. "So, even though you called me a not so nice name while I gave you a very thoughtful and sweet nickname, it was a pleasure talking to you."

Karen snorted. Of all the nerve. "I bet. If I'm lucky, that won't happen."

"That's one good thing about a town like Parker. It's so small running into you again is inevitable."

Karen pushed her cart past the obnoxious jerk and turned the corner as quickly as she could. What he said about running into her was true. And that was exactly what she was afraid of.

"So I met this girl." Brody and Breckin were facing each other in a booth at Sadie's Café. He hadn't seen Raven since running into her in Swanson's two days ago despite his best efforts to do so. He had perused all the small shops downtown—Pick Everything but Your Nose Flower Shop, Cure All Pharmacy, Nailed It Hardware, and more. No woman. He'd even taken a deep breath and gone in Wyatt's sister's new boutique clothing store, Hattie's Haute Couture, to see if she was an employee there. Raven looked like she would work in a fancy clothing store. Still nothing.

He finally decided to enlist his sister's help. He didn't want Raven to know he had been scouring the town for her. Desperation was not a look he wanted to portray. He was hoping his sister would know who the mystery woman was before he had to start hanging wanted posters on all the tele-phone poles in town. "A girl, huh? In the small town of

Parker? How on earth could she compete with all the women you canoodled in the big city?"

"Hey! I didn't *canoodle!*"

Breckin looked at him skeptically. "Come on, Brode. I saw the pictures you posted on social media. Living the highlife. A different woman on your arm every night. Don't lie to your sister."

Brody rolled his eyes. "Fine. I *might* have dated a few women."

She stared at him, saying nothing.

"*Okay!* Sheesh! I dated a lot of women. But I was always a gentleman."

"I bet you were," she scoffed.

"So anyway," he continued, avoiding her skepticism, "are you gonna help me figure out who she is or not?"

"Why not? It's not like I have anything better to do," she replied, taking another bite of her grilled onion burger. To be so little, his sister could always put away the food.

"Well for one, she's gorgeous."

"Gee, that really narrows things down."

"She's got jet black hair, green eyes, legs that go on for miles. And snarky as the day is long."

Breckin's eyes went wide and she snorted. "You've got to be shitting me."

"What? Why are you laughing?"

"Because there's no other woman in town who looks like that other than my friend, Karen. She's a teacher at the high school."

Why didn't they make teachers like that when *he* was in school? He had to look at ancient Mrs. Cochran with the bifocals and chin hair every day.

"That's great! You can get me the hookup then."

His sister rolled her eyes. "Hardly."

"Why exactly is that?"

"Because she's completely unapproachable, especially when it comes to men. It took me almost two years to befriend her and even now, she's really closed off. I'm basically her only friend. So you, Playboy, are definitely not someone she would give the time of day."

"What's that supposed to mean?"

"It means you're the definition of a person Karen avoids."

"What kind of person am I?"

"Loud, flirtatious, vivacious. You practically take up an entire room with your personality. At least now you do. Face it, Brother. You're a far cry from the nerdy bookworm you were in high school. New York changed you. I'm still trying to find out if that change is a good thing."

"Well, nice to know you still think highly of me."

"You're my brother. I'll always love you. And I'm happy you're home. But you can't say you're the same guy you were when you left town seventeen years ago."

Brody sighed. He really wasn't. "You're right. I'm not. I just didn't realize that wasn't a good thing."

"Maybe some time in Parker will bring back that somewhat humble guy I know and love so dearly," she said with an ornery grin.

"If by humble you mean completely awkward and a total dork, then I'm not so sure I *want* to return to that guy."

"Maybe you were a little nerdy. But you always made time for your family. Especially your kid sister. I feel like I don't even know you anymore."

"Ouch."

"You know I've always been truthful." Breckin swirled her last fry in ketchup and stuffed it in her mouth. "Now, I gotta go. Griff has Emma at the bar with him. There's no telling what she's heard by now."

"Griff doesn't strike me as a guy with a potty mouth."

Breckin rolled her eyes. "It's not him I'm worried about.

It's his crazy grandma and her horny boyfriend who are the problem. They have mouths worse than sailors and talk about sex in ways that would make porn stars blush."

"You think she can understand it?"

"I'm not sure. But I don't want Kelda's and Burt's colorful descriptors to be the first things my little girl understands."

Brody chuckled. "I don't blame you. I haven't seen them together in action, but I know on their own they're something else. I'm almost afraid of how they are as a duo."

"You have no idea."

Brody saluted his sister and watched her walk out the door. Breckin had been through hell and back with her last man. He was glad she finally found her happy ever after.

Brody took the last bite of his burger. He had forgotten how good Sadie's food was. Even though she wasn't professionally trained, her down-home cooking could rival any New York chef's. Her special of the day, a grilled onion burger and homemade fries, was really hitting the spot.

"How's the burger treating you?" Sadie walked up to his booth and sat down on the other side. Sadie had been serving customers in her café as long as Brody could remember. His very first meal in Parker was at Sadie's. Even so, she still looked the exact same as he remembered. Same white apron, same white shoes, same hair teased and sprayed within an inch of its life. The only thing that tended to change was the brightly colored glasses Sadie liked to sport. Currently, she was wearing a pair of lime green cat eye frames.

"Delicious as always, Sade," he said, pushing his empty plate back. "As you can see, I didn't have a problem finishing it."

Sadie shook her head and chuckled. "You and your sister sure can put the food away. I remember you two coming in here, tiny little things, and ordering from the adult menu.

Always cleaned your plates, too. I told my Clyde both of you must've had a hollow leg."

"I remember that," Brody said with a smile.

"But now here you are, all muscly and fine as a model on a New York runway. What exactly are they feeding you up there in the big city, Brody Cooper? And I just have to ask...*are* you a model? Because you sure look like you could be. And since no one in Parker, including your family, really even knows what you do for a living, I'm figuring model ain't outside the realm of possibility."

Brody snorted. "Why would you think I'm a model, Sade? That's ridiculous."

Sadie's eyebrow arched above the frame of her glasses. "Seriously, son? Have you *looked* at yourself in the mirror lately? If I were thirty years younger and single, I'd be crawling all over you like a spider monkey. Who knew behind those nerdy glasses of yours and that bad haircut would be such a stud?"

Brody could feel his face turning red. Talk about awkward. "No, I'm not a model. Not even close."

"Then what exactly *is* it you do? Are you a spy?"

"No."

"Member of the FBI?"

"Nope."

"Part of the President's Secret Service?"

"Afraid not."

"Running Google?"

"I wish."

"Well then, I'm all out of ideas," she said in exasperation.

"Let's just say I'm not doing much of anything right now," he said evasively. That was *sort of* the truth, anyway. "I needed a break. I took one."

"So how long are you in town?"

"Not really sure yet. I'm just going to go with the flow

for now and see how things go. I just know it was time to catch up with my family before they decided to disown me."

"Boy, I wish I had a job where I could call in when I wanted," she said, slapping the table with the rag that was thrown over her shoulder. "If I took off even a day I'm pretty sure Clyde would burn down the building."

If she only knew what *really* happened, Brody bet she wouldn't feel any envy at all.

"I've just felt disconnected from my family for a long time," he said, changing the subject. "I needed to make that right."

"You probably made the right decision. I heard your daddy talking to Harry the other morning over coffee about cuttin' you outta the will."

Brody choked on the coffee he was drinking. "Are you *serious?*"

Sadie winked at him. "Of course I'm not serious."

"That's not nice, Sade."

"You know what else isn't nice, Brody? You lookin' too cute for words. All the girls in Parker aren't like the big city girls. We don't have much time for playin' games. Our hearts break easy. Just keep that in mind before you try to charm the panties off some poor, unsuspecting innocent."

"Now why in the world would you think I would do somethin' like that?" Brody could already feel his Oklahoma drawl returning. It took years for his accent to disappear when he moved to New York. Now, after less than a week back in Parker, it was returning.

"Don't be coy, Brody Cooper. I've seen all those pictures you post on social media. A different woman on your arm every night, dressed all fancy. Those don't look like women you take home to your momma. They look like women just out for a good time."

"You sound like my sister. Guess it's a good thing I don't have a momma then," he mumbled.

Sadie's eyes softened. "Just promise me. You can have any woman you want when you go back to New York. You're in a different league now. Play nice while you're here."

Brody sighed. "Fine, Sadie. I'll play nice."

Sadie grinned before exiting the booth. She stretched, her joints cracking in response. "I swear, Brody, every day more and more pieces of my body start cracking. One of these mornings I'm going to wake up and crumble into a cracker."

"You still don't look a day over thirty to me, Sadie."

She lovingly hit him on top of the head with the towel she was holding. "There you go, bein' all charmin'. What did I say? Play nice."

"I didn't know it referred to you, too, what with you bein' happily married to Clyde and all. But I couldn't help myself. You were my very first crush, Sadie."

This time, it was the café owner who blushed. "You sure are somethin', Brody Cooper. But remember your promise."

Brody nodded. "I remember." He was just crossing his fingers his sister's friend wasn't that interested in playing nice. He needed a distraction from the turn his life had taken.

Karen was sitting in the back booth of Griff's bar, bouncing Emma Kate, her best friend's daughter, on her lap.

She had been sitting at her house, watching yet another episode of *House Hunters*, this time the International Edition, when Griff called in a panic. He told Karen Breckin wasn't answering her phone, his mother and Breckin's dad were in Lakeview Christmas shopping, and his meemaw and her boyfriend were causing a ruckus at the bar because Griff was out of onion rings. He begged

Karen to come to the bar and help him out by watching Emma until Breckin got finished eating lunch with her brother.

Karen chose to sit at the back of the bar to try and avoid the whirlwind that was Griff's Meemaw Kelda. The old woman gave Karen stress hives. She always asked too many questions and wouldn't take no for an answer. In Karen's world, nosey people meant nothing but trouble.

Thankfully, Kelda and Burt had stomped out of the bar after Griff told his meemaw he wasn't driving to Swanson's to buy more onions just so he could make her a batch of onion rings. Content with the smiling baby on her lap and not yet ready to return to her quiet house, Karen leaned back in the booth and looked down at her best friend's baby. She really was an adorable little thing. Soft black hair. Big brown eyes. Her daddy was going to be in big trouble when she was older.

"Well, well, well...what on earth did my husband do to get you out of your house?" Breckin walked up to the booth and plopped down on the other side.

Karen smiled and held Emma in the air. "He bribed me with your baby. How can I resist these chubby cheeks?"

Breckin's face softened. "She is pretty hard to resist, isn't she?"

"She really is."

"But why is she back here with you?"

Karen explained Griff's panicked call to her when he couldn't get in touch with Breckin. "I figured I would help him out, especially if it meant snuggling your little girl."

"Already tired of watching *House Hunters*?"

Karen rolled her eyes. "Hey! At least it was the international version."

Breckin laughed. "I prefer the renovation edition myself."

"So why weren't you answering your phone? I figured

you would have it right by your side knowing your baby was at the bar with your husband."

Breckin shrugged her shoulders. "I know, right? Totally unlike me. But my brother decided to drop into town unexpectedly a few days ago and we met for lunch. I figured it wouldn't be nice of me to check my phone every few seconds to see how my daughter was doing. I haven't seen him since Annie's granny died. Besides, I knew Miss Emma was in good hands with her daddy. I swear, sometimes I think he's better at this parenting thing than I am."

"You're a great mom, Breck. One of the best I've ever seen."

"Thanks."

"You're welcome. So? Your brother, huh? You hardly ever talk about him."

"It's because I hardly ever see him. He works all the time."

"Doing what?"

"That's a really good question. The sad thing is, Dad and I don't really know. We ask questions but he just gives vague answers. I know it's something that pays well because he always wears expensive clothes and lives in a fancy apartment, at least from what I can tell by the pictures he posts on social media."

"You haven't ever visited him? Where he lives?"

Breckin shook her head. "Nah. I always figured if he wanted me to come visit he'd one, tell me what he actually does for a living, and two, actually invite me. Since he hasn't done either, I took that as a hint to stay away."

"That's sad."

"My brother was always the quiet, nerdy type. As soon as he graduated, he left and never looked back. It was hard on him when my mom died. I was too young to remember her but Brody wasn't. My dad says Brody is just like my mom.

Bookworm, quiet, shy. Or he was, anyway. I don't really know who he is anymore. Every time I see pictures of him he has a new girl on his arm. But even with the new, outgoing version of himself, he's still the total opposite of my dad and his love of all things sports. I think he just wanted to get away."

"I can't believe I've lived in Parker for so long and never met him. Even though he is hardly ever here, it's really difficult to not notice someone new in town."

"About that. You actually have—"

"There are my two favorite girls in the whole, wide world! I've missed you so much!"

Griff walked up to the booth, a huge smile on his face, and kissed Breckin's forehead. When Karen first met him, she was a little scared. Well, a lot scared, if she was being honest with herself. The biggest muscles she had ever seen, tattoos up and down his arms, a wicked looking beard, and head shaved short. The definition of a bad boy. But when Breckin and Griff got together, Karen realized her first impression of Griffin Stephens was totally wrong. He was gentle, kind, and so in love with Breckin it made Karen's heart ache with longing. Their love was real and good and amazing. They were perfect together.

"Karen, thanks so much for coming to my rescue," Griff said. "I don't think I could handle everything by myself."

"No problem. I'll never turn down the opportunity to love on this little girl right here." Karen kissed the top of Emma's head and breathed in her smell. Babies always smelled so wonderful. She placed the baby in her father's massive hands, smiling at the look of adoration on his face. "Now that Breckin is here, it looks like I'm not needed."

"Where are you going? You don't have to rush off," Breckin said.

"I'm probably going to Swanson's to pick up a few things.

I need a few groceries to tide me over until school starts again."

"You never told me what your plans are for Thanksgiving. Are you going to spend it with family?"

This was always the part Karen hated. "Nope. Just me, myself, and I." Like always. Like her future.

Breckin shook her head. "Nuh-huh."

Karen arched an eyebrow. "What's that supposed to mean?"

"It means you aren't spending Thanksgiving alone. Or Christmas for that matter." Breckin got out of her side of the booth and grabbed Karen by the shoulders. "I don't know what you do with yourself during school breaks normally because you're so secretive about everything, but now that I know for certain you plan on spending it alone, I'm not letting it happen."

"Breck, it's fine. I'm used to—"

"Not. Another. Word. You're coming to our Thanksgiving. I won't take no for an answer. If you do, I'll just come to your house that morning, drag you out of bed, and hold you hostage at our house to celebrate anyway. So you might as well say yes."

Karen turned to Griff. "Is she serious?"

"Totally. Having a baby has really made her bossy."

Karen couldn't remember what it felt like to actually be around people during the holidays. It might be nice. "Tell me what to bring."

Breckin gave a victory shout. "Just yourself."

"Nope. If I'm coming I'm bringing something."

"Fine. Just bring something snacky for during the day. We don't eat our Thanksgiving meal until that night. And for Christmas, get a present. We play *Dirty Santa* and board games. You'll have so much fun!"

"Whoa, whoa, whoa. Don't be jumping the gun. I'm going

to see how Thanksgiving goes before I commit to Christmas."

"I have no doubt you'll have so much fun you'll be back. Christmas Eve and Day. The board games and *Dirty Santa* is Christmas Eve. We have a big meal at noon and open presents on Christmas Day."

"I'm not barging in on your family's present opening!"

"Well, I'm not letting you not get anything for Christmas! Everyone will love having you. Trust me."

"Just go with it," Griff whispered behind his hand. "This is a battle you're not going to win."

Karen sighed. "I guess I need to go shopping for some presents."

Breckin grinned. "It's going to be great, Karen. Promise."

With a wave, Karen walked out of the bar and into the frigid wind. Oklahoma wasn't playing this winter. It looked like the cold spell was here to stay. The weathermen were even predicting a large snowstorm on Thanksgiving in two days.

Karen knew it was early and she told her friend not to jump the gun, but if Breckin insisted she go to her family's Christmas, then Karen insisted she go prepared. And she had seen downtown at Christmastime. All the stores were packed with shoppers looking for a good deal. Karen wanted no part of the crowds. Since she had nothing but time on her hands, she decided to do a little shopping. And, if she were being honest with herself, she was getting sick to death of *House Hunters*.

A quick drive to the center of town had Karen parking her car on Main Street. First stop, Cure All Pharmacy. Not only did the pharmacy carry medical supplies and fill the townspeople's prescriptions, it also carried a variety of cute gifts. A person could buy home décor, adorable baby items, homemade soaps and lotions, and more. Karen figured this would be a good place to stop first.

Grabbing a handheld shopping basket, Karen walked to the back of the store. She mentally made a list of people in her head who needed gifts. Breckin, Griff and Emma for sure. A *Dirty Santa* gift. Kelda and her boyfriend, Burt. Breckin's dad and Griff's mom.

With a smile, she immediately spotted the perfect gift for Griff's mom, Susan. Because of Breckin's stories, Karen knew Susan loved all things chicken. On one of the home décor shelves was a whitewashed picture frame around a tin chicken silhouette in the middle of what looked like wooden shiplap walls. Placing it in her basket, she walked down the rest of the aisles.

In just a few minutes, she'd found almost everyone a gift. An Oklahoma City Thunder coffee mug for Breckin's dad. An extremely soft blanket covered in cat faces for Griff's grandma. A cuddly teddy bear that lit up in a variety of colors and played music for Emma. A Harley Davidson vintage tin picture for Griff. Breckin's favorite lavender and vanilla scented handmade soap and lotion. An oversized, incredibly soft blanket for *Dirty Santa*. The only person she couldn't find anything for was Burt. She decided to stop at the liquor store in town and buy a bottle of Crown Royal. She'd never met a man who didn't like it.

After a quick trip down the gift wrap aisle to get some paper, ribbons, and bows for her presents, Karen headed to the front of the store to pay for her items.

"Hey, Ms. Posey! I'll get ya over here." Jerica, one of Karen's math students, was behind the counter working one of the registers.

"Well, hello, Jerica. I didn't know you worked here," Karen replied, setting her basket on the counter.

Jerica removed the items one at a time. "My grandparents

own the place. I just help out around the holidays or when it gets really busy. Sometimes I work part-time during the summer, too."

"Do you get any lotion or soap free?" Karen asked with a smile. "If you do, where can I find an application?"

Jerica laughed. "They're the greatest, aren't they? My grandparents own a farm just north of the lake. They use their goats' milk to make the soaps and lotion."

"Well, whatever their secret recipe is, it's amazing. My skin is always so soft."

"I know. They're going to have a new scent in the spring. I'll bring you a sample to class."

"I believe that deserves some extra credit then."

Jerica placed Karen's items in one of the pharmacy's brown paper bags. "Here you go, Ms. Posey. I hope you have a Happy Thanksgiving."

"You, too, Jerica."

Karen made a quick stop at the liquor store and picked up a bottle of Crown Royal for Burt. She then headed to Swanson's to find something to make as a snack. It had been so long since she had cooked for more than one person she didn't know if she'd even remember how.

She wandered up and down the aisles aimlessly, hoping the Pinterest gods would send a recipe her way. She was standing in front of the cake mixes, trying to figure out if she could get by with making a box cake when she heard a familiar voice behind her.

"And we meet again."

Karen rolled her eyes. She knew that voice. And it grated on her damn nerves she recognized it so quickly. It was the same douche bag who had hit on her *last* time she had been in this very same grocery store. She turned and faced him. "You seem to be here an awfully lot. Did Mr. Swanson hire you as stock boy?" she asked sweetly.

He chuckled but ignored her comment. "You have a sweet tooth, Raven? Everyone tells me I'm pretty sweet. If you want to sample and see if they're right, you're more than welcome."

"I think I'll pass," she said, trying not to look him up and down but couldn't help herself. If she were a student in her class, she would have definitely gotten a big F on her test of no checking out the jerk standing in front of her. Today, the ass was wearing a pair of dark wash jeans that molded to defined thighs and a brown sweater that deepened the color of his eyes. His hair was a disheveled mess that looked too sexy for words. And that voice...sex and mischief and southern charm all rolled into one. Funny...she remembered the voice but not the drawl from their last encounter.

"That's not what your eyes say," he said with a wink.

"Oh, really? And what do my eyes say? I'm dying to know."

"Well, the way they just looked me up and down, they're telling me you'd like to see me without my clothes on."

"You are the most presumptuous man I think I've ever met," she replied with a sigh. "Do those lines have women falling at your feet?"

"If I said yes, would it work on you?"

Karen rolled her eyes again. She had a feeling if she ran into the infuriating man on a regular basis her eyes might become permanently stuck in the back of her head.

"Nope. Now, run along. I'm sure Mr. Swanson has some fruitcake you need to put on the top shelf."

He laughed a deep, throaty laugh that had her girly parts standing at attention. The man oozed sex appeal. Too bad she wasn't interested. Well, too bad she wasn't going to take him up on what he was blatantly offering.

"You have some spunk, Raven. I'll give you that. But are you ever going to tell me your name?"

"In a town as small as Parker, I thought you would have already figured it out by now."

"Maybe I have. Maybe I haven't. I'd still like to hear it from you first."

"Don't hold your breath for something that will never happen." Karen turned toward her cart and aimed it for the front of the store. It looked like she was going to take a platter of pre-sliced summer sausage, cheese, and crackers to Breckin's house. Forget about cooking anything. She just wanted to get away from the man before she did something stupid. Like take off her panties and throw them at him like a groupie at a concert.

CHAPTER 3

*B*rody didn't know why he didn't tell Raven he already knew who she was. Maybe it was because he didn't want to rat his sister out. Maybe he wanted to see if she would tell him her name on her own. If that was indeed his goal, it was an epic fail. Instead of Raven, he should have given her the nickname Ice Queen. Normally, her reaction to him would have him moving on to the next woman. They had a tendency to wait in line for him in New York.

However, it was Parker, and his choice of women was slim to none unless he wanted to pursue a woman of the elderly variety. But something told him his sister's friend had a story. A story he'd like to discover.

Brody's phone rang, breaking him out of his thoughts about the beautiful schoolteacher. "Hello?"

"Where in the hell did you run off to? I've been trying to reach you forever!" Jax Sanders', Brody's friend from New York, voice blared over the line. Brody held the phone away from his ear and shook his head.

"I've been gone less than a week, Jax," Brody said, trying

not to roll his eyes. "You probably haven't even crawled out of that socialite's bed I saw you in last."

Jax laughed. "She's a little tiger, that one. I figured she'd be up for some fun stuff, but man! She had a few surprises of her own. Did you know you can—"

Brody snorted. "Don't want to hear whatever freaky thing you did with a kitchen accessory, Jax. You've told one too many tales in the past. I feel my ears and memory will never recover."

Jax laughed again. "You know me too well. We had a fun time together but play time's over. I'm not interested in putting a ring on it, not with her or anyone. When she got that look in her eye, I hightailed it out of her apartment pronto."

"Look in her eye? After a weekend?"

"You know the look. I'm sure you've been given it a time or two."

Brody nodded. Like his friend, he had run quickly out the door.

"Imagine my surprise when I walked into work Monday and they told me you'd quit."

Brody started. "They told you I quit?"

"Yeah. Don't tell me you didn't and they have you hidden on some island, finding them some new ways to make hidden offshore accounts to make the company billions?"

Brody shook his head. "Not exactly."

He couldn't believe his bosses told his coworkers he *quit*. It couldn't be further from the truth. Escorted off the premises was more like it. He expected his name to be plastered all over the *New York Times* as soon as he tucked his tail between his legs and ran. But if it *wasn't*….there might be a way to salvage his name and reputation. Maybe all wasn't lost and he wouldn't be a Big Apple reject forever.

"Then what, *exactly*, happened?"

"Nothing much. I just told them I needed some time off. I was on a verge of a breakdown, man."

"You? Brody Cooper? Known for working eighteen hour days and sleeping with the most beautiful women in New York City? Not buying a breakdown. You better come up with something more plausible."

Brody sighed. He hated talking about his past. He wanted his coworkers and friends to think of him as sophisticated Brody, not the country hick Brody who arrived in New York almost twenty years ago with nothing but his summer savings from mowing lawns in his pockets. But maybe the truth would keep him out of everyone's thoughts while he figured out his next move.

"You know I hate coming home," he told Jax, making sure his Oklahoma drawl was well-hidden.

"I remember you whining like a little pussy every time you had to make the trip back," Jax responded. "Don't tell me you're there."

"My kid sister just had a baby. My dad threatened to cut me out of the will if I didn't come see my niece soon. It's been three years since I've been home."

Jax snorted. "And it's been five since I've been back to Florida. Who cares? You have your life up here. They don't fit in it. You said so yourself. Numerous times, if I remember."

Shame filled Brody at the words he remembered saying about his family. When he left town all those years ago, he was angry. Angry at his dad and life and the world. New York had given him the anonymity to make himself into whomever he wanted to become. Not the nerdy book lover. Not the guy who had to be gay because there was no other reason for a male, especially Donnie Cooper's son, to not like sports. Not the poor kid who lost his mom and stood in his kid sister's shadow his entire life. He had a chance to make himself into someone he *wanted* to be. Brody somehow felt by revamping himself he'd lost a part of the *real* him in the process.

"I did. I remember. But I don't want my niece growing up not knowing at least *who* I am."

"Who cares? She's a baby who won't even remember you in two days."

Brody sighed. His friend wasn't going to understand no matter how Brody worded it. "Okay, fine. You read through my bullshit. I had to get out of town for a little while because I slept with some dude's wife I met at the club."

"No. Shit! I knew you wouldn't go home to see some niece."

"Yeah, man. Turns out he works in our building. I didn't even know she was married. She told me she was divorced. But one day—I think it was the week when you were in Hong Kong—he came at me with a baseball bat. I figured it was time to get the hell out of Dodge and let things cool down before I came back."

Jax started laughing. "Was the sex good, at least?"

"Eh. I've had better."

"Man! I'm sorry I missed it. And really, I'm surprised I haven't heard anything about it."

"Tommy in security kept it pretty low-key. Didn't want it to reflect poorly on the company."

"I get it. James is a stickler for keeping his damn reputation intact."

"Yep."

"Well, are you at least on some tropical island being fed grapes by bikini-clad women?"

Brody was tired of talking to his friend. Conversation he usually enjoyed was leaving a bitter taste in his mouth. Maybe because it brought up all the memories of the bad things he had said about his family in the past. Or maybe it was because all of a sudden he realized how glaringly shallow his life really was. "Yep. Totally getting oiled down by a sexy little thing in a thong right now."

"Well then, I won't keep you on the line. You have a Happy Thanksgiving, Brode."

"You, too, Jax."

"Don't stay gone too long. I want to hear all about this baseball bat incident. Do I know the guy?"

"Nope. He was just a nobody," Brody said, hating himself for the words coming out of his mouth.

"Aren't they all?"

After hitting End, Brody put his phone in his pocket and sighed. He didn't realize what a douchebag he had become since moving to New York. But his sister and Sadie were right; he had changed...and he was beginning to think it wasn't for the better.

Absentmindedly, Brody hit the steering wheel of the rental car with his thumbs to the beat of Frank Sinatra's version of *Jingle Bells*. Christmas carols were the only music that had been playing on the local radio station since Brody rolled into town even though Thanksgiving hadn't even come and gone. And since the Focus he was currently driving wasn't equipped with Sirius, Brody was forced to listen. If he heard The Chipmunks sing *Please Christmas Don't Be Late* one more time he'd shoot himself in the pinky toe.

He made a mental note to himself to have his sister or dad follow him to Lakeview to drop the rental off at Enterprise tomorrow. If he was going to be in town for a while, he might as well quit paying for transportation. Everything in Parker was mostly within walking distance. If it wasn't, Brody was sure his dad still had Brody's 1991 black Chevy somewhere. Knowing his father, it was probably in pristine condition, too.

Taking his phone back out of his pocket, Brody pressed his sister's contact and waited for her to answer.

"What do you want?" she asked.

"Well, is that a way to talk to your favorite brother?" he asked.

"You're my only brother."

"Even if you had more than one, I'd still be your favorite."

He could feel his sister's smile through the line. "Seriously, Brode. What do you want? I'm up to my eyeballs in baby poop here. You're lucky I even answered!"

"One, gross. Two, that just *proves* I'm your favorite. You answered, baby poop and all."

"Hanging up now."

"No, wait! I really was calling for a reason."

"Then you better hurry up and get to telling me."

"What am I supposed to bring tomorrow?"

"*Seriously?* That's what you want to know?"

"What? It's a legitimate question!"

"You haven't been home in three years. When you were home all you ever brought was yourself. Now, when I'm covered in pea green baby poop, you want to know what to bring?"

"Again, *ew!*"

"Yeah, *ew!*"

"I don't know, maybe I want to participate instead of just showing up for once."

"Well, it's about damn time."

"What is that supposed to mean?"

His sister laughed. "It means the secretary at your office has sent both Dad and me the same cards on Thanksgiving every year. And she's sent the same cheese and fruit tray from Harry and David's for Christmas for the last five years. I'm getting tired of pears. If you stay through Christmas you have to get me something good to make up for all the pears.

Just don't buy me a diaper genie. I got five of them at the baby shower."

"I don't even know what a diaper genie is."

"It's a big, plastic tub that holds dirty diapers until you're ready to trash them. They're also supposed to seal in the odors of said diapers. Either they don't work as advertised or your niece has category five, grade A shit because those odors cannot be contained. We should sell her dirty diapers to the government. They could probably make bombs out of them."

"You've reached a level of disgusting I didn't know you had in you."

"Just wait until you get baby poop under your fingernail. Then you'll think disgusting."

"I'll pass. But seriously, I need some help. I have no clue what to bring tomorrow *or* what to buy for presents for Christmas because yes, I plan on staying, Punky Breckster. Or who the hell to even buy for. I know it's not just the three of us anymore."

"Funny how things change when you're gone for years."

"Ouch."

"Truth."

"Are you gonna help me or not?"

"Why are you buying stuff so soon, anyway? You have a month."

"Because I want to be prepared," he said. He was also bored out of his mind and needed something to do. Even if that something was Christmas shopping. "So? Help or not?"

He heard his sister sigh. "Fine. Have Sadie make some of her pumpkin cupcakes with cinnamon cream cheese frosting for tomorrow. If she can make them on such short notice, that is. I'm sure for you she'll make an exception. As for Christmas presents, Dad's been eyeing the new chainsaw Max just got in at Nailed It but is too cheap to buy it for himself. Susan likes chickens, Kelda likes cats. Burt still likes playing checkers and Griff likes Harley Davidsons. The pharmacy has a great selection of baby items. Just ask Jerica, the girl who works the register, what would be good. I'm pretty sure she hoards all the stuff she wants me to get Emma and stocks it on the shelf when she knows I'm coming in."

Brody laughed. "Seriously?"

"Seriously. Your niece is a celebrity in our small town."

"She is a pretty cute baby."

"The cutest."

"And what about yourself?" he asked.

"The biggest bottle of Pinot Grigio the liquor store has."

Brody laughed again. "So much for surprises."

"Screw surprises. I'm a mom. I need some wine in my life."

"Is there anyone else I should be buying something for?"

Dead silence drifted over the line.

"Hello? Breckin?"

"If I tell you, you better not make it awkward."

"What is that supposed to mean?"

"You know that pretty girl you met? The pretty girl who's my friend?"

"I remember. Karen, right?"

"Yep. She's coming."

"To Thanksgiving?"

"Thanksgiving *and* Christmas."

"Okay."

"Well, just Thanksgiving for now. She said maybe to Christmas. Which means…"

"What means, what, dear sister?"

"It means I want you to be nice."

"I'm nothing if not nice."

He could hear his sister's eyes rolling to the back of her

head. That's one thing she and her friend had in common, apparently. "Seriously. Be nice."

"I'm nice, I'm nice."

"Be Brody before New York nice."

"What's that supposed to mean?"

"I don't want Player Brody trying to play my friend. She's fragile. She doesn't need a man whore hitting on her. So be nice, nerdy Brody. The one you were before you left."

"*Fiiiiiine,*" he said with a sigh. "I didn't realize you liked me much better as a loser than who I am now."

"You weren't a loser. You were my sweet big brother. And I miss him."

"I said I'd be nice. I meant it," he said with a sigh. "Okay?"

"I'm holding you to it. And don't tell her you're coming or she'll probably back out."

"All these rules," he said. "Is there anything I *can do?*"

He was met with silence on the other end of the line. "Hello? Breck?"

"Just be…"

"I know, I know," he interrupted. "Be old Brody nice. So what should I get her? For Christmas? Because I plan on being on such great behavior she'll have no choice but to say yes."

"That you'll have to figure out on your own," she said with an ornery laugh.

"*What?* I don't even know her!"

"Aren't you the man of New York who is so popular with the opposite sex? I'm sure you've bought *lots* of presents for women you don't really know."

"Now who's being not nice?"

"I didn't say I had to be nice. That's your job."

"Come on, Breck. Throw me a bone. *Something.*"

"Fine. I'll give you a hint."

"Gee, thanks," he said sarcastically.

"Do you want it or not?"

"Beggars can't be choosers, I guess."

"Her favorite color is red."

"That's all I get?"

"Gotta go, big brother. Diaper *doody* calls." With a laugh at her own joke, his sister hung up the phone while Brody was left wondering what exactly he had agreed to.

KAREN LOOKED at the red wrapping paper, bows, and presents sitting on the coffee table in front of her. It had been so long since she had wrapped presents for anyone she had actually forgotten how. No lie. Had to look it up on Pinterest. And felt like an idiot the entire time.

Thankful to the Pinterest Karen who pinned an easy, step-by-step tutorial of how to make presents look like they were wrapped by an expert, Karen started cutting, folding, and taping. Before she knew it, all the gifts she had gotten at Cure All were covered in beautiful red paper bedecked in gold and white ribbons and bows.

"Not bad, Kare," she said to herself. "Not bad at all."

One by one, Karen took the gifts and placed them on the table around her tiny tree. She leaned against the couch and smiled softly. It was the first homey touch her house had seen in the seven years she had been in Parker. She'd forgotten how much she'd missed doing all the normal things people took for granted.

Almost as if her feet had a mind of their own, Karen walked over to the built-in bookcases on either side of the fireplace and opened the bottom drawer. Pulling out a small box, Karen open its lid and was assaulted with memories from a life she tried hard to forget but sometimes couldn't help but remember.

Karen took a worn photograph out of the box and lovingly caressed the two faces depicted, allowing herself to remember what she once had before she gently placed the photo back in the box, shut the lid, and closed the drawer. Before the tears could fall, Karen stood up and shook herself off. She had cried too many tears for what might have been. She refused to cry any more.

In the past when she was upset, Karen would bake. Feeling the need to shake off the nostalgia threatening to pull her under, Karen decided to head to the store. She didn't want to just take the meat and cheese tray she had grabbed the other day when she was in Swanson's because the asshole had her all flustered.

Feeling determined, Karen threw her *Nonchalance* sweatshirt identical to the one worn by David in *Schitt's Creek*, one of her favorite sitcoms, over her yoga tank and headed out the door. Thanksgiving was tomorrow and she was determined to wow her friend's family with a killer pumpkin roll.

In just a few minutes, Karen had parked in one of the front spots at the grocery store and hurried inside. The wind was even colder than usual. Karen hated the way Oklahoma wind seemed to cut right to the bone. She didn't think it was something she would ever get used to.

Grabbing a cart, Karen started typing a list on her phone of the items she needed to make her pumpkin roll. Once finished, Karen headed down the first aisle she came to and started filling her cart with the items she needed.

When she got to the baking aisle, she looked and looked for canned pumpkin to no avail.

"Seriously?" she said to herself. "You had to wait until the last minute to buy pumpkin for a pumpkin roll for Thanksgiving, Karen? Great idea. It's not like anyone else would want pumpkin for the holiday where the most pumpkin is used in the history of…well…probably ever."

As a last ditch effort, Karen scanned the top shelves for anything resembling a can of pumpkin. Jumping to see the very top shelf, Karen grinned. Unless her eyes were completely failing her, she saw one last jumbo can of pumpkin. Exactly what she needed. Now if she could just figure out how to get it.

Karen pushed her cart until it was wedged between the shelf and the display of flour stacked in the middle of the aisle. Taking a deep breath and crossing her fingers she wouldn't wind up on her ass, Karen placed one foot inside her cart and the other on the third shelf.

Moving super slowly so as not to disrupt the cart, Karen grabbed the can of pumpkin now at eye level. "Bingo," she said triumphantly.

It was at that exact moment Karen realized the wheels of her cart were moving.

BRODY WAS STILL *as sullen as a toad frog*, as his dad liked to say when he was a kid. Sadie had told him she didn't have time to help him make the cupcakes his sister told him to ask her for and no amount of cajoling could get her to change her mind.

So instead of delicious, homemade cupcakes Brody thought he was going to have for Thanksgiving, Brody had found himself pulling into Swanson's parking lot to see if he could walk the aisles to find anything to take to his sister's the following day. All the aisles had proven fruitless so far.

He only had a couple of aisles left. If Brody couldn't find anything, he already decided a trip to the liquor store was next on the list. Everyone loved alcohol. Especially him, especially in this situation. It was his first holiday with his family in years. And his family had grown substantially since he'd been gone. Something told him alcohol was probably not only justified but also needed.

Decision made, Brody turned down the only aisle he hadn't yet gone down in order to head out of the store. Imagine his surprise when he saw the woman with the raven hair who had been occupying way too many of his thoughts about to hit the ground ass first.

Without thinking, Brody started running toward the woman about to fall out of her cart, sliding on his knees the final few feet. Instead of hitting the hard concrete of the store's floor, Raven's tight little ass landed right on top of his thighs. And damn if that didn't make his dick do a happy dance.

"Well, well, well," he said, brushing her hair out of her face. "We have to stop meeting like this, Raven."

"Are you proud of yourself?" she said haughtily, managing to look down her nose at him even though he *literally* saved her ass just a few short seconds ago.

"You know what? I kind of am. That was a pretty athletic feat, if I do say so myself," he said with a wink. "And I think you owe me a thank you."

"And why would you think that?" she asked, jumping off his lap and dusting the nonexistent dust off her leggings. Her skintight, white and black striped leggings that left *nothing* to the imagination, even if she did have a baggy sweatshirt at least two sizes too big over them.

"Because your ass would have been a lot sorer tomorrow morning if it had landed on this hard concrete instead of my legs," he responded, picking himself off the floor. "I mean, I know my thighs are hard as rocks but they don't compare to literal concrete."

Brody shot her the smile that had most ladies in New York throwing their panties at his feet. To his surprise,

Raven-whose-real-name-he-knew-but-couldn't-say   just leveled him with a glare.

"I. Was. Fine," she said. "I wasn't going to fall. I had it handled."

"Tell that to the cart who was going one way while your body was going the opposite," he said. Good god, Ice Queen was a much better nickname for the woman standing in front of him. Would it hurt her to at least say a small *thanks?* He *knew* falling on that floor would have hurt like a bitch. No need for her to be one.

"Like I said, I had it handled," she replied, completely ignoring his comment.

"What in the world had you climbing in your cart and on the shelves of a store like a spider monkey, anyway?" he asked.

"That's for me to know and you to never find out," she called, pushing her cart around him and swishing that sweet ass of hers down the aisle toward the checkout.

Brody let out a chuckle. He couldn't wait to see her face the next day when she realized they would be under the same roof for several hours. Suddenly, he didn't mind his sister told him not to tell Raven he knew who she really was. This was going to be so much fun. He was going to make damn sure his was the first face she saw as soon as she opened the door.

"Happy Thanksgiving, Raven," he called softly. "I'll see you tomorrow."

CHAPTER 4

*I*f Karen had any free hands she would shake them in nervousness. Of all the places in Parker she had visited, she had been to Breckin and Griff's home the most. Once Breckin wormed her way into Karen's world, she realized she needed a friend in a desperate way. She treasured her friendship with Breckin and didn't know what she would do without her. Even Griffin had become an important part of Karen's life. His gentle, quiet, and welcoming nature made Karen comfortable the first time she met him.

Which is why Karen agreed to attend Thanksgiving at her friend's home even though she knew it wouldn't just be the three of them like Karen was used to. But even the thought of crazy Kelda and all her hijinks wasn't enough to keep Karen away. Once Breckin invited her, Karen understood how much she missed being around people during the holidays. And who better to be around than her best friend? Kelda or no Kelda, it was worth the risk. She just hoped Griff and Breckin would run interference if Kelda pushed too hard. They didn't know her story, but they both knew Karen was uncomfortable with too many questions.

Karen shivered as the frigid wind blew her black hair around her shoulders in crazy disarray. She turned the front door to no avail. It was locked. What the hell? They never locked their front door.

Just as she started to ring the doorbell, Karen heard the door open. She breathed a sigh of relief. It looked like help had arrived.

"Since when do you lock your do—"

Karen stopped in her tracks when she saw the person standing in the doorway of her friend's home. It was none other than the jackass from the grocery store. "Why are you here?"

"Told you we'd meet again, Raven," he said at the same time. With a smile, he crossed his arms over his chest and leaned against the doorframe. Another pair of dark wash jeans hugged his muscular legs and a hunter green corded sweater highlighted his broad shoulders. He was too sexy for his own good.

He moved out of the doorway and motioned Karen in with his hand. "Would you like to come in? It's pretty cold outside and your hair seems to be catching more than its fair share of the wind."

Karen rolled her eyes and tried in vain to brush some of her strands away from her eyes. Trying her best to ignore him, Karen walked by the man still standing in the doorway, a snarky smile on his face. All of a sudden, Breckin came running up to Karen, eyes wide.

"Hey, Kare! I tried calling you several times before you got here. Why didn't you answer your phone?"

"Guess I didn't hear it. Were you calling to warn me?"

Breckin raised her eyebrows. "Warn you about what?"

"About the—" Karen lowered her voice, "*Ass* standing in your doorway! Who *is* he? Other than the guy I'm pretty sure likes to stalk me in the grocery store."

Breckin laughed. "Stalker? No. That's just my older brother, Brody. He's harmless. Just ignore him. He thinks he's a lot cooler than he is."

Karen cut her eyes to the man still standing in the doorway. Harmless her ass. He was danger with a capital D. *"That's* your brother? Why didn't you *tell* me he was going to be here?"

"Because I didn't know he had been stalking you in the grocery store," Breckin said with a laugh.

"Well, he has. And it's annoying," Karen huffed, trying to hide how freaked out she was about her highly attractive stalker being her best friend's *brother.*

"Trust me, that's not a big deal," Breckin said, waving her hand. "He won't care about it at all."

"I thought you said he doesn't come home much."

"And that's true. I think he was last home three years ago for Sophie's funeral. But he came home this year for whatever reason. I'm sorry I forgot to mention it. Actually, I tried to tell you the other day at Griff's but then Griff came over to our table and I forgot."

"So where's he home from?" Karen asked. Breckin's brother oozed sophistication and wealth. If Karen were to guess, she'd say L.A. Some sort of fancy PR firm for celebrities. Maybe a model. Not that she cared. At all. She was just...curious.

"New York," Breckin said.

Karen felt herself blanch at her friend's words. "Did you say New York?" she asked nonchalantly, trying to calm the beating of her heart. Of all the places he could be from, it had to be New York.

"Yeah. He moved there right after he graduated from high school. I told you I don't really even know what he does other than make a lot of money and hardly come home anymore."

Breckin paused. "Hey, are you okay? You look pale."

Karen shook her head. "Yeah, I'm fine. I think I just forgot to eat today."

"I wish I had that problem. I *always* remember to eat. It's why I can't lose this baby weight!"

"You look great, Breck," Karen said absentmindedly. "But now that you mention it, I really am not feeling that great all of a sudden. I think I should maybe go home."

Breckin shook her head. "Absolutely not! I know you're nervous being around our family but I promise, you'll be okay. Griff has already come up with a plan to keep Kelda away from you and I'll make sure to keep close all day. You're not going anywhere."

"What are you doing?" Karen asked, feeling Breckin rummaging through Karen's coat pocket.

"Getting these," Breckin said with an impish grin. "To make sure you *can't* leave!"

"That's not cool, Breck," Karen said. "You're not my friend anymore."

"I better be."

"Why is that?"

Breckin winked. "Because I'm your only friend."

To Karen's horror, Breckin tossed the keys to her brother. "Brode, would you mind keeping these for me? Karen thought she was feeling sick and wanted to go home. But she'll be all lonely if she goes home so we want to make sure she stays."

Brody grinned and stuck the keys in the pocket of his jeans. "Something tells me they'll be safe in my jeans. Unless, of course, you want to come get them?" he asked Karen.

Rolling her eyes, she didn't even answer. Instead, she followed Breckin into the kitchen and set her cracker, cheese, and summer sausage platter as well as the homemade pumpkin roll on the island in the center of the room. "Why didn't you tell me about your brother?"

Breckin shrugged her shoulders. "I'm sorry. I meant to tell you about him. I just forgot. I got all caught up in Christmas shopping and cooking for this week and it just slipped my mind. But he told me you guys met."

Breckin opened the platter and made herself a summer sausage, gouda cheese, and cracker double decker sandwich. "Don't worry. I told him you wouldn't be interested."

Sitting on one of the stools at the island, Karen proceeded to make her own cracker sandwich. "When did you tell him that?"

"The time I went to eat lunch with him and he told me about this girl he met. After his description, I knew it was you. I told him to keep his hands off."

"So he's known who I was this *entire time?*" Karen squeaked.

Breckin laughed and popped another cracker sandwich in her mouth. "Since the day you took care of Emma at the bar, yes. Same day I forgot to tell you about him."

Karen rolled her eyes. "Let me guess. He knew my name, too."

"Of course. What has he been calling you?"

"Raven."

Breckin snorted. "Oh, brother. He might be all model-y and buff now but deep down he's still the dork I know and love. Just give him some time back in Parker. I have a feeling he'll be back to the old Brody and less of the rich, snooty Brody in no time."

"So he's staying here? For good?"

Breckin shrugged her shoulders. "I'm not sure. He just said he'd gotten a break from work and decided to come home since he hadn't seen us in so long. I joked I was going to send his bosses a thank you card but he just ignored me. I'm beginning to wonder if he works for the mob."

"I don't work for the mob." Brody walked up behind Karen's stool and reached over her shoulder for some cheese and sausage. "I just work a boring desk job. Normal nine to five like everyone else."

Karen took a deep breath as his arm grazed her shoulder, a strand of her hair tickling her face in the process. Traces of sandalwood and cedar wafted under Karen's nose. He smelled like he'd just hiked across a trail in the Alps. Karen wanted to pull his sweater close to her nose and breathe him in again. It was divine.

"Like what you're sniffing, Raven?" he whispered in her ear, sending a shiver down her spine. "Be careful you don't breathe too deep and get dizzy."

Karen jumped out of her seat. Damn the man. He smelled just as good as he looked, maybe better. Laughing at her reaction, he took another piece of cheese and popped it in his mouth. "So, I guess you now know I know your real name is Karen. Nice to officially meet you."

"That was a very *Friends* comment," she said, ignoring him saying her name out loud. She didn't know it was possible for a name as simple as Karen to sound so sexy. Damn him again.

He raised one eyebrow. "Come again?"

"They don't know we know they know we know," she said. "Don't you watch *Friends*?"

"Not much for television. I like to do other things to occupy my time," he said, blatantly looking her up and down. Heat ran a blazing trail through her body. She was pretty sure if she looked in a mirror her face was pale no longer. Her guess was confirmed by his shit-eating grin. "Well, well. I guess you're not as immune to me as I thought."

"Whatever," she said, marching past him and into the living room. "I'm going in here."

To her chagrin, Brody grabbed the tray off the island and followed Karen into the living room. Griffin was sitting in his oversized recliner with Emma perched in his lap. She looked adorable in a burnt orange tutu over a pair of brown ruffled tights and a cream, brown, yellow and orange striped onesie emblazoned with the words—*Gobble, Gobble*—underneath a turkey. On her chubby baby feet were sparkly gold Mary Janes.

"Oh, my lord. She looks so adorable!" Karen said, grabbing Emma off her dad's lap and kissing her chubby cheeks. "What are you doing, Miss Emma Kate?"

The baby grinned and grabbed Karen's face. "Yes, I've missed you, too. You should tell your momma and daddy to let me watch you more often."

"Tell that to your friend," Griff replied. "It was like pulling teeth getting Breckin out the door the other night. I don't know why she thinks she'll be able to go back to school next semester."

Breckin plopped down on the arm of Griff's recliner and kissed him on the cheek. "Because I know she'll be in good hands with your mom. And I'm tired of smelling like baby poop and vomit and not having adult conversations. It's time. I'll appreciate her more when I'm away for a little bit during the day."

"You say that now. Tell me if you still feel that way when you're away from her eight hours at a time."

Breckin bopped him on the head. "Buzzkill."

Griff grabbed Breckin's hand and kissed the top of it. "Realist."

All of a sudden, Griff and Breckin's front door blew open and banged against the wall. Kelda Vanderburgh stormed in, her hair dyed a normal brown. However, the red, yellow, and orange feathers woven through her hair at random left no doubt what holiday was being celebrated.

"Sorry we're late! Burty had to take a shit. He took so long on the toilet because of playing that damn crossword puzzle on his phone that his foot went to sleep and he couldn't walk. I had to rub it for about ten minutes to get the feeling back into it so he could get to the car!"

"Dammit, woman! I told you *not* to tell your family about my bowel movements!" Burt said, following closely behind Kelda through the front door. "You promised! A man's bathroom business is his own business! Besides, I wasn't going the whole time. I just couldn't figure out the clue to thirty-seven down. How the hell was I supposed to know an eagle's nest was an aerie?"

"I might have had my fingers crossed when I said I promised," Kelda said. "Besides, I'm sure everyone within a ten mile radius of our house could hear you farting and blowing it up. I told you not to eat any more of those protein bars. They're eating your insides!"

Karen hid a smile behind her hand. Kelda was something else.

"Well, if it ain't the schoolteacher," Burt said after catching a glimpse of Karen sitting on the fireplace ledge. "What the hell is she doin' here?"

"Burty! Don't be an ass! She's obviously here because she don't got no friends 'cept Breckin, so Breckin invited her so she wouldn't be alone," Kelda whisper-shouted loud enough for the entire room to hear. "Don't you know suicide is the highest around the holidays? I'm sure Breckin don't want that on her conscience."

"Aren't you glad you came?" Brody walked up and sat down next to Karen, his thigh touching hers. Karen couldn't help but think he was doing it on purpose. "Your keys in my pocket now guarantee you won't be another holiday suicide statistic. Unless, of course, you commit suicide because of having to spend the evening with Kelda and Burt. Being with them is enough for anyone to contemplate it at least once."

Karen tried not to smile but failed miserably. He was spot on in his assessment of Kelda and Burt. They were a lot for anyone to handle.

"Well, I have to say, a smile fits a lot better on your face than the death glare you're usually sporting," he said with a grin. "Did I also detect a twinkle in your eye or was that just the light playing tricks on me?"

"Definitely the light," Karen replied. "No twinkles in these eyes."

"So sorry we're late!" Breckin's dad and Griffin's mom followed closely behind Kelda and Burt. "I was trying to get Donnie to hurry but you know how men are," Susan said.

"Was he takin' an elephant-sized shit? That was Burty's problem," Kelda remarked, pointing her thumb her boyfriend's way.

"Damn it, woman!" Burt yelled.

"Language, Mother!" Susan yelled at the same time.

Kelda held up her hands. "Good lord! A woman isn't even able to speak her mind nowadays without someone comin' unglued. You'd think I'd be respected and all, especially since I'm pushing a hundred. But *no!* I still get treated like a damn baby."

Kelda threw her purple velvet coat on the coat rack next to the door and walked over to Karen. "Okie dokie, teach. You've had her enough. Give me my great grandbaby."

Kelda grabbed Emma out of Karen's hands. Before Kelda could even sit down on the couch, Emma had puckered up her little face, her lower lip quivering.

"Don't be cryin' now," Kelda said. "Breckin, she sure has been cryin' a lot lately. She's probably teethin'. I got some whiskey in my purse."

Kelda motioned to Burt, who was still by the front door. "Burty! Get me that bottle of Fireball that's in my purse! I need to rub some on Emma's gums to numb her teethin' pain."

"No, no, Kelda!" Breckin said, whisking her daughter out of Kelda's arms. "I think she's probably just hungry. No need for whiskey."

Breckin shot a look at Griff before heading into the kitchen with her daughter.

"Meemaw," Griff said, rubbing his head with his hands, "how many times do I have to tell you Breckin knows how to raise our child?"

Kelda harrumphed. "Well, it's plain to see she *don't* know how to help a baby soothe her teethin' woes. As soon as I took Emma from the teacher she started wailin'!"

Kelda turned toward Karen and squinted her eyes. "Did you do somethin' to that baby? Pinch her? Pull on her diaper? Whisper some sort of witch chant in her ear?"

Karen's eyes widened. "No! Why would I do any of that?"

"A woman as pretty as you without a man? Something fishy about that picture is all I'm sayin'," Kelda replied, continuing to stare holes in Karen's forehead.

"Who says she's not with a man, Kelda?" Brody asked, wrapping his arm around her shoulders suggestively.

"Not even in town a week and already has the ladies dropping their panties for him," Burt muttered. "I remember those days."

"I drop my panties for you plenty, Burt Gallagher!" Kelda said. "If you weren't so busy sittin' on the toilet all the damn day, you could get in my panties any time you wanted! Free pass!"

"Burt! You can't say things like that to Karen! She's a guest in my home," Griffin said, rubbing his head again.

"Mother! Not everyone wants to know all about your sex life!" Susan cried.

"I'm not dropping my panties for anyone!" Karen yelled.

Brody laughed. "I hate to break it to you, Raven, but no one is paying attention to you anymore."

Karen looked around the room. Sure enough, everyone was involved in different conversations all around the room. Breckin's dad was trying to break up an argument between Susan and Kelda. Burt was pointing his finger in Griff's face. Griff looked like he was trying not to break Burt's finger.

"Now I'm beginning to remember why I haven't come home for the holidays in so long," Brody said.

"Are they always like this?"

"I don't know. When I used to come home regularly, it was just Breckin, Dad, and me. I've heard there's never a dull moment since Griff and Breck got together and Kelda's entered the picture."

"Well, thanks for putting her laser beams on *me!*" Karen protested, shrugging Brody's arm off her shoulders.

"You should be *thanking* me, Raven."

"What is that supposed to mean?"

"It means she was calling you a witch and acting like you did something to make Emma cry when we *all* know it's Kelda's crazy that makes that baby cry. Hell, she makes *everyone* cry. I simply defended you."

"By insinuating you're *with* me."

Brody held his hands up in innocence. "Honestly thought I was doing you a favor. And we've already determined no one is paying attention to you anymore. I'm betting Kelda and Burt are also getting the *Be nice to our guest or you're never coming back to the holidays at our house* talk. All is right in the world. Like I said, you should be thanking me."

"You and your need for thank yous."

"What is that supposed to mean?" Brody asked.

"You wanted a thank you last night for supposedly saving me from falling on the ground at Swanson's. Now you want a thank you for telling everyone we're in a relationship."

"Your butt and lack of people currently talking about you right now would justify a thank you if you asked them," he replied.

Karen rolled her eyes. "Fine. Thank you."

"It was my pleasure. Want to know something?"

"I'm not sure I do."

"Well, I'm going to tell you anyway," he said, an impish grin on his face.

"Fine."

"We're sitting on the fireplace," he said.

"I know this."

"My sister always decorates her fireplace mantle for Christmas."

"It's Thanksgiving."

"I guess she decorated it early. But guess what she always decorates it with?"

"I've never been much for guessing games."

"Mistletoe. You know what that means?"

"I'm almost afraid to ask."

Brody put his finger under Karen's chin and tilted her face up. "It means you owe me a kiss."

BRODY LOVED the way Karen's vivid green eyes went wide. He had gone out with hundreds of women in New York, all beautiful in their own right, but none of them held a candle to the natural beauty of the woman sitting beside him. He knew her hair would feel like silk running through his fingers. He could taste the sweetness of her skin.

With a slow smile, Brody leaned his head down toward

hers. To his surprise, he was met with a hand on his chest, pushing him away. What. The. Hell?

"One, that's *not* mistletoe. It's...well, I don't know what it is. But I know it's *not* mistletoe. I'm not an idiot. Two, what makes you think I'd even be *interested* in kissing you?"

"Why *wouldn't* you be interested in kissing me? It's not like there are many eligible bachelors in Parker, Oklahoma."

"I know it might be hard for you to get this through your thick skull, but maybe I don't *want* or *need* a man in my life."

"Are you a lesbian? Because that's hot."

Karen rolled her eyes. "No, I'm not a lesbian. But I'm not surprised you would think that."

"What is that supposed to mean?"

"It means a man as full of himself as you are couldn't possibly fathom why a girl wouldn't be dropping her panties for you as soon as you look at her with that look of yours."

"I have a look?" Brant grinned at the blush that crept up her neck and face.

"Never mind," she said. "You wouldn't understand."

"Try me."

"So why doesn't your family know what you do in New York?" she asked, totally changing the subject.

Brody shrugged. "I don't know."

"Think they're too dumb to understand?"

"What? No! I just—"

"You just what?"

Brody sighed and ran his fingers through his hair. "I don't know. I was pretty miserable in Parker. We moved here after my mom died and I never really fit. I didn't play sports. I was more comfortable with a book in my hand. As soon as a graduated, I left and never looked back."

"Weren't you scared?"

Brody shrugged again. "A little. But the fear of staying in

Parker for the rest of my life outweighed the fear of the unknown."

"So why New York?"

"It was the Big Apple. The city that never sleeps. Where dreams are born. I figured it was as good of a start as any."

Brody had no idea why he was telling the girl sitting beside him his life story. It was almost like his brain had a life of its own. He hadn't ever told his story to *anyone*. Maybe Kelda was right. Maybe the pretty lady beside him *was* a witch because she had definitely cast some sort of spell on him.

"I know what you mean," she said with a sad smile.

Brody raised his eyebrows. "Are you from New York?"

"What? Why would you think something like that?" she asked. All the color had drained from her face. Brody could tell he had hit a nerve.

"I don't know. You just seem too sophisticated to live in a small Oklahoma town like Parker. I've seen a lot of them. You're a city girl at heart."

"That's where you're wrong," she said, shaking her head. "I'm small town through and through."

Brody leaned over until their lips were almost touching. "It's okay, Raven. Just keep telling yourself that. But I know it's a big, fat lie."

"Is everyone ready to eat?" Breckin walked into the living room, an apron wrapped around her waist.

Karen jumped up like someone poked her with a hot fireplace poker. "I'll help you set the table," she practically shouted. Brody grinned. She definitely wasn't as immune to him as she desperately wanted him to believe. And that was something he could work with.

～

KAREN JUMPED up from her perch on the fireplace. "I'm starving."

She followed her friend into the dining room and started setting the placemats out on the table. "I still can't believe you didn't tell me *he* is your brother," she muttered.

Breckin laughed. "What's the big deal? Unless you're attracted to him."

"*What?* No. Absolutely not," Karen replied, slamming down the plate she had in her hands a little harder than she intended. "Not interested."

Her friend had a gleam in her eye. "I don't know. He sure has you all flustered. Maybe you deserve to go out on a date. Have some fun. Lord knows you haven't since you've been here."

"Not happening."

"What's not happening?" Brody asked, walking behind Karen and grabbing a plate from the stack before setting it on an empty placement. "Surely it's not going on a date with me. Because I plan on asking."

Breckin snorted. Karen shot her a death glare. She was so dead.

"Don't bother. I'll say no," she said to Brody.

To her annoyance, Brody shot her a wink. "Maybe at first. But I'll wear you down."

"Not likely."

"What are we eating? Will it be gentle for my Burty's stomach? You know he had the runs before we got here," Kelda said as she plopped down in a chair at the table.

"Annndddd...I'm no longer hungry," Brody whispered in Karen's ear. She couldn't help it. She laughed. Damn him.

"What's so funny?" Breckin asked, an ornery smile on her face.

"Your face," Karen said. She was surprised she didn't stick

her tongue out at her friend. Brody Cooper did *not* bring out the best in her.

Breckin laughed. "Nice one, Kare. Way to revert back to middle school. I can see my brother brings out the best in you."

Karen was saved from hurling another completely childish insult at her friend as everyone else gathered in the dining room.

Once everyone was seated around the table, Griff stood up and clinked his spoon on Breckin's wineglass. Even though he was a bartender and owned a bar, Griff didn't drink. He always said his dad was an alcoholic and he didn't want to follow in his footsteps. It only made Brody like him more.

"First, I'd like to tell everyone thanks for coming to our house for Thanksgiving this year. We know it was new to everyone and a lot to ask, so it really means a lot to us that none of you made a fuss about it."

Kelda started to interrupt. Before she could say anything, however, Brody heard a loud bang under the table, saw Susan shoot her mom daggers from across the table, and Kelda sporting a scowl on her face.

"Why you gotta kick me under the table, *Susan?*" Kelda said. "I was just gonna say it was no problem."

Griff rolled his eyes. "Anyway, thanks. It is the best Thanksgiving I think I've ever had. My mom is the happiest she's ever been, I have a beautiful baby girl, and Breckin took pity on me and decided to share her life with me. There's only one thing that could make it better."

Everyone around the table gasped as Griff got down on one knee in front of Brody's sister and pulled a ring box out of his pocket. "I know we started things kind of backward, Jelly Bean, but I'm living my dream. The only thing that would make it complete is if you were my wife. What do you say?"

Even Brody got choked up when he saw his sister's eyes fill with tears. "Yes, yes, yes! Griffin, I'll marry you!"

Breckin wrapped her arms around his neck and planted a kiss on his lips, tears spilling down her cheeks. "This is *definitely* the best Thanksgiving ever. Karen is here, my brother is home, my dad is happy, I have a beautiful daughter, and I'm getting married to the love of my life!"

Without thinking, Brody put his arm around Karen and pulled her close. He was surprised when she didn't pull away. "Pretty sweet, huh, Raven?"

Tears were flowing down her face. "Pretty sweet indeed."

Burt cleared his throat and stood up, holding his own wine glass. "Well, Griff stole my spotlight but I'm gonna go ahead and do what I was planning anyway. I can't get on my old knees, but whaddya say, Kelda? We don't have many years left, I figure. Want to spend them married to me?"

Kelda grinned and grabbed the ring box he had taken out of his pocket. "Hot diggity dog! Look at the size of this thing! Of course I'll marry you, Burty! And you know what that means?"

Everyone at the table shook their heads.

"It means me and Breckin get to have a double wedding! Ain't that something? You're right, Breckin. This is definitely the best Thanksgiving ever."

CHAPTER 5

"*W*elcome back, everyone. I hope you all had a wonderful Thanksgiving break."

Karen was standing in front of her first period math class trying not to smile as her students groaned collectively. Karen herself wasn't as pumped as usual to return to the classroom. For the first time in ages, she had actually enjoyed her break. It had definitely been eventful. Even so, she was glad to be back within the normalcy of her boring, everyday life. A life that didn't include Brody Cooper.

"I know you've probably forgotten everything I taught you before the break, so we're going to review quadratic equations before heading into chapter seventeen. Go ahead and open your books."

Karen began to review the lesson, placing emphasis on the difference between real and complex solutions of discriminants. She never thought she would ever be a math teacher but it had always come naturally to her. Yes, she had been a math major in college, but only because it was dependable. Safe. She imagined herself working a regular eight to five, Monday through Friday job in a bank or some sort of financial firm. Nothing exciting, but something stable enough to pay the bills. Turned out teaching had been her lifesaver.

A knock sounded on Karen's classroom door, breaking her out of her memories. Her students were working quietly on the equations she had assigned them, a fact that surprised as much as it pleased her. Usually her students were antsy on the first day back, already ready for Christmas break. She guessed modern technology had done her a favor. They probably knew everything about each other's breaks already.

"Come in," she called from her perch at her desk.

The door opened and in walked Brody Cooper, looking deliciously yummy in a pair of the dark wash jeans he tended to favor, a tight, black Johnny Cash t-shirt that emphasized his cut biceps and washboard abs, and a worn NYU ball cap. He had donned a pair of extremely sexy, tortoiseshell glasses that made him look even more scrumptious then he already was. Karen felt her lady parts dance a jig. She was also pretty sure she heard her female students' heartbeats immediately quicken as he sauntered into the room, looking like the picture of every girl's fantasy...including her own.

"What are you doing here?" she asked. "And how did you get in?"

"Easy. The secretary in the office was the secretary when *I* walked these halls," he said with a dimpled grin. "All I had to do was throw a little charm her way and...*voila*...here I am."

"Who *are* you?" Daisy, the head cheerleader, homecoming queen, and girl definitely not lacking attention from her male peers, piped up from the back of the room.

"I am Mrs. Henderson's brother. Brody Cooper. Just here to visit your lovely math teacher. Don't let me interrupt your..." Brody looked at the smartboard that was still projecting Karen's lesson. "Fascinating discussion on quadratic equations."

Daisy giggled and pulled out her phone from under her leg where it had been hidden. Her fingers flew over the screen. Karen was pretty sure she was texting all her friends about the hottie who had appeared in Karen's room. Usually Karen didn't let her students use their phones unless they were finished with their assignment, but she let it slide this time. If she was a teenage girl, she'd probably be texting her friends, too.

All of a sudden Karen noticed the vase of red roses Brody held in his hands. "What are those?"

"These are called roses," he said impishly. "Men suitors with any romantic bone in their bodies usually buy them at one time or another for the woman they're trying to woo. So here I am…wooing."

A collective gasp of teenage girls filled the room. Karen looked up to see every female student in her class texting away. She shook her head. She was going to be the subject of student gossip for the entire week.

"Well? Don't leave me hanging, Raven. Is it working? The wooing?"

Karen shook her head. *"Don't* call me that in front of my students!"

"Why?"

"Because it's not my name and I don't want them talking about me more than they already are! Look at their fingers flying over their screens."

Brody glanced around the room before grinning. "Good. The more people who know, the better."

"Know what?"

Brody sat on the corner of her desk, placed the vases of roses beside him and leaned over to whisper in her ear. Karen tried to appear unaffected but knew he heard her breath catch. "That I have the hots for the sexy math teacher."

Karen was saved from replying by the bell sounding in

the hall. "Don't forget. If your equations weren't finished, you need to have them to me in the morning," she said as her students filed out of the classroom, the girls giggling and blushing as they passed by Karen's desk.

"Well, you successfully caused a ruckus," Karen said. She secretly wished she had more students filtering in her room but second hour was her planning period. She hoped she could find some way to usher him out of the front doors before third period arrived.

"Did I? And here I thought I was being all romantic. Don't women like gestures like this? I'm pretty new at the whole wooing concept."

"You haven't had to woo because women throw their panties at your feet? Or because you haven't gone on more than one date with the same woman in several years?"

"Something like that," he said, pushing a strand of hair behind her ear.

Damn, he smelled good.

"You haven't even read the card," he said, taking it out of the tiny envelope and handing it to her. I came up with it myself. I'm no Keats, but I thought I did pretty good, all things considered."

"Considering what?" she asked skeptically.

"That I'm no Keats," he said with a grin that had Karen wanting to throw *her* panties at his feet.

Karen grabbed the card from his hand and read the words he had written. *To Raven, I can't get you out of my head. Your smell, your smile, the way your eyes dance when you laugh. You should laugh more, Raven. You're breathtaking when you do.*

Karen felt her heart skip a beat as she locked eyes with Brody and felt the heat in his gaze. If any man had perfected the art of smoldering, it was Brody Cooper. And damn if he wasn't smoldering at her now. In her own freaking classroom.

"Well? What do you think?"

"Huh?" Karen asked. Her thoughts were making it hard to concentrate.

"Of the card. I know it's not a poem but I thought it was decent."

Karen felt herself shaking her head. "Uh huh," she said, trying and failing to form a coherent sentence. "It was good."

"Was it enough to get you to go out on an official date with me?"

"I'll think about it." The words exited her mouth as if they had a mind of their own. A date. In public. With Brody Cooper. She was going to be the talk of the town.

"Well, that was easy. I figured you'd put up more of a fight. Guess I'm a better writer than I thought."

Brody leaned over and kissed her sweetly on the forehead. "I'm guessing it will be a busy week since you're back at the grind. What about Friday night?"

"I said I'll think about it."

"I'll pick you up at six," he said with a wink. "You best get to work, Ms. Posey. Those papers won't grade themselves."

At his words, Brody got up from her desk and left her room, the smell of his cologne trailing him out the door.

Karen couldn't help it. She read the note again, took a whiff of the roses, and smiled from ear to ear.

"So I heard you caused quite the commotion today at Parker High." Brody, Breckin, and Griffin were sitting around his sister's kitchenette table eating chicken tacos. His sister had become quite the cook since he'd been gone. He guessed miracles did still exist since she was one rung below horrifically disastrous in the kitchen as long as she'd been his sister.

"Completely different from the shy, quiet kid who used to walk the halls."

Brody shrugged. "All I did was take a pretty woman some flowers. What's the harm in that?"

"You know what the harm in that is," she said, throwing her napkin across the table at him. "You went to school here and lived in this town during your formative years. You know how people talk."

"And what are the fine folk of Parker saying about me and the pretty math teacher?"

"Well, for one, there's a poll going around on social media about you two."

"About what?"

"If you've slept together yet."

Brody choked on a piece of chicken. Grabbing his glass of water, he took a big gulp before shaking his head. "Seriously?"

"Seriously," Breckin said sternly. "And it shows seventy-eight percent of the town believes you have."

"Well, that seventy-eight percent is sadly mistaken," he replied. "Maybe I should get in on this poll. Is there money involved for the winner?"

Breckin threw a tortilla at him. "That's not funny, Brode! We're talking about my friend here! My very private, very closed-off friend! This might run her out of town."

"I don't think that will happen since she agreed to go on a real life date with me this Friday," he said with a grin.

"A date? Nice!" Griff looked up from the bottle he was feeding his daughter and held out his fist for a pound. "I don't think I've seen Karen go out on a date since I've known her."

"Not nice!" Breckin exclaimed, slapping both Brody's and Griff's hands as they pounded fists. "Not nice at all!"

"Why not?" Brody asked his sister, still marveling that she

was the one who made the tacos he was eating. They were damn good. "And honestly, did you *really* make these tacos? No judgment if you didn't. They are seriously delicious."

"Yes, I made them. They're really simple. You just take…" Breckin frowned. "Stop trying to change the subject!"

"I wasn't." Brody held his hands up innocently. "Just complimenting my sister on her newfound cooking abilities."

"It's *not* nice because chances are, Karen doesn't know about the poll. Once Karen *knows* about the poll, she's liable to pack her bags in the middle of the night and leave for who knows where!"

"She is a really private person, isn't she? Why do you think that is?" he asked, trying for nonchalance.

"I don't know. I think something in her past really spooked her and she just wanted to start over."

"Who comes to *Parker, Oklahoma* to start over?"

"I don't know," Breckin said with a shrug of her shoulders. "Someone who needed out of the big city?"

"Do you know where she's from originally?" he asked.

"No, but I've always imagined a big city. She seems too sophisticated for a small town her entire life. Heck, maybe you crossed paths in New York and didn't even know it."

Brody shrugged. "So what else are people saying about us?"

"Oh, everything. But it doesn't matter. You should've heard the rumors about me and your sister when we were dating," Griffin said.

"Such as?"

"Nothing you need to know about," Breckin said, shooting her husband a dirty look. "Well, if you insist on taking her out, have you even thought about what you're going to do with Karen on Friday?"

"You mean you approve of me taking her out on a date?"

"I'm warming up to the idea," she replied.

"I don't know. I haven't decided yet."

His sister started laughing. "Oh, my god."

"What?" he asked with a frown.

"She didn't say yes."

Brody tried to play it off. "Of course she did."

Breckin shook her head. "No, she didn't. If she had, you'd already have a date planned out to impress her. She probably said she'd think about it just to get you to leave her alone."

Brody tried to keep his expression neutral. How the *hell* did his sister *do* that?!

"Yep. I'm right," she said, slapping her fiancé on the arm. "Look at his face. He's always had a horrible poker face."

"I have not!"

"Ha! And now he's being defensive. She totally didn't agree," she said with a laugh.

"*Fine!* She said she'd think about it. Which we all know in women's talk means yes."

"*Sure* it does," Breckin said with another laugh. "Whatever you have to tell yourself."

"It does. And I'll prove it to you. Karen Posey is going to go out on a date with me this Friday."

Breckin raised her eyebrows. "We shall see."

"We shall," he agreed.

"So when are you going to hold my kid again?" Breckin asked, changing the subject completely. "I'm starting to get offended and thinking you don't like her."

"How could I *not* like her? She's adorable. Just look at her," Brody replied. His niece was sporting a sequined black Harley Davidson shirt he was pretty sure came from her father and a pair of hot pink pants with ruffles all along her diapered bottom. He was probably biased but he thought she was the cutest baby he'd ever seen.

"I'm just kind of worried I'm going to do something to hurt her," he admitted.

"Babies are practically indestructible," Breckin replied. "Now hold her."

"Fine!" Brody said with a laugh. "Give her up, Dad."

"I just burped her so she shouldn't puke on you," Griffin said.

Brody looked down at his niece and grimaced at the thought of *baby puke on his sweater. But his grimace soon turned into a smile.* She really was something else, even if she didn't do much. As soon as he had the thought, Emma looked up at him with her big eyes, cooed and gurgled, and then gifted him with a double-dimpled smile.

"Well, look at that," he said softly. "You must really like your Uncle Brody, huh, kid? I *am* pretty cool."

"See? I know you think she doesn't do much, but that smile could melt anyone's heart," Breckin said with a big smile.

"I totally agree, sis. You and your fiancé sure made a pretty baby."

"Prettier than all those models you paraded around with in New York City?"

"No comparison."

"I like that you finally decided to come home, Brody."

"You know what? I am, too."

"HE *PROPOSED*?" Breckin's friends, Annie Holloway and Colleen "CC" Chandler were squeezed in the other side of the booth at Sadie's Café. Annie, Breckin, and CC had known each other since elementary school and were still best friends. Every now and then Breckin convinced Karen to meet them at Sadie's for their weekly Wednesday sundae date. The trio always shared a banana split. They tried to get Karen to add her own favorite, which she had done one time, but she usually preferred to eat a simple strawberry cone.

Instead of their usual Wednesday date, however, Breckin had called Karen and begged her to meet her other friends at the café this evening. She said it was easier to meet in the evening rather than the middle of the day because Griff could be home with the baby. Not feeling the current episode of *House Hunters* on her DVR, Karen had agreed.

Breckin held out her hand for Annie and CC to see. "Yes! It was so sweet!"

"I can't believe we missed it!" CC pouted. "I can't believe we didn't even *know!* He didn't even ask our opinions on the ring or anything."

"Well, I think he did a fantastic job picking out the ring," Annie said. "It's *gorgeous!* But I can't believe *you* waited this long to tell us! Why didn't we get a call the day after it happened?"

Karen agreed with Annie. Breckin's center-cut diamond was a nice size without being ostentatious, the small diamonds lining the band sparkling in the light. It was a beautiful ring. Even better was the fact it looked just like something Breckin would pick for herself. If ever there were soulmates, Breckin and Griff were it.

"Because," Breckin said, pulling her hand away from Annie's to stare at her ring. Again. "Something bad happened."

"What could possibly be *bad* about being proposed to?" Annie asked.

"Well, you know Kelda and Burt came to Thanksgiving."

CC groaned. "Don't tell me Kelda did something crazy. Like take the ring and run."

Breckin shook her head. "Nope. But it's almost as bad. Isn't it, Karen?"

Both of Breckin's friends turned their attention to Karen.

She wanted to hide under the booth. *Why* did Breckin have to bring her into it?

"What does that mean? Were you there when it happened?" CC asked. "If you were, you have to tell us the details in your viewpoint. Breckin sometimes tends to skew things to fit her story."

"Hey! I do not!" Breckin said.

"Remember the one time in junior high and we played *Seven Minutes in Heaven*? You had to go into the closet with Neal Matthews."

Breckin groaned. "Don't remind me."

"You told us how amazing your first kiss was. How he was such a wonderful kisser."

Annie started laughing. "Yeah! I remember that. We believed you until we went to school that Monday and heard him telling everyone you had knocked yourself out on one of the shelves in the closet. He spent six of the seven minutes trying to get you to wake up!"

Breckin crossed her arms over her chest. "I was embarrassed to be the *last one* to be kissed. Both of you had been kissed by super hot guys and there I was…the kissless virgin."

"Last I heard, Max Gibbons is working the night shift at a convenience store in Lakeview and only bathes once a week, so I'm thinking *my* first kiss isn't something I want to admit to," CC said with a laugh.

"Don't you remember what happened after that? Neal wouldn't shut up about what happened. When Brody caught wind of it, he threatened to beat Neal within an inch of his life if he didn't stop making fun of you. He probably couldn't scare high school kids, but Neal about wet his pants when Brody caught him in the hall," Annie said.

"Your brother is a good one," CC said. "He was always taking care of you, even when you didn't want it."

"You should've seen the way he followed Karen around all evening," Breckin said, a gleam in her eye. "He's smitten."

Annie's and CC's focus went back to Karen. "Whatever does she mean?" CC asked.

"I sense a story," Annie added. "So spill."

Karen shrugged her shoulders. "Nothing really."

"Nothing? Really?" Breckin said, eyebrows raised. "That couldn't be further from the truth, Kare! In fact, I know he caused quite a scene at school today bringing you flowers!"

Annie and CC gasped. "No way! Brody brought you *flowers?*" CC squealed. "Oh, he must have it *bad!*"

"Right after Griff proposed to Breckin, Burt proposed to Kelda. And Kelda wants to have a double wedding," Karen blurted. She had to take the focus off herself. There was no way she wanted Breckin's friends asking questions about her personal life.

Karen hid a smile behind her hand when Annie's and CC's attention turned yet again to Breckin.

"What. In. The. Hell?" CC said. "Is this for real? Tell me it's not for real, Breck."

Breckin banged her head on the table. "It's for real."

Both Annie and CC started laughing so loudly all the other patrons in the café turned and stared at their booth. "Are you serious?" Annie asked, tears streaming down her face. "I'm so going to help plan this wedding."

Breckin put her head in her hands. "What do I do? I can't tell her no. She'll make my life a living hell. A shared wedding won't be worse than a horrific existence for all eternity!"

"Can't Griff talk her out of it?" CC asked.

"Have you ever talked Kelda out of her outrageous hair colors? She dyed it orange for Halloween and made you braid feathers in it for Thanksgiving!"

"Fair point," CC said. "I don't know, Breckin. Maybe try

to make it as small an event as possible. Only close friends and family."

"Kelda will swear the entire town is close friends of hers. And the more of a spectacle it is, the happier she will be. Don't you remember her ninetieth birthday party?"

Karen couldn't help but smile. Kelda's ninetieth birthday was what brought Griff and Breckin together. He had asked Breckin to help him plan the party. It was cat themed, big, raucous, and a *definite* spectacle. Her friend was screwed.

"I'm so screwed," Breckin said, echoing Karen's words.

"What could make you possibly screwed?" Sadie, the owner of the café, walked up to their table, a rag thrown over her shoulder. "You got a fine man, a beautiful baby, and the best friends a girl could have. Seems like you're living the dream, kid."

"Griff proposed to me, Burt proposed to Kelda, and now she expects to have a double wedding."

Sadie pulled up a chair from a nearby table and sat down at the end of their booth. "Oh, honey. You are totally screwed."

Breckin banged her head against the table again. "What am I going to do?"

"Try to make it the least ostentatious as possible?" Annie suggested.

"I'll try to tone down her hair color choice," CC added.

"I'll try to convince her no cat cakes like her birthday party," Sadie said.

Breckin raised her head off the table. "What about you, Kare? What are you going to contribute?"

"How about I make the invitations and accidentally forget to ask Kelda for her input? And I'll do it close enough to the date I can't change them."

Breckin's eyes shone with tears. "You guys are the best. But I need to ask you a question."

They all looked at her expectantly.

"Do you think we should just elope?"

"Honey, if you don't think *that* will bring down the wrath of Kelda Vanderburgh quicker than Satan fell from heaven as an angel, then you know nothing about your fiancé's grand-mother," Sadie said.

Breckin sighed. "You're right. I guess it's just wishful thinking."

"There is *another* solution," Annie said.

"What?" Breckin asked. "I'm willing to try anything."

"Just wait until she dies. Kelda is ancient. Surely her years are numbered."

A laugh escaped Karen before she could help it.

"What?" Annie asked with a shrug of her shoulders. "She's ancient."

"She's also mean as shit," Sadie replied, "which only means one thing."

"What's that?" CC asked.

"She's probably going to outlive us all."

CHAPTER 6

"*H*ey, Sis. Do you love me?"

Brody and Breckin were at Sadie's eating the special of the day, chicken spaghetti. And, as always, it was delicious. Sadie was a damn fine cook.

Since Brody had been home he had settled into a routine. Sleep late, get dressed, and meet a family member for lunch. Yesterday it was his dad. Today it was his sister. He had even eaten lunch with Griffin. Well, he had sat on a barstool while Griff was behind the bar but still…it counted.

Brody was so used to the hustle and bustle of New York City he just knew he would go crazy being back home with nothing to do, but his time off had actually been nice. He had gotten to catch up on some of the books that had been sitting unread in his Kindle forever, become more comfortable around his niece, and had even reconnected with some of his friends from high school. Being back in Parker was not the nightmare he thought it was going to be. Maybe he should have gotten fired a long time ago.

Brody laughed when his sister rolled her eyes so far back in her head he thought she might pass out from the effort.

Always the dramatic one. "Yes, I love you. No, I won't do your dirty work."

"Who said anything about dirty work? Maybe it's not even work at all."

"What do you want?" Breckin asked with a sigh.

"You see…it's Wednesday."

"Brody Cooper, if this is a Hump Day joke I swear—"

"It's not a Hump Day joke!" he exclaimed. "At least give me a little credit."

"I'm holding my breath in skepticism," she said with another eye roll.

"I need Karen's phone number," he replied, refraining from commenting that if she was indeed holding her breath she wouldn't be able to talk to him. He needed to stay in his sister's good graces.

"And why do you think I would give that to you?"

"Because you want to see your friend happy, and going on a date with me this Friday will make her happy?"

Breckin laughed. "Not until you admit she didn't agree to go out with you."

"I'm not telling a lie!"

"Fine. No number then." Breckin made a show of taking her phone and placing it in her purse before taking another bite of her spaghetti.

It was Brody's turn to roll his eyes. "Fine," he said with a sigh. "She didn't agree to go out with me. But I know she wanted to. And I haven't heard from her since I gave her the flowers, so I need to know."

"How does she have your phone number?" his sister asked.

"Because I put it on the card I put in the flowers," he said.

"And she hasn't called?" Breckin smirked.

"If she had would I be groveling at your feet for her number?" he said, refraining from rolling his eyes. Nothing like his kid sister subtly insulting him to keep his ego in check.

"Fair point." With a grin, his sister pulled her phone out of her purse and her fingers flew over the screen. When Brody's phone dinged with his sister's ringtone, he smiled. Brody now had the pretty teacher's phone number.

"Thanks, Punky Breckster," he said, leaning over the booth and kissing her on the cheek.

"That was too easy, big brother," she said. "You've gone soft in your old age."

"Honey, your brother might have done a lot of things but gone soft is *not* one of them." Sadie walked over to their table and sat down in one of the empty chairs. "Have you *seen* those abs he has hidden under that shirt of his?"

Breckin rolled her eyes and took a bite of the homemade garlic bread Sadie served with the spaghetti. "Not you, too, Sade. I swear, a boy gets big muscles and all logical thought flies out the window. And anyway, come to think of it, when did *you* see Brody's muscles?"

"Let's just say I happened to walk by CC's gym the other day to see your brother lifting weights," Sadie said, waggling her eyebrows. "Without his shirt on."

Brody could feel his face turning red. "I feel violated."

"Honey, the entire female population, with the exception of your sister, walked by that window at least fifty times while you were in there. How did you not notice? I think Kelda even posted some pictures on her social media pages."

Breckin snorted with laughter.

"That's not funny, Punky!" Brody said, throwing a chunk of bread at his sister. "Again, feeling a little...no, a *lot*... violated now."

"It's your fault for not having a shirt on," Breckin said.

"You need to tell your friend to tint the windows or something," Brody muttered. "Give a guy a little privacy."

"They were tinted when she started," Sadie replied. "But then Jimmy Cooper's kid accidentally threw a baseball through it at the Fourth of July celebration this summer. CC got the new glass installed but there's been a delay with the shipment of the tint she ordered."

"That's a long delay," Brody grumbled.

"Honey, it's Parker, Oklahoma. What do you expect?"

"That'll teach you to wear a shirt from now on," Breckin said.

"Don't you have *any* sympathy for your brother who was ogled like a piece of meat?"

Breckin looked at him and smiled. "Nope. None whatsoever."

"When did my sister get so mean, Sade? Can you tell me that?"

Sadie laughed. "It really was your fault for not wearing a shirt, Brody Cooper. How do you expect any hot-blooded woman *not* to want to look at you? New York turned you into a hottie deluxe."

Brody leaned over and kissed the café owner's cheek. "You'll probably be the first and last woman I ever love, Sadie."

He grinned when a blush flushed her cheeks. "And New York taught you how to flirt, too. Tell me again how you're single?"

"He's probably *not* going to be single if he has anything to say about it," Breckin said, taking the last bite of her spaghetti before throwing her fork on the table. Brody tried to shake his head before she could tell Sadie he had gotten Karen's phone number but his sister didn't look his way.

"He just got Karen's phone number from me," Breckin continued.

Sadie shot him the *look*. The look he got as a kid when she caught him doing something he shouldn't have. Since he grew up without a mom, Sadie had taken it upon herself to serve as his substitute.

"Remember what I said, Brody Cooper. You better be nice."

"I remember, Sade. And I promise I'll be nice."

"Oh, he *better* be nice," Breckin said, also staring him down. "Karen is one of my best friends. If he breaks her heart he'll also have to answer to *me.*"

"Ladies, I haven't even asked her on a date yet. She might say no. I already asked her once and she said, "We'll see.' That doesn't bode well for me."

Sadie rolled her eyes. "Honey, she's gonna say yes."

"I don't know. Her maybe was pretty wishy washy."

"Brody, if a woman can turn you down over and over the way you look it only means one thing."

"Oh, yeah? What's that?"

Sadie patted him on the cheek. "That she's probably a lesbian."

Karen frowned at her phone. She didn't recognize the number and that meant one thing—she wasn't answering.

Pressing the decline button on her screen, Karen stirred her microwavable macaroni and cheese and sighed. Sometimes she really wished someone else was living with her just so she would have an excuse to cook an actual meal.

Her phone dinged to tell her she had received a text message. It wasn't Breckin's text tone, so she had no clue who it could be. Breckin was the only person who ever texted her. Karen sighed again as Radiohead's *Creep* ran through her head. She really was turning into a pathetic weirdo-ooo.

Picking up her phone, she hit the home screen and opened the message.

BRODY

Hey, Raven. Avoiding my calls already?

Karen tried to keep the smile from forming on her face but failed miserably. How the hell did Brody Cooper get her phone number? Karen's eyes narrowed. Her friend was getting an earful the next time Karen saw her.

I don't answer numbers I don't recognize.

Well, now you know who it is.

Actually, I don't. Karen smirked. Who is this again?

That hurt, Raven. You're a mean girl. Who the hell else calls you Raven?

All the boys.

She responded with an upside down smiley face. As soon as she sent it, Karen groaned. She was *flirting* with Brody Cooper. What the hell did she think she was doing?

Ha! I know that's a lie.

Oh, really? And how do you know that?

Because I talked to my sister. And Sadie. They apparently know all your secrets.

Karen rolled her eyes. Guess she had to add the café owner to the list of people getting an earful.

> Fine. Suppose I do know who this is. What do you want?

Karen watched as the bubbles showed up on her phone. What could he possibly be typing?

> You promised to go out on a date with me. It's time I collected.

> I did no such thing.

> You said maybe. That's the same thing.

> IT IS NOT!

> Shouty caps! Not the shouty caps. I'm really scared now.

Karen rolled her eyes. Damn him for being sarcastically cute. That was her weakness.

> If I agree to go out with you will you leave me alone?

Karen's grip tightened on her phone as she waited for his reply. Damnit to hell. Against her better judgment she really wanted to go on this date. And knew her reply was going to be yes no matter where he planned on taking her. She blamed the jeans. His ass looked amazing in a pair of jeans. And the dimples. God, she was screwed.

> Absolutely not. You're too pretty to be left alone, Raven. So whaddya say? Wanna have some fun?

Karen's hands shook in nervousness as she quickly typed one word.

Sure.

She looked down at her phone, her finger hovering over the send. Should she really do this? As if it had a mind of its own, her thumb hit send, whooshing her message to Brody.

Almost immediately, a smiley face appeared on her screen.

Great! Now you just have to do one thing.

What's that?

Dress for cold weather. It's been ridiculous outside lately.

Okay. When? Friday?

Nope. I'll pick you up in ten.

Ten what?

Ten minutes, silly. Don't worry. If you have to get pretty I'll wait. But I think you're beautiful with no makeup on. Like the first time I saw you in the grocery store.

Ten minutes? Karen's breath hitched. How in the hell did he expect her to be ready in ten minutes? With a sigh, she headed upstairs to dress for the frigid weather outside. Maybe if she didn't put forth any effort and looked a hot mess, Brody Cooper would leave her alone.

But you don't want that to happen, Karen's inner voice said. Karen shook her head, told her inner voice to shut up, and went upstairs to *not* put on makeup.

〜

BRODY KNEW Karen was wracking her brain trying to think of where he might be taking her. Taking him at his word, Karen had indeed dressed for cold weather. Which was good, considering they were supposed to get even more snow and an ever bigger temperature plummet overnight.

One thing about the state where he had lived the majority of his life—the weather was an unpredictable bitch. A snowstorm had blown in overnight and blanketed the town in snow. And since the temperatures had been below freezing for a few days Brody figured the snow would stay.

Brody snuck a peek at Karen, who was sitting as close to the door of his old Chevy truck as possible. It wouldn't have surprised him if she opened the door, jumped out, and ran back to her house. He didn't know if she did it purposefully or not, but Karen did not have one speck of makeup on her face. And he was right. She was just as beautiful as she was with the minimum amount he had seen on her. Maybe more so.

After eating lunch at the café with his sister, Brody had killed time around town until he knew Karen would be home from school. His first instinct was to ask her out for Friday but quickly changed his mind. Something told him if he allowed her to stew on her decision for two days she would have talked herself out of it by the time Friday rolled around. So he came up with something on the fly.

Brody had been trying to think of a place to go in their small town that would impress Karen. While they had been texting back and forth, Brody had thought of the perfect first date. Time was on his side, too, since there were still a couple of hours left until the sun fell below the horizon.

Brody drove slowly through town to get to his spot, a small pond right on the edge of Sophie Cleaver's land. Annie's grandmother had let him walk through the field close to her house all the time as a kid and teen to get to the pond. He knew she only let him because he was Breckin's brother, but he didn't care. The pond was his sanctuary. He would go there when he was having a bad day. To be alone, to help himself manage the loss of his mom. To escape the reality of his life in a small town where he really didn't fit. He had been to his pond more times than he could count, which is why he knew it would be completely iced over and perfect for skating.

They had stopped at his dad's house on the way, Brody discreetly grabbing his and his sister's old ice skates from his dad's shop before heading to their destination. As they got closer to the pond, Karen remarked, "Isn't this where Annie's animal sanctuary is?"

"It is. You know, I haven't been back home since she and Wyatt opened it. I guess I should make a trip."

Karen nodded her agreement. "You really should. It's amazing."

"Do you have a favorite animal?"

"Yep. The yellow python named Banana."

"Seriously?"

"Seriously. Why is that so hard to believe?"

"You're so…well, *pretty* and *dainty* I figured you for the cutesy animal type. Sloths, lemurs, baby bunnies."

"Ew. Sloths. They give me the creeps with their long claws, slow movement, and beady eyes." Karen shuddered.

Brody grinned. "You're cute when you're grossed out, Raven."

Karen wrinkled her nose in response. "So if we're not going to Sophie's Haven," Karen said, referring to Annie's animal sanctuary, "where *are* we going?"

"Right…here," Brody said, pulling up to the edge of the pond and putting his truck in park.

"A pond?"

"A pond."

Karen met his eyes, a question on her face. "Why?"

"Because this…" he said, motioning to the pond in front of them, "is my pond."

"Really?"

He chuckled softly. "No, not really. But it *was* the place I would always go when I was having a hard time with something and needed to think. I spent lots of my teenage years out here, just me and my thoughts, struggles, and dreams."

"Sounds lonely," she said softly.

"Sometimes it really was. It's why I had to leave. Parker, that is. I needed to find myself."

Karen nodded. "I get that."

"Have you ever left a place? To find yourself? New York, maybe?" Brody asked. He didn't figure she would answer but wanted to try anyway.

"Not by choice," she replied softly. "Definitely not by choice."

Brody started to ask another question but before he could, Karen had gotten out of the truck and walked to the edge of the pond. "It's frozen!" she called.

"I know!"

"Then why did you bring me here? I've seen frozen water before."

"But have you *skated* on it?" he asked, holding up the ice skates he had gotten out of his dad's shed.

"I've skated Rock—" she started to say before shaking her head. Brody was pretty sure she was going to say Rockefeller Center but he wasn't going to ruin the day by asking.

"I've skated on ice before. But I'm horrible."

"I haven't done it since I was a teenager. Well, I skated in New York all the time. But I haven't skated in Oklahoma for a while. It doesn't usually get cold enough to freeze the entire pond here. It's a small pond, so I took a chance since it has been so cold recently. Guess we're in luck today," he said, winking her way.

"This is going to be ugly," she muttered.

Karen grabbed Breckin's worn skates from Brody's hands and sat on a log to put them on her feet. Brody followed suit. Within minutes, they were both standing at the edge of the pond looking down at the ice.

"Are you sure this is frozen enough for us to skate on it?" she asked incredulously. "It looks pretty thin."

"It looks the total *opposite* of thin!" He laughed. "Look at how thick that ice is!"

Karen shuddered before taking a tentative step onto the pond. Instead of following, Brody stood still and watched her hobble onto the ice. Her hands were held out at her sides, she was hunched over like an old lady and lifting her feet up and walking instead of *gliding* on the ice. It was quite possibly the cutest thing Brody had ever seen.

"Are you coming?" she asked. "I'm not here for your entertainment."

Brody figured it was time to show off a little. One of his favorite times of year in New York was around Christmas. The tree, skating, all the lights. He took many, many women skating. For some reason, they thought it was romantic so he had become quite the prolific skater through the years. When the women saw him gliding smoothly across the ice, it was almost like they wanted to throw their panties at him right on the rink.

Pushing off, he skated effortlessly toward her and skated ahead of her before spinning in a circle and facing her with a bow.

"Show off," she huffed.

"Come on, Raven. Take my hand and let me teach you a thing or two," he said with a smile, holding out his hand.

With a sigh, she took his hand tentatively in hers. "You better not make me fall, New York."

"Why, Raven, have you given me a nickname?" he asked impishly.

"Don't make me call you something worse," she said. "I may be a teacher, but I know a few cuss words."

"Like what? Meanie? Stupid-head?"

"Hey, I've listened to some Eminem songs. I know how to drop the F bomb with the best of them."

Brody couldn't help but laugh. She was too adorable.

Karen blessed him with one of her rare smiles. The one where her eyes twinkled and she looked like a carefree teenager. He wished he could see it more often.

"I do. Really good," she said, her tongue peeking out of the corner of her mouth in concentration. "You better not let me fall. I don't want to get a concussion. I need my brain to keep my job. Math isn't easy."

"I was surprised when my sister said you teach."

"Why did that surprise you?" she asked, throwing out her arm to steady herself when they took a turn around the southern end of the pond.

"I don't know. I can tell you're smart. You just struck me as an English lover."

"I was an English major in college for a little while," she said with a smile. "But I changed it to math."

"Why?"

"Which would you rather grade? A five page essay or thirty-two algebra problems?"

Brody laughed. "That's some good logic right there. Did you always want to be a teacher?"

Karen shook her head. "No. Not always. I just kind of… fell into it, I guess."

"What did you want to be then?"

The light dimmed in her eyes. "It was so long ago I don't even remember," she said softly.

Brody knew better than to push her. Her hand gripped his harder as they navigated a turn on the ice. "You're doing great," he said with a smile.

"I thought you said you didn't lie."

Brody chuckled. "Fine. You're not the best skater in the world. But you're not the worst, either. Basically, you're a step above atrocious."

Karen started to stick out her tongue at him but she tripped on a chip in the ice and went crashing to the ground. Since Brody was still holding her hand, he followed closely behind, landing on top of her with an *oof.*

"Ouch," she said with a chuckle. "You weigh too much."

"Are you calling me fat, Raven?" he asked, raising his eyebrows.

"No. But you could get off of me instead of staring at my face like a weirdo."

Brody grinned before kissing her on the forehead and rolling onto his back on the ice. "Do you want to keep going? We haven't been skating long."

"I guess so. But next time you have to keep me from falling."

Brody helped Karen to her feet and they slowly made their way across the ice again, hand in hand. They skated until Karen's cheeks and the tip of her nose were a rosy pink and the sun was starting to set. She sniffled before releasing his hand, navigating a *slow* turn on her own.

"Ha! Look at what I did!" she said with a smile.

"Lookin' good, Raven. But your face is pink and you look like you're pretty cold."

"I can't feel my toes...or my fingers," she said with a grin.

"Then let's go. The sun is starting to set, anyway."

"Go where?"

"Back to your place. I was thinking we could order some pizza from Lickety Split and watch a movie."

"What makes you think I want to spend more time with you?"

"Call it a hunch."

Karen sighed. "Fine."

Brody started his truck to warm it up before helping Karen remove her skates. "Let's drop these off by my dad's house before heading to yours."

"How is it? Being back in your childhood home?"

"Weird," he said, backing carefully out of the field and onto the gravel road. "Everything looks the same but it doesn't have any of the noises from growing up."

"Like what?"

"Games on the television. Breckin blaring her loud music as she straightened her hair. Annie and CC storming through the house. Now it's just silent. I don't know what to do with silence from the home I grew up in."

"Does your dad not watch television anymore?"

Brody shook his head. "Don't you know?"

"Know what?"

"He moved in with Griff's mom, Susan. They got married at the courthouse in secret."

Karen grinned. "Isn't it a little odd? Your dad and Griff's mom together while your sister and Griff are getting married?"

"A little? How about a lot!" he replied. "The first day I was home she walked in, called him honey, and *kissed* him. I was shocked."

"I can imagine."

Brody pulled into the driveway of his dad's house and put his truck in park. "Let me throw these in here and then we'll head to your house."

"Okay."

Leaving the truck running, Brody put the skates in their original place before hopping back in the truck. "I think it's gotten even colder since we left the pond. I knew New York temperatures are usually colder than Oklahoma's, but I don't think they can compare to the wind chill."

"No doubt," Karen said. "It took me forever to get used to the change when I moved here."

"From New York?" Brody asked, trying to sound nonchalant.

"Nice try. From somewhere."

"Why so secretive, Raven? Have something to hide?"

It seemed as if Karen hesitated before responding. "No. I just haven't thought about my past in a long time."

"Bad memories?"

This time, she did hesitate before answering. "Too many."

Brody decided not to push his luck. He didn't want this day to end. He was having too much fun. "So what kind of pizza do you like?"

"Hawaiian. Supreme. Pepperoni. Basically any kind."

"I'm a fan of Hawaiian myself. My dad and Breckin didn't like it so I didn't get to eat it much growing up. Now I over-compensate and eat it every chance I get."

Brody grabbed his phone off the dash and handed it to Karen. "Why don't you call it in so we can just pick it up and not have to wait?"

Karen looked up the number to the convenience store before placing his phone against her ear. She ordered a large Hawaiian and an order of garlic cheesy bread.

"Cheesy bread, huh?" he asked as she pressed end.

"It's the best. *Almost* better than their pizza."

"That must be a new item on their menu. They didn't have it when I walked there every day for lunch when I was in school."

"Sometimes I order it instead of a pizza it's so good."

A few minutes later Brody pulled into the store's parking lot. "You want to come in?"

Karen shook her head. "And have people talk even more? No, thank you. I'll just be hiding in the floorboard."

Brody laughed. "Suit yourself. Do you want anything else?"

"Some of their cinnamon almonds."

Brody saluted her before exiting his truck and heading inside. Stomping his boots on the mat in front of the door, Brody opened it, the bell above his head jingling his entrance. To his surprise, Sal Sanders, the owner of the store, was working the register.

"Well, well, well. Look at what the cat drug in," Sal said. "I haven't seen you since you were a scrawny, gawky kid who walked in here for lunch every day. How've you been, Brody?"

Brody walked over to the register and shook Sal's gigantic hand. He had played lineman for the University of Oklahoma in college in the seventies and even spent a couple of years playing for the Cowboys in the NFL. A knee injury, however, had him retiring early. With his earnings playing football, Sal returned to Parker and opened Lickety Split. Now, he owned several of the convenience stores in surrounding towns.

"Not too bad," Brody replied. "How about yourself?"

"I can't complain."

"Why are you working behind the register? I figured since you're the boss you'd just be making the work schedule, not *working* yourself."

Sal waved his hand in the air. "I work every now and then. Susie Mayfield is pregnant and usually works the register this time of day. I didn't want her driving here on the ice with her being 'bout to pop and all. I live two blocks over from the store. Told her I'd cover her shift."

"You've always been a good man, Sal."

"Not a big deal. I don't want a pregnant worker of mine getting in a wreck and causing brain damage to her baby," Sal replied, his ears turning red at Brody's compliment.

"Well, I'm sure Susie appreciates it. Tell her I said hello. We graduated together."

"Will do."

Brody grabbed a bottle of pink Moscato and the cinnamon almonds Karen wanted before asking Sal for his order.

"Wine and pizza, huh? Putting the moves on some lucky lady?"

"Why would they be lucky?" Brody asked.

"All the women in town have been abuzz with news of you being back," Sal replied, waggling his eyebrows. "You sure don't look like you did when you left, all hundred pounds, shaggy hair and nerdy glasses. I think they're taking bets on who's goin' to bag you first. Looks like you already have someone in mind, though."

Brody shook his head. "Nope. I just like a little wine with my pizza."

"Don't tell that to the pretty schoolteacher in your truck," Sal said with a wink. "She might be offended."

Brody rolled his eyes. He should have known the rumor mill would have already been going about his return. Now Karen, who cherished her privacy, was going to be dragged right through the middle of it.

"Don't worry," Sal said. "Your secret is safe with me."

Brody blew a sigh of relief but it was short-lived.

"Besides, Kelda was in here the other day telling Netty Delphino about you two sharing some "smoldering" looks at Thanksgiving." Sal finger-quoted the word smoldering.

"Is nothing private in this town?" Brody groaned.

"You should already know the answer to that, sonny. This ain't the big city where you've been for so long. This here is rumor city. What ain't true is and what's happening tomorrow is already yesterday's news."

IF KAREN HAD TOLD herself when she met him at the grocery store she would be sitting on her couch eating pizza and watching TV with Breckin's brother, she would have laughed her future self out the door. As she glanced out of the corner of her eye, however, she saw him sitting. On her couch. His sock-clad feet were currently propped on the chipped coffee table and his elbows rested on his knees as he stared intently at the screen. He had shucked his boots the minute he walked in her door and had found one of the latest comic books-turned-movie for rent on her satellite. Tom Hardy was currently battling with the alien form, Venom, for possession of Tom's body.

Karen was only halfway watching. Her thoughts were keeping her preoccupied, although she had to admit Mr. Hardy was definite eye candy. She kept going over and over in her mind how hers and Brody's relationship had evolved into him sitting on her couch eating pizza. He had been such a pompous, snarky ass the first time she had met him. In just a short time, however, she had gotten a glimpse of the shy, insecure high school student growing up in a town where he didn't really fit he once was. And damn if it didn't send her ovaries into a tailspin.

As if he could feel Karen staring intently at his profile, Brody turned to her and grinned. "What? You don't like Tom Hardy? I thought everyone with a vagina had thoughts of having his babies."

Karen shrugged. "Never been much for comic books."

Brody grabbed his chest. "Tell me you're kidding."

"'Fraid not."

"That's like a dagger to my heart, Raven. Nerdy teenage me read every comic book known to man."

"Seriously?"

"Seriously."

Karen laughed. "I still can't really picture you as a nerd. Not looking the way you look…now."

She felt her face turn red as the words slipped from her mouth.

"Are you saying you think I'm attractive?" he asked with a grin.

"Brody Cooper, you *know* you're attractive. You don't need a woman to tell you that."

"Maybe I don't want to hear just any woman tell me. Maybe I want it specifically to be *you.* Come on…give nerdy me a break."

Karen rolled her eyes. "Fine. You're attractive."

"How attractive on a scale of one to ten?"

Karen just raised an eyebrow in response.

"Okay. I'll take that raised eyebrow as an eleven," he said, taking a bite of the pizza slice in his hand. "But seriously. What were you thinking just now? Because I know you weren't paying attention to the movie."

"I was just thinking about Christmas break in a couple of weeks," she said. There was no way she was going to tell him she was thinking about him. His ego would be uncontrollable. "The kids have already checked out so it's really pointless to do anything. I'll just have to review it after the New Year."

"You teachers have it easy."

"Excuse me! We do *not* have it easy! I'd like to see you be responsible for fifteen teenagers every hour all day long. Or grading papers until the wee hours of the morning. Or trying to make math fun for kids who think it's pointless because they all have calculators on their smartphones."

Brody shuddered. "No, thank you."

"That's what I thought."

To her surprise, Brody grabbed her calves, swung her legs around and placed her feet in his lap.

"What are you doing?" she asked.

He didn't answer. Instead, he began rubbing the arch of her foot. A groan escaped her lips. She couldn't remember the last time someone had rubbed her feet.

"Does that feel good?"

She couldn't muster anything but an, "Mmmmhmmm."

Brody smiled softly. "Good. Something tells me you don't get pampered near enough."

Karen leaned back on the arm of the couch and closed her eyes. If his hands could work such magic on her feet she couldn't imagine how pleasurable they would feel on her... nope. She willed her mind not to go to a place where Brody's capable hands roamed her body. She was just going to relax and enjoy the foot rub. Karen felt her body melt back into the couch's worn cushions. Forget managing hedge funds or modeling or whatever Brody did in his real life in New York. He could make a living being a personal foot masseuse.

"So what are you going to do with yourself now that you're not working?" she asked, sounding more relaxed than she'd been in years.

"I haven't really thought that far ahead. Maybe babysit Emma?"

"Ha!" Karen said with a chuckle. "That's funny."

"What's so funny about me watching my niece?"

"Your sister *barely* lets your dad watch her and he raised two kids. Why do you think she'd let *you*, New York's bachelor of the year with *no* babysitting experience...well, unless it includes babysitting models...watch her *only* child?"

Karen let out a yelp when Brody grabbed her middle toe

and pulled, its knuckle popping with a loud click. "Ow! What was that for?"

"For saying I babysat models!"

"Well? Didn't you?"

"If I did it was reverse babysitting because it was the most expensive babysitting I ever did," Brody complained.

Karen laughed. "Don't tell me you had something in common with those half-dressed nitwits who walk the runway. I'll be disappointed in you, Brody Cooper. And just when I was starting to think you're not half bad."

It was Brody's turn to laugh. "You're right. I didn't have much in common with them. Except the fact we were all eye candy. And you *know* that's right," he said, waggling his eyebrows. "After all, you *did* say I'm an eleven on a scale of one to ten."

"I did *not* say that! You gave yourself that particul—"

Brody cut off the rest of Karen's statement by pulling her across the couch and onto his lap.

"It's okay, Raven. I think you're an eleven, too. Maybe a twelve when you smile at me instead of frown. Your face lights up and that's all I can think about," he whispered, his mouth inches from hers.

Karen's breath hitched as the smell of the mountains wafted under her nose. Heaven help if he ever left town. She'd have to take up mountain climbing to try and get him off her mind. Brody's lips almost touched hers when she heard a knock on her door.

Brody groaned. "Seriously? Are you expecting company?"

Karen shook her head. "No. No one ever comes over to my house unless it's your sister. And she usually just walks in."

"I have a feeling we're not going to like who is on the other side of the door," he grumbled.

"Why do you say that?"

"Because," he said, pointing to the open blinds on the window by the front door. "I would know that brown hair filled with feathers anywhere."

"Yoohoo! I see that teacher in your lap, Brody Cooper! All the while my titties are freezing and I could break a hip on this ice. Would you like that on your conscience? Open the damn door!"

Karen moved off Brody's lap and headed to the front door. Before she could open it, however, the door flew open and Kelda Vanderburgh came trouncing into Karen's living room. "Well, if I had *known* you didn't lock your door, missy, I woulda just come on in instead of freezing my ass off on your porch. I'm an old lady, ya know. Haven't you ever heard of brittle bone disease? Old people's bones snap like turkey wishbones!"

"What are you doing at my house, Kelda?" Karen asked.

"Why are you being rude, *Karen?*"

Karen stared at Brody, but he just raised his eyebrows and shrugged his shoulders. She sighed. "I'm sorry, Kelda. I wasn't trying to be rude. I just know the roads are bad and it is dark and...isn't your license revoked?"

Kelda rolled her eyes and shook her head, the little bells placed in her green hair jingling at the movement. "Dale Matthews is such a fuddy duddy. He thinks he can keep me down! Nobody can keep *this* lady down! Down with the *man* is what I say!"

Karen could see Brody trying to hide his smile behind his hand. At this point, Karen knew he was going to be no help. All she wanted to do was try to get the human tornado that was the ninety-two-year-old in front of her out the door. "Okay, okay. Down with the man. Again, can we help you with something, Kelda?"

Kelda reached in her purse and pulled out a bright red piece of paper. "I was delivering a party invitation. I like to hand deliver mine instead of putting them in the mail. Gives it a more personal touch, if you know what I'm saying."

Karen knew that Kelda probably decided to hand-deliver Karen's invitation to whatever was announced on the red paper as soon as she saw Brody's truck in Karen's driveway. "What is it, Kelda?"

"Well, *you're* the teacher. I assume you can read," Kelda said, waving her hand at Karen as she started walking around the living room. "Huh. How long have you lived in our town? Seven years? It looks like you just moved in or are 'bout to head out in the middle of the night. You running from the law? In witness protection? I can keep a secret, ya know."

Karen almost choked on...well, on *air*...at Kelda's words. "Nope. None of that," she said with a cough. Brody raised his eyebrows her way. She pretended she didn't see.

Karen looked down at the paper. A picture of a cat sitting in a litter box was in the top right of the page, *There's litter on the floor after the potty,* written underneath. Karen chuckled. She had to admit it was a funny play on Taylor Swift's latest song.

"Burty and I are hosting a New Year's Eve party at the senior citizens'," Kelda said.

"Kelda, we haven't even had Christmas yet. Isn't it too early to be sending invitations to a New Year's party?" Brody asked.

To Karen's shock and amazement, Kelda slapped him on the back of the head. "Don't backtalk your elders, Brody Cooper. I'm sending the invitations *now* so people don't have a reason to back out. Plenty of advanced notice. Duh."

It was Karen's turn to hide a smile behind her hand at the look on Brody's face. "Who all is going, Kelda?" she asked.

Kelda looked at Karen like she had horns on her head. "Who's going? Who's *going*? I can't believe you're asking me that!"

"It's a valid question," Brody said, this time ducking quick enough to dodge another slap to his head.

"Everyone! Everyone is comin'! It's the talk of the town, I'm telling ya. Me and Burty know how to throw a party, that's for sure! I'll take it as a personal affront if you don't come."

Karen sighed. She had to go. Otherwise, Kelda would make Karen's life a living hell. "I'll be there."

Kelda grinned like the cat who ate the canary. "Good deal. But you can't come without a date. It says so right on the invitation."

Karen hadn't read all the details. Sure enough, in fine print at the bottom of the paper it stated, *If you're single, you can't mingle. This party is for lovers only.*

"Isn't that kind of discriminatory, Kelda?" Brody asked. "What if a single person *wants* to come?"

"And see all the couples dancin' and makin' out? That's pretty pathetic if you ask me," she muttered. "Besides, I don't know why y'all are complainin'. You're lookin' at your date right now."

Brody raised one eyebrow and grinned Karen's way. "Whaddya say, Raven? Want to be my date to the…"

"New Year's Cat's Meow," Karen deadpanned the name of the party.

"Of course. Why wouldn't it be?" Brody said with a grin.

"Kelda!" Karen heard an old man's voice yell from her front porch. "What in tarnation are you doing? All you said was you were gonna deliver the invitation and try to catch them doin' the nasty!"

Kelda let out a sigh and rolled her eyes. "Forgive my Burty. He doesn't just have diarrhea of the ass…he's got it of the mouth, too."

Before Karen or Brody could reply, Kelda had stomped to Karen's front door and opened it wide. Burt was standing in the doorframe, the tips of his ears and nose a bright red. "I'm freezing my ass off in the car! Hurry up, woman!"

"Why'd you turn it off, dummy? Don't you know it's like, ten degrees outside? I'm not takin' care of you if you fall and break a hip or get hypothermia."

Burt rolled his eyes. "You *took* the keys!"

Kelda reached into her purple coat's pocket and pulled out a keychain with more cat baubles on it than actual keys.

"Huh. What do you know? I guess I did. Force of habit, honey bun. Let's let them get back to what they were doing."

"Did you catch them doing the nasty?" Burt asked.

"No!" Karen yelled.

"Unfortunately not," Brody said at the same time.

"Almost," Kelda replied. "If I had been a minute later I would've seen some good action!"

Karen put her head in her hands. She didn't know how Breckin survived.

"You kids have fun now. Don't do anything we wouldn't do!" Burt called.

Kelda stopped at the threshold of the door. "Oh! I almost forgot. The even finer print said there's a fifty dollar cover charge for each couple. Tata!"

"Fifty dollars to attend a party?" Brody asked.

"We're old and on old people assistance," Kelda said. "We don't have disposable funds and I gotta raise the money to pay for my wedding *some* way! I love her and all, but Breckin is *not* going to outshine me on my special day."

With a slam of the front door, Kelda and Burt were gone. Brody sighed. "Well, I guess there's only one thing we can do now."

"Not go?" Karen said hopefully.

"Nope."

"Then what?"

"Call my sister and give her the good news."

CHAPTER 7

"*P*lease tell me my brother didn't screw things up royally enough that you don't want to come to my house for Christmas?"

Karen and Breckin were sitting in the teacher's lounge sharing a pizza from Lickety Split for lunch. Karen had twenty minutes to eat before her next class. It was nice of her friend to drop by and eat with her. Karen had gotten lonely in the time Breckin had been gone on maternity leave.

"Why are you here again?" Karen asked, completely ignoring her friend's question. "You're not supposed to be back until *after* Christmas break, silly. Go be with your kid."

Breckin waved her slice of pizza at Karen. "She's fine. She's at the bar with her daddy."

Karen chuckled. "That sounds so wrong. You have a baby. In a bar."

Breckin laughed. "*Sweet Home Alabama!* I love that movie!"

"Me, too."

"Don't think I don't notice you trying to change the subject," Breckin said, taking a bite of her pizza. "So? You? Christmas? My house?"

Karen rolled her eyes. "Yes, I'm still planning on coming to Christmas. I even bought all the Christmas presents already. Except Brody. I have no clue what to get him."

Breckin squealed in glee. "Yay! I'm so glad you're coming! I wish I had known you didn't do anything for the holidays all this time. I would have invited you way sooner."

Karen took a bite of her pizza. "I've been fine."

"Do you not have family you go see?" Breckin asked.

"No."

"Oh, Kare," Breckin said, a trace of sadness in her voice. "Why did you never say anything?"

"Because I said I was fine. Now, instead of feeling sorry for me why don't you go ahead and ask me how the date went already? I know you've been dying to."

Breckin grinned. "Finally! I didn't want to push you but I *really* wanted to know!"

"Why didn't you just ask your brother?"

"Because he would probably tell me how amazing it was...even if it wasn't. You know how it is. The male ego and all that. So...how was it?"

Karen couldn't keep the smile from forming on her face. "It was...nice."

"That smile makes it seem like it was more than nice."

Karen shrugged her shoulders. "Your brother is...well... he's not what I expected."

"Yeah, he became pretty pompous after living in New York for a while and quit coming home. But the longer he's been back the more of the older Brody is showing himself. I'm glad you guys had a good time. What did you do?"

"Well, he took me ice skating at some pond—"

"*Sophie's* pond?" Breckin screeched.

Karen raised her eyebrows. "Wow. That's some reaction."

"You don't understand. That's *Brody's* pond. He didn't think we knew about it...that he was being super secretive.

But my dad and I always knew he went there to think. My brother has always been an old soul."

Breckin took another bite of her pizza. "You know, I don't really remember my mom. I was really young when she died. But Brody does. So moving here…growing up without a mom…was really hard on him. Sophie, Annie's grandma, would let him go to the pond. I think she knew he needed a place. Just for him."

"I know. He told me," Karen said, taking her empty plate and Breckin's and throwing them in the trash.

"He told you?" Breckin said, her eyes wide. "Man, he's got it bad."

"What are you talking about?"

"He didn't even tell *me* about that pond, Karen. But he *took* you to it. And that, my friend, is a big deal."

Karen shook her head. "We're just having…I don't know. We just had fun. That's all it was."

"Whatever you have to tell yourself, Karen."

Karen rolled her eyes and ignored her friend's comment. "So, are you going to help me out?"

"With what?"

"I have no clue what to get your brother. For Christmas. I got something for everyone else but I didn't even know he was your brother when I went shopping and now I have to get him something."

Breckin grinned. "Get him something comic book related."

"Even now? But he's a grown man."

"He may be grown but he still geeks out at anything having to do with Marvel characters. Trust me."

"I saw an Iron Man coffee mug at Cure All when I was buying everyone else's presents. Would that work?"

"Uh…yeah. I'm pretty sure my brother has coffee running through his veins instead of actual blood. He'll be even more smitten than he already is."

"He's not smitten!" Karen protested.

"Oh, really? Then why is he standing in the doorway looking at you like you're the last piece of his favorite birthday cake?"

Karen's eyes widened at her friend's words. *Surely* Brody didn't have the balls to show up at school to talk to her *again.* All the commotion he had caused when he walked into her classroom last time had just died down. She turned in her chair and swore under her breath.

There the bastard was...wearing an NYU hoodie, a pair of navy blue sweats that hugged his thighs in *all* the right places and...those glasses. Again.

"What are you doing here, New York?" she said through clenched teeth. "Did you not cause *enough* commotion last time you were here? The kids just stopped texting about it!"

"Aw, you called me New York," he said, sitting in the chair beside her. "You must really like me."

Karen rolled her eyes. She started to reply but before she could, Breckin jumped out of her chair and headed toward the door. "I'd love to stay and chat with you, big brother, but I have a baby. In a bar. I need to go check on her."

"Breckin, you better not..." Karen's words were met with a finger wave from her friend as she walked out the door.

"You really need to leave," she said, trying to put some distance between herself and the delicious man sitting in the chair beside her. "I'm serious, Brody."

"You know what I'm serious about, Raven?"

Brody's cologne wafted under her nose and she could feel her lady parts liquefying in response. Her high school libido response to him was ridiculous. Unable to form coherent words, she just shook her head.

"I'm serious about the fact that I can't get you out of my

head. And ever since that almost kiss we had on your couch yesterday all I want to do is kiss those beautiful lips of yours."

"We didn't almost kiss," she breathed. "You just got all up in my personal bubble without my permission."

Brody scooted his chair close enough to hers that their thighs were touching, sending heat up her thigh straight to her vajayjay. "Oh, Raven, but we did. And it would have been amazing."

Brody leaned toward her, his lips, again, just a breath away from hers. All of a sudden, the bell for class rang. A startled Karen jumped off her chair. "Well, that's the bell. Gotta go…you know…teach the kids and everything."

Karen turned to leave and groaned. Several of the cheerleaders were standing in the doorway of the teacher's lounge, their phones out and focused on Brody and Karen.

"Hey, Ms. Posey," one of them said innocently. "Whatcha doing?"

"We're not doing…I mean *I'm* not doing anything," Karen responded. "Mr. Cooper here was just…uh…just looking for his sister."

"Doesn't he know she's not here because she had a *baby?*" the cheerleader asked. For the life of her Karen couldn't remember the girl's name. Damn Brody Cooper for rendering her brain useless.

"He does. He just forgot. But now he's leaving. Isn't that right, Mr. Cooper?" she asked, turning toward Brody.

"I actually came to see Ms. Posey," he said with a cocky smirk. "I don't know why she thinks I wanted to see my sister."

If looks could kill, Karen was pretty sure he'd be on the floor dead because…lord have mercy. The looks those cheerleaders were giving the two of them had Karen shaking her head. She was definitely going to be the talk of the halls until Christmas break.

All the cheerleaders giggled as their fingers flew over their phone screens. Yep. He was definitely dead.

"Girls, you better get to class. You're going to be late," she said, shooing them out of the doorway. She heard their laughter echoing all the way down the hall.

"I can't believe you told them that!" she said, turning to Brody and leveling him with what she thought was her best glare. "They're never going to settle down now. The days leading up to Christmas break are going to be awful!"

To her horror, Brody walked up to her until their bodies were touching chest to chest. She gasped when he tucked a strand of her hair behind her ear. Leaning down, he whispered, "If I remember correctly, you're the one who told me the kids have already checked out, anyway."

Nibbling on her ear, Brody breathed her in and sighed. Placing his forehead on hers, he looked her dead in the eyes. "What are you doing to me, Raven?"

As if on cue, the last bell rang. She was officially late for class. "I have to go," she managed to say as she pushed away from him. "I'm late for class. And you…"

"Yeah? And me what?" Brody asked with a grin.

Karen shook finger at him. "You…don't come back here again. Or I'll put you in detention."

"Is that a promise?"

Karen rolled her eyes but couldn't help the smile from creeping on her face. Damn Brody Cooper. He was trouble with a capital T.

~

"So I hear you've been putting the moves on the pretty teacher in town."

Brody and his dad were sitting at a back booth in Griff's bar sharing a huge plate of nachos. His dad had Emma, who was playing with some sort of colorful toy, on his lap. Breckin was right. She did indeed have a baby in a bar just like in *Sweet Home, Alabama.* Brody would never admit it to anyone but he had always liked that movie. Reese Witherspoon was a cutie.

"Why do you think I'm putting the moves on Karen?" Brody asked, taking a nacho off the plate and popping it in his mouth with a crunch.

"Because Kelda has a poll going to see if you two have already slept together. And last time I was in Nailed It Max asked me if you two were getting hitched."

Brody choked on the chip he was chewing. Taking a large pull on his beer, he hit his chest and tried to dislodge the chip from his throat. "Why in the hell would he ask you that?"

His dad shrugged his shoulders. "I don't know. Maybe because Kelda posted a picture of you two on one of her social media pages that had you guys up close and personal on Karen's couch."

"How do you know it was Karen's couch?"

"Because it wasn't my couch," his dad said, grabbing a nacho off the plate. "So? What's the deal? She's a nice girl. I don't want you and your...well...*wayward* ways...to cause problems between Breckin and one of her best friends."

Brody rolled his eyes. "What the hell is that supposed to mean, Dad?"

Brody laughed when his dad covered Emma's ears with his hands. "Don't cuss in front of your niece!"

"Dad! Seriously? She's three months old. What could she possibly understand yet?"

"I don't know, but I don't want your sister to blame me when Emma's first word is hell. She's totally put a ban on cursing in her house so she won't blame Griffin."

"If Emma's first word is hell, Dad, I'll take complete blame for it."

"I'm holding you to that."

"Holding him to what?" Griffin walked up to their table, picked up his daughter and held her above his head, laughing with Emma gurgled a smile.

"Holding him to the promise he will admit he was the one to say hell in front of Emma if it's her first word."

Griffin laughed. "I think he's safe for now. We have a while until she says her first word. Unless she's a baby genius."

Brody's dad grinned. "She's pretty smart."

Brody chuckled to himself. His little niece, in her three short months of life, had already managed to wrap the two most manly men Brody knew around her tiny little finger.

"So what is the deal with you and Karen?" Griffin asked. "I've seen all my meemaw's posts about you two."

"Oh, my god. Your meemaw is the nosiest person on the face of the planet," Brody grumbled. "I'm pretty sure she took pictures of us through Karen's blinds."

"She totally did," Griff agreed. "You can see the lines of the blinds in the pictures."

"Can't the police chief do something about her? Throw her in jail for a night or something for invasion of privacy?"

"Would *you* want to be the cop who had to put up with my meemaw in jail? Even for a night?"

"You have a point."

"Dale just lets her do what she wants and hopes too many people don't get offended," Griffin said. "I can't wait for the day when she can't drive."

"Didn't Dale revoke her license some time ago?" Brody's dad asked.

Griff snorted. "Like she listened."

Brody shook his head. He felt sorry for Griffin. He didn't know what he would do if he had a grandma like Kelda. Probably crawl in a hole and become a hermit until she died.

"Seriously, though. What are you doing with Karen? I'm curious," Griff asked.

"Don't act like my sister didn't put you up to asking just to see if I would tell you anything different than I told her."

Griffin grinned. "You know your sister too well."

"I don't know. We're having fun, I guess. She's fun to be around. And beautiful. But definitely has some walls up."

"That she does. Even Breckin doesn't know her story. And I'm pretty sure if you found out before her, my soon-to-be wife would be greatly offended."

"Then if I do find out before her I'll definitely keep it a secret. At least until Karen spills to my sister."

"I'm glad you're back, Brody. For your sister and your dad. They've missed you."

Brody's dad held up his beer bottle in agreement. "That we have. I honestly didn't know if you'd ever come back home."

His dad's words bothered Brody more than he cared to admit. In his effort to escape everything that had caused him grief as a teenager, he really had abandoned his family. For the first time since he left New York, Brody was glad he had been fired or forced to take a leave of absence or whatever it was that happened to him. He really didn't know. And ironically, he didn't much care, either.

"Give me that baby," he said, taking Emma from her dad and smiling at her. "If her first word is going to be a cuss word and I have to take the blame for it I'm going to teach her the good ones."

CHAPTER 8

*K*aren took a deep breath before walking through the door of her best friend's house. She didn't know why she was nervous. She had been here hundreds of times before. But knowing Brody Cooper was behind that door had her stomach aflutter.

Brody had made himself scarce ever since he showed up at school for the second time and the cheerleaders had caught them together in the teacher's lounge. Karen didn't know what she did or didn't do, but she hated the fact it bothered her he hadn't come back. And then she kicked herself for caring because she was the one who *told* him not to come back. Ugh. She was even annoying herself.

But now here she was. A week and a half without Brody Cooper in her life had come and gone and she had survived. Now she was about to see him for Christmas at her best friend's house. Just as she started to open the door, it swung open wide. And lo and behold, there was the guy she was obsessing over, looking ridiculously good in a cream sweater that brought out the color of his amber eyes and enhanced his olive skin.

"Well, hey there, Raven. Can I help you with those presents?"

Before Karen could even answer, Brody took all of Karen's packages out of her hands and headed in the house. With a sigh, Karen followed. She had a feeling Breckin's family, most importantly, Kelda, would be watching her and Brody's every move.

"Get yourself together, Karen," she muttered to herself.

"What was that?" Brody asked.

"Nothing."

"It didn't sound like nothing," he said with a grin, placing Karen's presents under the large Christmas tree Breckin had placed in front of her living room window.

"Why haven't you called, huh? Or even tried to come around?" The words slipped from Karen's lips. Ugh…so much for getting herself together.

To her annoyance, Brody smiled in the way only Brody Cooper could. The smile that could make her heart skip a beat.

"If I remember correctly, did you or did you *not* tell me *not* to come back to the school?" he asked with a wink.

"I did. But…" Karen paused.

"But what?"

"I didn't think you'd listen to me," she said, hiding her eyes behind her hands.

Brody chuckled. "Just like a woman," he whispered.

"And what is *that* supposed to mean?" she asked, holding her breath as he totally invaded her personal space.

"It means you're hot, you're cold. I picked up my phone to text or call you a hundred times in the week I haven't seen you but I didn't want you to get mad at me. One minute you tell me to leave and then, when I do, you get mad and want to know why I quit coming around. What's up with that, Raven? Why can't you just admit you want me?"

"I didn't say I was mad. I just asked why you didn't come around or where you've been."

"The face you're making says you're mad."

Karen rolled her eyes. "I'm not mad."

Brody inched even closer until they were chest to chest. Leaning down, he whispered in her ear, "Prove it."

Before Karen could answer, the front door flew open and the tornado that was Kelda came barreling in the house.

"It's colder than a witch's tit out there!" she yelled. "Hot damn! I'm not made for this weather. I can't even feel my doodah. I need to move to the beach."

"Why don't you quit your grumblin' already." Kelda's fiancé followed closely behind carrying a laundry basket filled with presents. "It was hotter than hell in the car. You can't be *that* cold. You just walked from the car to inside."

"Don't you be tellin' me what I can and can't feel, Burt Gallagher!" Kelda hollered. "I'm cold and that's that. I don't tell *you* when you stink up the entire house with all your big, stinky turds, do I? No, I don't. Because that's not polite. And I'm a lady."

Brody snorted in laughter. Kelda turned and shot daggers his way. "What's so funny there, mister? Did you snort because you don't think I'm a lady?"

"I think nothing of the sort," Brody said, clearing his throat. "I…uh…I sucked a piece of Karen's hair up my nostril. Her hair smells *really* good. You should smell it."

Karen stared at him in horror. Because she knew Kelda had absolutely no boundaries whatsoever. She wouldn't blink an eye at sniffing Karen's hair. Kelda marched over to Karen and pulled on Karen's arm until her hair was within smelling-distance of Kelda's nose. The old woman inhaled loudly.

"Well, it's not Suave coconut, but I guess it's all right," Kelda said, letting go of Karen's arm. "You probably pay too much for that expensive shit when you could get the ninety-nine cent bottle of Suave that works just as well, missy."

Karen shook her head. "I'll make note of that, Kelda. Thank you."

"Where's my great grand-baby? I haven't seen her for nearly a week. Breckin! Are you hiding that baby from me?" And as quickly as she arrived, Kelda was gone. Karen watched her walk to the back of Breckin's house, the Christmas bells and red mini ornaments jingling in her Christmas tree green hair, probably to yell at Breckin for something...or to steal her baby.

Karen turned to Brody. "I can't believe you *told* her that!" she muttered. "That woman has no concept of personal space. And I like my personal space!"

Brody quickly moved right into her personal space and smiled. "You don't seem bothered when I enter your personal space, Raven. Why is that?"

"Would you two move outta the way?" Burt pushed between Karen and Brody with a huff. "First, you didn't offer to help an old man by taking this basket off my hands. Now, you're right in the way of where they need to go. What if I had collapsed from a heart attack because of all the effort it took holding up these presents, huh? All you millennials are damn disrespectful."

"But we're not millen—" Karen began but Brody just shook his head. Of course it wouldn't be smart to argue with a man as old as Methuselah. She'd rather bash her head into the fireplace.

"So sorry, Burt," Brody said. "That was really inconsiderate of us."

Burt stared at both of them before giving a *hmpf* of agreement. "You're damn right it was. So, tell me. Have you two done it yet? I'm tired of Kelda trying to catch you in the act. It's exhausting enough trying to keep up with the woman in the sack. Now I gotta try to keep up with *her* and while she's trying to catch *you* in the sack! So next time you do it, do this guy a favor and give me a call beforehand."

"Oh, we're not doi—" Karen began but was interrupted.

"Yeah, yeah, yeah. Of course you're not, girly. A girl who looks like you and a guy who looks like him, both at the peak part of your sexual lives? Why in the hell would you want to pleasure each other? Not buying what you're selling."

Karen could feel herself turning red all the way to the tips of her ears. She was doomed.

Just then, Burt let out a fart loud enough to rattle the front windows. Karen couldn't help it. She laughed out loud.

"We'll see if you're laughing when you're my age and have to eat that she-devil's cooking," Burt said, leveling her with a glare. "Get outta my way. I gotta make a pit stop."

Karen could hear him muttering something about Kelda and her chili on his way. Turning, she saw Brody leaning against the wall, staring at her intently. Karen's breath hitched for the millionth time in the short while she had been at Breckin's house. If she didn't find a way to stop that she was going to hyperventilate.

"Why do you keep staring at me?" she asked him. "It's weirding me out."

"Because you're breathtaking."

Karen rolled her eyes. "Hardly."

Brody took his hand and ran it through her hair. Despite herself, she sighed.

"Very," he said, his thumb caressing her cheek. "I tried to stay away from you, Raven. Just like you wanted me to. I was trying to be good. But…shit. Look at you. I don't know how I'm going to be able to keep my hands off you."

Karen pulled away from his touch. "Well, you're going to have to."

"Why is that?"

"Because I don't want to be on all of Kelda's social media pages tomorrow morning. You know her laser beams are going to be focused on us the entire night."

"Is that such a bad thing?" he asked with a smirk.

"Yes," she said. Too bad her internal demon disagreed.

BRODY COULDN'T KEEP his eyes off Karen the entire night. He did as she wished and tried to stay away from her as best as he could but damn…it took a lot of effort. All he wanted to do was run his fingers through her silken hair. Smell the faint traces of citrus and honey that wafted off her skin. Make her smile.

Even though she told him to keep his distance, he had managed to snag little moments with her through the evening. Grabbing her hand when he walked by the table laden with food. Playing footsie under the table with her when they were eating. Tugging on the end of her hair when he thought no one was looking. He felt like he was in junior high again.

When she had told him to leave her alone the second time he had visited her at the school he had taken her at her word. Despite her opening up to him, he knew Karen had secrets she wasn't ready to share. The last thing he wanted to do was scare her off or be accused of playing her by his sister or the nosy café owner. Besides, he had things he had to figure out about his job or lack thereof.

Jax was correct about one thing. No one at the company knew he was basically fired. They all thought he had simply taken some time off. Which, to Brody, meant all hope wasn't lost about salvaging his job. He'd heard through the gossip grapevine via Jax that Sebastian had lost even more money than he had but was still working. That boded well for him.

He already had some feelers out about the next step in the process. Now he was just waiting.

But currently the last thing on his mind was work because he was sitting next to Karen on the fireplace. The exact same place they first sat together on Thanksgiving Day, in fact. And just like that day, Brody made sure to be close enough that his thigh was touching hers.

"Why are you sitting so close to me?" she said through her teeth while avoiding eye contact. "I told you we should keep our distance."

"*You* said that. *I*, however, did not agree. And look, no one is even paying attention to us."

Brody looked around the room. Kelda was sitting on the couch, arms crossed over her chest and a frown on her face. Burt was sitting beside her, looking equally as grumpy. Griff was perched in his recliner and Susan and his dad were cuddled up on the opposite end of the couch. So. Weird. He didn't think that was something he'd ever get used to seeing.

His sister walked around the corner. "Anyone ready to play *Taboo*?"

Karen stood up so fast her forehead almost smashed into his. "I'm ready!" she yelled at Breckin, who was standing in the middle of the room, holding Emma.

"Might as well," Kelda grumped. "As long as I don't have to be partners with the shitter."

Brody held back a laugh. Burt had to run out of the dining room during dinner to...in his words, have a *sit down*. Kelda took that time to announce to the entire room the problems Burt was still having with his digestive tract. Only she didn't use tact to describe it. Brody was pretty sure no one took another bite of food the rest of the night.

"Kelda, you—" Burt began.

"Sounds great!" Breckin said, interrupting another squabble in the making. "Let's just play girls against boys.

That way, everyone who is sitting by each other can make sure the other person doesn't say any of the buzzwords."

Burt pulled a glasses case out of the front pocket of his shirt. Unsnapping it, he pulled out a pair of hot pink and lime green polka-dotted frames.

"Nice glasses, Burt," Griff said with a grin.

Burt shot Griff the bird. "Kiss my hairy ass, beard boy. They were the only pair the pharmacy had in my prescription. Kelda's devil cat, Diablo, got ahold of my other pair and scratched the lenses all up."

"That cat isn't dead yet?" Brody whispered to Karen. "It was alive when I was in Parker. That thing has to be nearly twenty-five years old."

"I think it's holding on by sheer will alone. Its sole purpose in life is to torment others. Kind of like its owner, now that I think about it."

Brody laughed. "Look at you, cracking a joke. You *do* have a sense of humor."

He was granted a small smile. "Don't get used to it."

Breckin placed Emma in a turquoise swing next to Griff's chair. "Griff and I will go first."

"No, *I* want to go first!" Kelda said. "I'm the oldest. Haven't you been taught to respect your elders?"

Breckin sighed. "Fine, Kelda. You can go first." She got out the cards and placed them in the holder before handing it to Kelda and the buzzer to Burt.

"Do you know the rules?" she asked.

"Of course I know the rules," Kelda said. "I'm not an idiot."

"Okay, then. Give us some good clues, Kelda. Annnddd…go!"

Kelda flipped the first card over. "Oh! This one is easy. You make it out of snow."

Burt pressed the buzzer right in Kelda's ear. "Nope!"

"What? I didn't say one of the bottom words, ass wipe!"

"But you said snow, *idiot!*" Burt retorted back. "The word is snowball. You can't say part of the damned word!"

Kelda threw the card on the ground before flipping the next card over. "Fine! Oh! This one! I was just talking about it earlier. It was what Burt was doing while he was blowing it up in the bathroom!"

"A crossword!" Breckin yelled.

"Always about the toilet," Burt grumbled. "Last time I'm trusting you with any of my bowel movement secrets."

Kelda gave her a thumbs up and flipped the next card. "Ah! It comes in apple, blackberry, peach. It's sweet and has a crust. It's not pie."

"Cobbler!" Susan said with enthusiasm.

"Yes!" Kelda cried.

"No!" Burt said, buzzing the buzzer in Kelda's face.

"What do you mean, no?"

"I told you to get a pair of glasses, too," Burt said. "It said *clobber,* not cobbler."

Kelda took the glasses off Burt's face and held the card up. "Well, what do you know? You're right. It's about time that happened. I'm tired of being the only one ever right in this relationship."

"Time!" Griff called, holding up the timer. "No more clues."

Kelda pulled the glasses off her face and threw them at Burt. "You're such a cheating McCheater Face, Burt Gallagher!"

"How the hell did *I* cheat? I can't help it your verbiage isn't as large as mine! You should do more crosswords. Maybe then you wouldn't *suck!*"

"*Okay!* Time for Burt to give the clues!" Breckin said, taking the card holder from Kelda. "Ready to give the clues, Burt?"

"I think I need a break," Burt said. "I gotta go to the bath-room. Y'all can come back to me when I get back."

"Are you takin' your phone? Because if you are, I know you'll be playing your crossword and taking a shit. Just know I'm not rubbing your feet if they go numb!" Kelda yelled at him.

"At least I know the difference between clobber and cobbler," Burt muttered.

"Can you believe him?" Kelda asked, pointing with her thumb toward the bathroom. "You agree with me, don't ya? He's nothing but a cheater."

Everyone else in the room gave a series of unrecognizable words and nods of their heads. Anything to appease the crazy ninety-something-year-old woman.

"Aren't you glad you didn't stay home?" Brody asked Karen. "You'd be sitting in the quiet, eating all by yourself watching Hallmark Christmas movies."

"I just love how you think you know me," she said. "It's cute."

"You think I'm cute, Raven? Nice to know you're finally being honest."

Apparently forgetting her rule, Karen patted his cheek. Brody started at the zing of electricity he felt as her hand touched his face. He was immune to zings. Or so he thought. If one touch on his face from this woman could make him feel this way, he could only imagine how good it would feel with her hands *all* over his body. Damnit to hell. He didn't care what she wanted. Some way, he had to convince this woman sitting beside him how good of an idea it would be to touch *all* his parts.

"Just you wait. I'll worm my way under your skin, Raven. It's inevitable."

"Prepare for failure, Brody Cooper. I've told you it's not a good idea. The sooner you get that through your head, the better."

She rolled her eyes before smiling. "We shall see."

"Yes, we shall." Brody returned her smile. He had always loved a challenge.

CHAPTER 9

*K*aren let out a sigh of relief when the game playing part of the night was finished. She usually enjoyed game night at Breckin and Griff's. She even managed to have fun when Breckin had a girls' night with Annie and CC. But game night with Kelda was too much.

After arguing about *Taboo*, Kelda and Burt got into it when he couldn't guess her clues for donut and worm on *Guesstures*. About half an hour ago, Burt told Kelda she was giving him the stress runs and made another beeline for the bathroom. No one had seen him since. He had either fallen in the toilet, escaped out the window, become engrossed in his latest crossword, or fallen asleep. Maybe even died. Whatever the case, Karen didn't really care. Kelda was quiet for the first time that night.

What she *did* care about, however, was the fact Breckin's brother had been attached to her side all night long. He was like the annoying little brother she never had. Although the thoughts running through her head about him were definitely *not* brotherly at all.

He constantly found ways to touch her, catching her off

guard every. Damn. Time. A brush of the hair out of her eyes. A hand placed gently on her lower back as she walked into the kitchen to get something to eat. Almost like he was marking her as his. Which was a ridiculous notion, because she *told* him they needed to keep their distance.

Karen rolled her eyes and let out a sigh. At least it was only for two days. Tonight and tomorrow on Christmas day. Then she could avoid him like the plague...like he had done to her when she...well, when she told him to leave her alone. Heck, he'd probably get tired of Parker and run back to New York before the New Year. To canoodle with all the models she knew were probably always perched on his arm.

Of all the places the damn man would live, it had to be New York City. Karen counted her blessings New York was the biggest city in the United States. Surely he didn't know who she was. He couldn't possibly. Still, the thought he would figure it out eventually set her stomach rolling. It couldn't happen. Not after all these years. She was finally settled.

"Is everyone ready to play *Dirty Santa?*" Griff asked. Breckin had stepped out to put Emma to bed. Her eyelids had drooped about an hour before as Karen was rocking and humming gently to her. Even so, she continued to hold the precious baby in her arms until her right one fell asleep. Then she reluctantly gave Emma back to her momma. Breckin had grinned down at her child, sending a ping of sadness through Karen's heart. The look reminded her too much of her past.

"Aren't we going to wait on my Burty?" Kelda asked. "We can't start without him."

"Do *you* want to be the one to interrupt...whatever he's doing in my bathroom?" Griff asked.

Kelda shrugged. "Nothin' I've never seen...or smelled...before."

Griff shuddered and rolled his eyes. "Fine. Be my guest, Meemaw."

With an oof, Kelda pushed herself off the couch and sauntered down the hallway. It was the first time Karen noticed the old woman's shirt. How she had missed it before, she had no clue. Maybe because she was so distracted by the nuisance sitting beside her. Kelda's sweater was bright purple with silver strands woven throughout. On the front was a cat's body with the face of the kid from *Home Alone.* The cat-kid was wearing a Santa hat with the words, *Merry Christmas Ya Filthy Animal,* emblazoned on the front.

"Just now noticing her sweater, huh?" Brody asked, grinning at her as he popped a purple grape in his mouth. "Where does she even *get* those things?"

"I have no clue. But there can't be many people in the world who would want to wear that hideous thing."

"It would totally win my office's ugly sweater contest if I were to snatch it from her."

"You wouldn't live to see—" Karen paused.

"See what?"

"I'm trying to figure out your age."

"Thirty-six."

"You're closer to forty now, mister."

Brody shrugged his shoulders before popping another grape in his mouth. "Eh. Age is just a number. And let me tell you, Raven, I may be thirty-six, but I have the stamina of an eighteen year old."

Karen rolled her eyes. "You are insufferable."

"Admit it. You're picturing it now. You. Me. Together. Don't think we wouldn't be anything other than amazing."

Karen hated him. Hated him because he was totally, absolutely, undoubtedly correct.

"Don't worry, Karen. You don't have to answer. Your face says it all." Brody got up. "I guess I better help my brother-in-law get everything ready for *Dirty Santa*. Just so you know, I don't hold back. I steal presents. I play dirty. No one is safe with me. No matter how cute she might be."

"I'll be sure to tell Kelda you said that."

Karen watched Brody walk away, now hating herself for staring at his delicious backside. He really was a beautiful man.

"I've seen you eyeing my brother all night." Karen started as Breckin plopped down beside her on the fireplace. "Funny. Out of all the men I thought would finally catch your eye, I didn't think for one second it would be my brother. Of course, I never thought you would ever meet him, either, so..."

"I haven't been *eyeing* him," Karen huffed. "I've been *trying* to get him away from me."

Breckin looked at her pointedly. "Sure you have. Just be careful. I saw Kelda staring over at you two for quite some time. If you don't want to be the talk of the elderly rumor mill of Parker the day after Christmas, I'd avert my eyes more often than not."

Karen sighed. "Duly noted."

"Are you going to go on another date with him?"

"I shouldn't," Karen replied.

Breckin quirked an eyebrow. "Why not?"

"Because...well...I'm sure he's going back to New York eventually."

"So what?" Breckin said. "You obviously had fun. And like it or not, it is quite apparent you two have chemistry. Might as well have a good time while he's here. But that's my two cents. Do what you want, love. It's your life. It just makes me happy seeing you...and my brother...smile."

Burt finally returned. Apparently he didn't die, fall in the toilet, or escape out the window. To be honest, Karen wouldn't blame him if he had done any of them. Why the man wanted to marry Kelda was anyone's guess. She must be great in bed for an old lady. Karen shook her head at the image in her head. Ew.

Griff began explaining the rules of *Dirty Santa*. To Karen's surprise, Kelda didn't interrupt him once. Then Griff had everyone draw a number out of a cup. Brody grinned when he pulled his. He had annoyingly returned to his seat beside Karen as soon as he finished helping Griff separate the *Dirty Santa* presents from the real ones. Karen had tried to stealthily scoot down on the brick so their thighs weren't touching but there was no point. He had just scooted right along with her. Karen had caught a glimpse of Kelda pulling out her phone and facing it Karen and Brody's way. She had a feeling the elderly rumor mill would be atwitter come the twenty-sixth.

"Number one. The best one of all."

"Why is that best?" Karen asked him.

"Because I get last pick of *all* the presents because I have to go first."

"It figures your first Christmas back in years you'd get the best number," Breckin complained.

"Hey, I can't help it if I'm good." Brody grabbed a present from the coffee table and unwrapped it.

Karen started laughing when he pulled out a bright pink, see through, lace lingerie set. That had Kelda written all over it.

"Just so you know, I'm stealing that Brody, and you better not fight me for it," Kelda said. "I ordered that on the internet and it cost me a pretty penny."

"Then why did you put it in *Dirty Santa*, Kelda?" Brody asked, putting the scrap of lace back in the bag. Karen loved the look of shock on his face.

"We couldn't get to the store due to the fact my Burty has been having..." Kelda looked at Burt, who shot her the death glare. "Well, he hasn't been feeling so hot. I've been takin' care of him. I ordered this as a present to myself about a month ago but since I didn't have nothin' else to bring I just threw it in a bag. Like I said, nobody else better touch it."

"Yeah!" Burt agreed. "I have plans for that little number."

Brody shuddered. "I am going to be traumatized forever," he whispered in Karen's ear. "Will you help me get the image out of my mind?"

"Not a chance."

The game continued. Donnie opened a Pioneer Woman bowl set, which Susan stole from him with a wink and a smile. Griff took the blanket Karen brought from Burt and promptly handed it to his wife. His next selection had him stuck with Monkey Butt powder.

"You owe me," he told her amid the laughter of the room.

"Don't act like you won't use it," she replied impishly, kissing him on the cheek. "I know how you get chafed on those long bike rides."

Finally, it was Karen's turn. She had gotten the last number. Looking around the room, she finally decided to choose the final present on the table. Unwrapping it carefully, she knew her face turned all shades of red when she saw what was inside.

"You have to show us!" Breckin said. "Those are the rules."

"I know what it is," Kelda said with an evil grin. "I bought them for my Burty the same time I got the pink lacy number."

"Oh, now I *have* to see it," Brody said, stealing the package out of Karen's hands.

"Hey! Give it back."

Brody died laughing when he saw the present. "This is even better than I thought it would be," he said. He held up a tiny Speedo. Karen didn't even know how the maker printed the words to fit, but on the underwear were the words, The

Man, The Myth, The Legend. After the word man, the arrow pointed up. After the word legend, the arrow pointed down to what was definitely the area that held a man's…well…his parts gifted by the Man upstairs.

"I'm so taking these," he said with a laugh. "You'd smell better with the lotion I got stuck with, anyway."

Kelda was complaining that she should be the one who got to keep the Speedo since she was the one who purchased it. Griff was explaining to her that wasn't how the game worked, especially since she stole the lacy pink number from Brody. No one was paying a bit of attention to Brody and Karen.

With a grin, Brody leaned over and whispered in her year, "These underwear are definitely on point for their new owner. Care to witness me model them?"

Absolutely, the devil on her shoulder whispered in her other ear.

"Not interested," she said out loud. Now if only her willpower could hold steady.

BRODY WATCHED as Karen grabbed her coat and made a beeline to the door. She wasn't as immune to him as she wanted him to think. Otherwise, why would she look so flustered?

Too bad for her he ran in the New York Marathon the last four years. She wasn't about to outrun him before he got a chance to say goodnight.

"Going somewhere, Raven?" he asked, casually leaning against Breckin's front door just as she placed her hand on the knob.

"Yes," she said, blowing a strand of that gorgeous, silken

hair of hers out of her eyes. "Home. That's usually what a person tends to do once the festivities are over."

"But without even saying goodbye? I'm hurt," he said, holding his heart.

Her green eyes rolled. "I bet you are. Now, please move."

"Not yet."

Karen removed her hand from the doorknob and placed it on her hip. "And just why not?"

"Because this," Brody said, pointing above their heads, "is most *definitely* mistletoe. Which means you owe me a kiss."

"You are *not* going to kiss me," she breathed.

"And just why not?" he asked, echoing her words. He leaned in closely, the smell of citrus and honey wafting under his nose. She smelled good enough to eat.

"Because....we..."

"We what, Raven?" he asked, tucking a strand of hair behind her ear.

"We have to keep our distance."

"Hurry up and kiss her, ya fool! I have plans for this little number."

Brody sighed and turned to the sound of Kelda's voice. Sure enough, the old woman was in her purple velvet coat, standing behind Karen and holding the lacy pink piece in the air.

"I'm trying my best, Kelda. But you trying to hurry things up isn't doing anything for me."

Kelda harrumphed. "Sure don't look like she's dropping her panties for him like ya thought, Burty," she whisper-shouted in her boyfriend's ear.

"Whaddya say, Raven? As soon as you let me give you a chaste little peck on the lips you can be on your way."

"That's not a good idea to do in front of Kel—"

Before she could argue more, Brody placed his hands on both sides of her face, leaned down and pressed his lips against hers. Her skin was silk, her lips rose petals that tasted faintly of grapefruit. It was a heady combination. One of his hands moved to cusp the back of her head to pull her closer.

"What was that you were saying about not droppin' the panties?" Burt said loudly. "Looks to me like those underoos will be off as soon as they walk through her door."

Karen jumped out of Brody's embrace and touched her lips like they had been scalded. Her cheeks were flushed pink and her hair where his hand had been was a tangled mess. If she looked this good from just one kiss, he could only fathom what she looked like covered only in his bedsheet.

"I...I...I need to go," she said breathlessly before grabbing the doorknob and rushing out the door.

Breckin walked up to him and hit Brody on the back of the head. "Way to go, idiot!"

"Ow! What was that for?"

"For kissing her! Now I'll probably have to wrap her in chains and haul her back to the house tomorrow for Christmas!"

"Hey! I wasn't the one talking about her panties dropping! You can blame that on *those* two!" Brody replied, pointing his finger at Kelda and Burt. For once, the duo had the decency to look guilty.

"How was I to know she'd run as soon as we said something?" Kelda asked. "Lord knows if this eye candy was kissing *me* I'd have my clothes off in *seconds*, not just my panties!"

Burt threw his hands in the air. "Always after the young pups! You know what, Kelda Vanderburgh? I think I just might tell my dealer I don't need any more little blue pills, if you get my drift. You can go get you a young buck. Good luck and good riddance!"

"Looks like you need to handle this fiasco," Brody whispered in his sister's ear. "Why don't I go out and make amends with Karen?"

"You better fix this, Brody! You aren't going to ruin my friend's Christmas!"

Brody saluted his sister before jogging out into the frigid weather. The sounds of Kelda and Burt's bickering faded into the night as he crossed the yard toward Karen's old Mini Cooper. He really needed to think of something witty and charming to say because, if the way she was looking at him was any indication, he'd need a miracle to get her to his sister's house Christmas morning.

KAREN DIDN'T THINK she'd stopped touching her lips since she ran out of Breckin's house like a teenage girl out past curfew. Her lips were still burning and she could still feel the calluses on his fingertips caressing her face. Brody's scent would be forever burned into her nostrils and her hormones were still stampeding through her stomach like a herd of wild buffalo. Damn the man. Why'd he decide to come home for Christmas? Why'd he have to be from New York? Why'd he decide to set his sights on *her*?

She kicked the tire of her old car in frustration. When one kick wasn't enough, she pictured Brody Cooper's head in the middle of it and aimed again. Unfortunately, she realized too late she was standing on a slick patch of ice. Her feet went out from under her, the lotion she won in *Dirty Santa* flew out of her hands and her head banged against the hard asphalt of the road. Stunned, she lay on the ground, eyes blinking to hold back the tears as she tenderly felt the knot forming on the back of her head. Finally, with a groan, she tried to sit up but her stomach rolled at the movement.

"Whoa, whoa, whoa. Easy there, Raven. You knocked

yourself out pretty good. Probably shouldn't be moving too quickly."

Karen started to roll her eyes but grimaced at the movement. Brody must've seen the entire debacle. Of course. Because that's how her luck worked. "I'm fine, really," she said. "What are you doing here, anyway?"

Again, she tried to sit up. Again, a wave of nausea roiled through her stomach. This was so not good.

"I came to apologize for surprising you with that kiss but now that I'm out here, I can't lie. Because I'm not sorry at all," he said, bending down and smiling softly. "That was the best kiss I've had in a long time."

"I have a hard time believing that," she whispered. Her head began pounding even harder the longer she stayed on the ground. Karen hated the tears that began to spill out of her eyes and down her cheeks.

Brody gently ran his thumbs down her cheeks to wipe away the tears before tenderly probing the back of her head with his fingers. "One thing you can ask my sister about, Raven. I don't lie. Which makes me hate what I'm about to say."

"What's that?"

"I'm pretty sure you have a concussion."

Karen's eyes widened. "What? I can't have a concussion. How do you know I have a concussion?"

"Are you dizzy? Nauseous? Ears ringing? Headache?"

Karen nodded and then held her head. Even that small movement sent sparks of pain shooting through her head.

"You have all the classic symptoms. Plus you have a wicked bump on the back of your head. But good news! I know what you need to do to treat it."

"What's that?"

"Go to bed. Be still. Take Tylenol. But here's the most important thing."

"I have a feeling I might not like this part."

"You can't be alone. Looks like you're spending the night at my house or I'm going to yours."

Karen's felt all the blood drain from her face. That was *so* not a good idea. "Not going to happen," she said.

"Where else are you going to stay? You don't need a crying baby to wake you up all hours of the night. Breckin told me how fussy Emma can be. And Breckin will be up at the crack of dawn cooking for tomorrow. It's too late to call anyone else. Your only other choices are Susan and Donnie or Kelda and Burt."

Karen sighed and let out a small groan. She hated that he was right. "Fine. But you're sleeping on the couch."

CHAPTER 10

*K*aren gingerly sat up slowly, Brody's hand at the small of her back to steady her movement. She fought the nausea threatening to spill the contents of her stomach all over the sidewalk.

"Easy does it, sweetheart," Brody said softly. "Don't move too quickly. You don't want to upchuck all over yourself."

Karen smiled softly. "That's exactly what I'm trying *not* to do. I've already humiliated myself enough in front of you by busting my ass on the ice."

"Technically, you busted your head more than your ass," he replied. "Besides, I've already seen you bust your ass when we went skating."

Karen took a deep breath as she finally sat completely upright.

"Okay?" he asked.

"I think so," she whispered. She touched the back of her head, wincing at the knot she felt on the back of her head. "Ouch."

"It's a big one."

"That's what she said."

Brody grinned, his eyes twinkling. "Another joke. I believe this hit on your head has improved your sense of humor."

"Haha."

"Think you're ready to stand?"

Karen nodded before quickly stilling her head. That was not a good idea. "Now is as good as ever, I think."

Brody grabbed one of her hands and kept the other on the small of her back. He gently raised her to her feet. Karen hated the way she had to lean into him to steady herself. The more she leaned, the more she smelled the deliciousness that was Brody Cooper. She wanted to blame it on the concussion but couldn't. It was just him.

"Thanks for helping me. I can take it from here," she said, moving toward the driver's side of her car.

"What do you think you're doing?" he asked.

"I'm driving home."

Brody shook his head. "Not happening."

"Why not?" Karen felt like she had been asking him that question an awful lot in the last few minutes.

"Because passing out is also something that might happen when you have a concussion. I don't know about you, but I don't want to die or be seriously injured on Christmas Eve."

"How do you explain how we get to my house then?"

Brody took her keys out of her hands. "Easy. I'm driving. Good thing I chased after you, huh? Otherwise, you would've had to go back inside and hear Burt and Kelda talk about your panties."

Brody led Karen to the passenger's side of her car and opened the door for her. "Careful now. We don't want you knocking your head on the roof trying to get in."

To Karen's chagrin, Brody wouldn't even let her buckle her own seatbelt, claiming he didn't want any more movement to *jar her brain.* If it didn't hurt so much, she would have rolled her eyes.

"Be careful with my car. She shifts hard when switching gears."

"I'll say," Brody mumbled as he pulled away from the curb and pushed down on the gas. "It feels like this thing is on its last leg. No offense."

"None taken," she replied. "Sea Breeze has been with me a long time. I figure I'll drive her until she clunks. It's not like I have to drive long distances. I don't really leave Parker."

"Sea Breeze?"

"For her color."

Brody chuckled. "Creative."

Soon after, they pulled into Karen's driveway. Brody killed the car, wincing as the engine sputtered before shutting down. "You really need to take Sea Breeze in to be checked out."

"Maybe," she said evasively. Mr. Big Bucks sitting beside her didn't realize how far a teacher's budget *didn't* go. Why would he? He was used to the opulence of New York.

Before she could open her door, Brody had run around the front of her car to open it for her. "Who says chivalry is dead?" he asked.

Karen slowly got out of the car with his help, her stomach protesting the movement. "My house keys are in my coat pocket."

Holding her breath, she felt Brody's hand graze her hip as he felt for the keys. His steel-gray eyes held hers with an intensity she didn't want to name. He had felt the connection of his hand on her hip as well. Even through the fabric of her coat, it had sent a zing of electricity through Karen's body.

Brody cleared his throat. "Which one is the key to the front door?" he asked, his voice cracking.

"The blue one."

"All right. Let's get you up these steps." Brody helped her up the wooden steps and across the wooden slats of her front porch. It really was a cute little house. The outside brick was painted cream, her front door a dark, almost eggplant, purple. The beams holding up the porch were wood stained dark to match the porch and the shutters on either side of the picture windows.

"I didn't tell you this the other day, but I remember this house," Brody said. "It was Mason's grandmother's home. She had a large table sitting on this porch. During the summer she would make homemade lemonade and give it to all the kids who walked or rode their bikes down the street. It was on the way to the community pool so I'm pretty sure every kid in town stopped by here all summer. No telling how many pitchers of lemonade she went through over the years."

"That's a great story," Karen replied. She wished she knew other memories of the house. Maybe it would help her feel like it was a home rather than just a place to rest her head at night. Brody opened the front door with her key and helped her over the threshold.

"I only made it to the living room last time I was here. Just point me the way of the bedroom."

Karen motioned up the wide staircase to her left. "It's the first door on the right when you turn left down the hall," she said.

"Of course there would be stairs. We'll just go slowly."

After what seemed like an eternity, Karen stopping a few times to take some steadying breaths, they made it to her room. In here, a little more of her personality showed. A little bit of her old self came to life. It was the only way she could sleep at night.

An antique cherrywood dresser sat under the window, its ornate, brass handles worn with age. Sheer white curtains hung on the window, which let in plenty of natural light. Her brass bed, also antique, hinted at its age, the ivory balls at the top of every rail on the headboard and footboard decorated with hand-painted bands of ivy. A pale green Oriental rug covered the wooden floor. A white comforter with twines of ivy to match the ones on the porcelain balls covered her mattress. A hunter green, tufted velvet chair and ottoman sat in the corner, a tall lamp she left on before leaving the house casting shadows on the wall. Brody hadn't turned on the lights when they entered the room. Even without the lamp, the full moon shining in the window was enough light to see the silhouettes of the furniture.

"This is...well...different from downstairs," he said. "I actually feel like a person lives in this room."

"I found that I couldn't sleep without *something* of myself in here. I decided I had to put something in this room that reminded me of my old life," she said softly.

As soon as the words left her lips she realized her mistake. She never should have mentioned her old life. Mentioning her old life made people ask questions. Questions she couldn't answer. Didn't want to answer. Especially if it was Brody Cooper asking them.

Thankfully, either Brody didn't hear her or was choosing not to probe. "Let's get you out of these clothes and into something more comfortable," he said.

"You're not going to help me change," she shrieked, wincing at the pain that shot through her head. Concussions could kiss her ass. They sucked.

"Raven, I saw what one kiss did to you. I'm not about to see what the result of you undressing in front of me would be. I just want to get them for you so you have to move as little as possible. Then, if you'll tell me where your bathroom is, I'll get you some Tylenol for your head. Do you have a cup or anything in the bathroom I can fill with water?"

"I have a bottle of water on my nightstand."

"Okay. Now just tell me what drawer you keep your pjs in."

"Top right," she said. "They're basically just oversized t-shirts."

"Any one in particular that's your favorite?"

"The blue NYU one."

Brody pulled the shirt out of the drawer and laughed. "It's seen its fair share of washes, hasn't it?"

Karen looked at the shirt and saw what Brody saw. The navy blue faded to a denim color. The U worn almost completely off. The unraveled hem. To him, it looked worn and tattered. To Karen, it held precious memories she would never, ever let go. Sometimes, if she held it to her long enough, she could almost smell Jeremy's cologne. Almost.

"It's special," was all she said. "Are you going to give it to me or not?"

Brody handed her the shirt and took a step away from her. "Get dressed. I'll be right back."

As soon as he walked out the door, Karen let out the breath she had been holding. Concussion or not, she didn't think she was going to sleep a wink.

BRODY LOOKED DOWN at a sleeping Karen. She was curled in the fetal position on her right side, snoring softly. He smiled. Something told him she would be mortified if she knew she snored in her sleep.

Gently, he pulled the covers over her bare legs until they were tucked under her chin. He had the desire to trail his hand behind the covers and touch her skin. He knew it would feel as soft as it looked. But he refrained. Brody knew he had to approach Karen with caution. She had a story to tell. And by the way she skirted the issue every time he asked a question, he knew it was probably a story no one knew. Not even his sister.

"What's your story, Raven?" he asked softly.

As if she heard him, she let out a soft sigh and rolled onto her back. Her hair fanned out across her pillow, her long eyelashes resting on her porcelain skin. She really was breathtaking.

Brody rubbed the back of his neck. He didn't want to sleep downstairs. It would be incredibly annoying to run back and forth to check on Karen throughout the night. Besides, he knew from experience the couch downstairs was not the least bit comfortable. He knew Karen would freak if she woke up to find him in her bed. Brody eyed the chair in the corner. It looked like the velvet chair and ottoman was his only option. He took off his shoes before removing his jeans and sweater and folded them neatly on the floor next to the chair. If she truly had a concussion, Karen would be none-the-wiser. It was a compromise for Brody since he usually slept in his birthday suit.

He quietly tiptoed into the hallway and into the bathroom he found when he was waiting for Karen to change. Opening the medicine cabinet, he crossed his fingers and then grinned when he found what he was looking for—an unopened toothbrush. Grabbing the toothpaste in the cabinet, he ran the brush over his teeth and threw some water over his face. He had a feeling it was going to be a long night.

Brody walked back into Karen's room to see her tossing and turning, a frown on her face. "Jeremy," she whispered. "Jeremy, no."

Brody didn't know what to do. Should he wake her? She was obviously having a dream. What he didn't know was if it was a nightmare or would simply go away on its own. Karen's tossing and turning became more agitated.

"Bella! Bella, where are you?" she shouted. Brody could hear the panic in her voice. "Bella!"

Brody couldn't take it anymore. "Karen," he said softly, brushing the hair out of her eyes. "Karen, wake up."

Brody noticed the sweat beading on her forehead. Definitely a nightmare. She needed out of whatever was filling her head.

"Karen," he said, this time louder and with more force. "You need to wake up. You're having a bad dream."

At his words, Karen's eyes popped open. Brody hated the fear he saw in them. They were glazed and unfocused, locked on some nightmare he couldn't see but knew was part of her past. She sat up and shook her head, her eyes focusing as she looked around her room.

"Hey," he said softly, sitting on the edge of the bed and taking her hand in his. "You okay? That was quite a dream."

Karen turned to him. "I'm okay," she said, taking a deep breath. "Did I say anything?"

Brody started to tell her the names she mentioned but then stopped at the fear he saw in her eyes. To mention Jeremy's and Bella's names, whomever they were, was probably not a good idea. "Nope. No names. Just a lot of screaming. Were you dreaming of me?"

He sighed in relief when she rolled her eyes. "Hardly. Just a bad dream about…"

Karen hesitated. "About falling. I have a lot of dreams about falling."

"Falling's pretty scary stuff," he said. "Here's a secret for you."

Karen looked at him, one eyebrow cocked. "What secret?"

"I'm terrified of heights."

"Really?"

"Really. My office is on the twentieth floor of my building. I'm pretty high up in my company so I have an office that looks out over Manhattan. It's not a corner office but it still has those floor to ceiling windows you see in the movies. And they terrify me."

"Are you serious?" she asked with a small smile.

"Totally. I made sure my back wasn't to the windows when I moved in. My desk is on the solid wall on the left side of the room. I wanted floor to ceiling curtains covering the glass so I didn't have a panic attack but my boss vetoed that idea. Now I just avoid them like the plague."

Karen's smile grew wider, her grass-green eyes twinkling with laughter. "That's funny."

"Not really. I begged for an office on the first floor but again, my boss vetoed that idea."

"You must be pretty important, whatever it is you do."

"I was," Brody said.

"What's that supposed to mean?"

"I was a stock broker for one of the biggest firms in New York," he said, surprising himself. He didn't tell anyone what he did. "One slip up lost a lot of money for many, many, many of our clients. Needless to say, my boss wasn't very happy with me. I was told I needed to take a mandatory break. I still haven't been informed if my *mandatory break* is permanent."

"Oh," Karen said softly. "That sucks."

Brody let out a breath. "Yep. Totally sucks. Since I was pretty much shunned by everyone I thought were my friends, I tucked tail and ran to the only place I could think of where I would still be loved despite my incredible screw up."

"Home."

"Home," he agreed. Which he realized was true. All of a sudden, he didn't know why he had been running so hard from his life in Parker. It was good to be home. With people who loved him no matter if he were rich or poor. Successful or an epic failure. Which was a good thing, since it was beginning to look like he was the latter.

"Why haven't you ever told any of your family what it is you do?" she asked.

"I don't know. I guess it was just a part of me I wanted to keep for myself. I never really fit the mold of what a guy in a small town should be."

"Meaning?"

"A jock. Member of Future Farmers of America. *Something* considered appropriate."

"I take it you weren't?"

"I liked to read. I was a loner. Didn't really mesh with the rest of the male population of Parker. When I went to New York, I finally found my niche. Took out student loans and paid for NYU so my dad didn't have to foot the bill. I found sophistication. A will to succeed. I got hired right out of college. It didn't take long for me to show my willingness to work hard and show I was a quick learner. I caught my boss's eye and moved up fairly quickly."

"You'd think you'd want to share that with your family."

"You'd think. But I knew my dad wouldn't understand. So I kept it to myself. And stayed in the place where I fit in."

"Makes sense."

"I've told you my story, Raven. Want to tell me yours now?"

"I don't have a story," she said softly. "Just saw an opening for a teaching job in Parker and wanted a change."

"I think that's bullshit," he said, leaning in until his lips were close enough to touch hers. He could smell the citrus and honey on her skin, could see her pulse beating a frantic rhythm in throat.

"Well, you're wrong," she said breathlessly. "I'm boring."

"Too bad I don't believe a word that's coming out of your mouth right now."

Karen leaned back as if she realized how close they were. All of a sudden, her eyes widened as she looked him up and down. Her breath hitched and the pulse in her throat noticeably increased. "Brody Cooper, want to tell my why you're naked? In my bed?"

Brody grinned before shooting her a wink. "I'm not naked, Karen. I'm wearing boxers. But thanks for noticing."

CHAPTER 11

*K*aren couldn't believe Brody Cooper was in her bed. Naked. Well, not *totally* naked. If he was…well…she had no clue what she would do. Because Brody Cooper looked just as good with the majority of his clothes off as he did with his clothes *on*. Probably better, if she were being honest with herself. Smooth, olive skin over toned muscles. A trail of hair leading to anatomy Karen hadn't seen in person for so long she didn't know if she remembered what it looked like. A large tattoo of an eagle, its wings outspread, spanning the width of his chest. And that hair on top of his head…god, she wanted to run her fingers through it.

"I did notice," she said haughtily, trying to calm her pulse. "And you need to put some clothes on. *Now.*"

To her annoyance, Brody just grinned that crooked smile of his she had gotten used to in the short time she had known him. "How was I to know you were going to have a dream about me and wake up? I was just trying to get comfortable so I could sleep in your comfy chair."

"I have a couch downstairs."

"Which is incredibly uncomfortable."

Karen tried to hide her smile but failed. "That's fair."

"And I didn't want to run up and down the stairs all night. I figured if I slept in the chair I would be able to monitor you easier."

"I really am fine if you just want to go—"

"Not going home, Karen. So don't suggest it."

"I'm fine, Brody. I've been on my own for a long time."

"Well, tonight you're not going to be. End of story."

Karen sighed. "Fine."

"Now, since I'm going to be taking care of your every whim throughout the evening, I need you to tell me one thing."

"What's that?"

"Tell me your middle name."

"It's O'Conn—" Karen realized her mistake as soon as the words came out of her mouth. She almost said her *real* last name instead of her middle. A name she hadn't uttered for over seven years. A name she thought she had erased from her system. "Uh, Sue. Karen Sue Posey."

"Were you about to say O'Connell?" Brody asked. "That's an awfully weird middle name, Karen Sue."

Karen willed her hands not to shake. What an epic mess up. It had to be the concussion messing with her brain. She never would've said it otherwise. "No. I was going to say Connelly. It was," she said, trying to shrug her shoulders nonchalantly. "It was...it was..."

"It was?" Brody asked.

"My maiden name," she blurted out. "I was a Connelly before Posey. This concussion has messed with my brain."

"You've been married before?"

Karen couldn't believe she was such an idiot. That was the only excuse to come up with? She had to make sure Brody didn't say anything to his sister. She'd be a dead woman. Breckin had been trying to get Karen to open up about her past *forever.*

"For like, a week. Maybe not even that long."

"It had to be long enough for you to change your name."

Karen figured the only way to go without digging herself into an even deeper hole was to tell the truth. Or at least some semblance of it.

"I married my high school sweetheart right after we graduated. He enrolled in...school...and I went with him. I thought we were going to be together forever but then something happened and it ended. It wasn't pretty. But I already had changed my last name so...I just kept it. That was easier than to try and change everything back."

Karen crossed her fingers, toes, and everything in between Brody would buy her story. A lot of it was the truth...just skewed a little bit. After what felt like an eternity of him boring holes in her forehead, he finally nodded.

"I guess that would be easier than to try and change everything back."

Karen let out a breath.

"How long were you married?"

"Five years."

"I thought you said you were married for a week. Five years is a lot longer than a week."

The lies were already jumbling into one big mess in Karen's head. "We were just *together* for a week. Then I left and he wouldn't sign the divorce papers. Just like the guy in *Sweet Home Alabama.*"

Brody whistled. "Did you go to school in New York?"

"How did you know I was from—" Karen's eyes widened as she realized how he tricked her.

"I *knew* you were from New York! I could tell. What part? Brooklyn? SoHo? Manhattan?"

Karen shook her head, wincing at the pain. "I'm not from New York. I told you that already."

"You can't fool me..." Brody's words trailed off as he looked at Karen's face. "Karen, are you okay?"

"Yeah, I'm fine." But she was not fine. The more she shook her head, the more it started to pound. A wave of nausea overtook her and she swayed in bed.

Brody wrapped his arms around her and pulled her to his chest. Karen inhaled the scent of cedar and sandalwood and sighed at the warmth of his skin. Just once. Just this once she'd let someone comfort her.

"You're okay," he whispered. "You just need some sleep."

Brody released her and she tried not to let her disappointment show. Her eyes widened when he walked around the other side of her bed, pulled the covers down, and crawled in.

"What are you doing?" she whispered.

In response, Brody gently grabbed her arm and pulled her to him. "You have a concussion and I'm being an ass and asking you all these questions you don't need to answer. I know your head is pounding. I know you're dizzy. Fortunately, I have just the cure."

Again, Karen found herself wrapped in Brody's arms, her head on his chest. He leaned back on her pillows, rested his chin on the top of her head and started running his fingers through her hair and softly down the side of her face.

Karen couldn't help the sigh of contentment that slipped from her lips. She could feel the throbbing in her head subsiding the more he ran his fingers through her locks.

"Just rest, Raven," he said into her hair. "You're safe. No nightmares will get you while I'm here. And you won't have an asshole asking you any more questions, I promise."

As Karen felt her eyes drifting shut, she couldn't help but

realize this was the first time in over seven years she hadn't felt completely alone.

KAREN SQUINTED her eyes at the light filtering in through her bedroom window. A dull throb echoed through her head and she winced. She wasn't sure how long concussions were supposed to last, but it hadn't even been twenty-four hours and she was already over the feeling.

She rolled over and ran into a solid, warm object. Karen opened her eyes and found herself looking at smooth, olive skin. All of a sudden the night came back with startling clarity. Her nightmare. The comfort of Brody's arms. His near naked body enveloping her in its warmth. What in the hell had she done?

She stared at his sleeping form, his chest rising and falling in a steady rhythm. Long, blond lashes rested on his cheeks. Of course. God always gave the males the amazing lashes. She also noticed a small mole on his chin she hadn't seen before. Since she had tried to avoid eye contact with him as much as possible, that wasn't surprising. He really was a beautiful man.

Karen tried to blame her concussion on the fact she let her guard down last night and took comfort in Brody's arms. But deep down, she knew that wasn't it. For some reason, she felt a connection with the man sleeping beside her she hadn't felt in over seven years. Even for all his sarcasm and teasing, she knew he had a good heart. She could sense it when he was telling her his story. His broken heart might not be like hers as far as circumstances went but it had been hurt nonetheless.

As quietly as possible, Karen tried to push back the covers and crawl out of bed. When her feet hit the floor, she became extremely aware of how *little* her t-shirt covered and how *much* her legs were showing.

Good thing you decided to shave last night before going to Breckin's, she thought before shaking her head. Why should she care if her legs were silky smooth? It's not like she had any intention of letting Brody Cooper touch them.

She had just taken her first step when a distinct male voice, still gravelly with sleep, said, "Going somewhere, Raven?"

Karen immediately crouched down and tried to stretch her shirt to cover as much of her legs as possible. Her eyes widened as Brody sat up and reached for the ceiling in a yawn, his ab muscles rippling at the movement.

"Huh?"

"I asked if you were going somewhere," he said, sending that half-cocked smile her way while brushing his hair out of his eyes. Could he *be* any cuter?

"I…I…" Why wasn't her *brain working?*

"Because if you were, I was going to say I'd have what you're having."

"I was…um…going to make coffee," she finally uttered.

"Can you make me a cup?" he asked, sending her a wink.

Karen nodded her head before grabbing it gingerly. To her horror, Brody flipped the covers off his body, started *walking her way,* and placed his hands gently on the back of her head.

"Still tender, huh? You still have that knot," he said softly. "But some color has returned to your face, so that's good."

"You don't have any clothes on," she breathed.

"Again with that?" he asked, rubbing gentle circles on the back of her neck with his thumbs. "I'm in my underwear, not nude. And I believe you're showing as much leg as I am, Karen."

She wanted to crouch down lower and cover her legs

with as much fabric of her shirt as she could but...those *thumbs.*

"I can put these fingers to good use in other places, too," he whispered into her hair. "Just say when."

Karen tried to pull away, but before she could Brody had successfully trapped her between her dresser and his body. His smooth, tan, lick-worthy body. "Me...kitchen...coffee," she whispered.

"In a minute," he whispered back.

Before Karen could raise her voice to argue, Brody cupped her face in his hands and smoothed a strand of hair out of her eyes. "You are the most beautiful woman I've ever seen," he whispered before his lips crashed against hers.

Karen moaned at the contact. He coaxed her mouth open with his tongue and began exploring. Her tongue followed his in a gentle, steady rhythm as his hands caressed her face in the most gentle way possible. His hands drifted down her face and traced the outline of her collarbone before running down her arms. Linking her fingers with his, he took her arms and looped them around his shoulders. They were so close Karen didn't know where she ended and he began.

Karen gasped as his lips traced the outline of her jaw and made their way down her neck. This was so not going how she had anticipated.

As if Brody could sense her hesitation, he pulled back, took a deep breath, and smiled. "Merry Christmas, Raven."

"Merry Christmas, Brody," she said, trying to get her breathing under control.

With another grin, he ran his fingers through his hair and pushed it back from his forehead. "If you'll tell me where your coffee pot is, I'll make the coffee," he said. "After all, you're the one with the concussion. I'm supposed to be the one taking care of you."

"On the counter in the kitchen next to the fridge. Creamer's in the fridge and sugar is in a canister in the cabinet above the pot. So's the coffee." Karen knew she was touching her lips that were still swollen with his kisses. At this point, she didn't even care. Her body had come alive under his touch.

Karen let out a little squeal of shock when Brody slapped her playfully on the butt and said, "Now, please put some pants on. You're making me uncomfortable showing all that leg."

She openly stared as he walked out the door. His backside in those navy boxer briefs were looking awfully nice. She was suddenly glad he took off his jeans and got into her bed the night before. It was the best night of sleep she'd gotten in…well, seven years.

With a grin, she got back in bed and pulled the covers up to her chin. They weren't supposed to be at Breckin's house until eleven and it was only eight. Plenty of time to drink a cup of coffee and relax. Maybe even read a couple of chapters in her latest romance novel before getting in the shower.

A few minutes later Brody walked back into her room carrying two steaming cups of coffee. "I didn't know how you took yours so I just brought the sugar canister and creamer to you."

"Thanks," she said.

"I didn't see any pumpkin spice creamer," he said with a grin.

Karen wrinkled her nose. "That's because pumpkin spice is overrated and stupid."

Brody let out a deep laugh that crinkled his eyes in the corners. "Not a fan?"

"Every time fall arrives the social media memes about pumpkin spice start. It's the time of year I roll my eyes the most."

"What's your name? I'll add you."

"Add me on what?"

"Facebook. Instagram. Snap. Whatever you're on."

Karen shook her head. "I don't have any social media accounts."

"Really? Why not? I thought everyone did."

There was no way Karen could tell him the real reason she couldn't post pictures of herself for the world to see. It would lead to nothing good. "I just don't like it. It takes up too many people's time and energy that could be used on other, more productive things."

"Then how do you see the pumpkin spice memes?"

"I look over your sister's shoulder."

Brody laughed again. "The more I learn about you the more interesting you become, Raven."

"I'm not interesting. I'm boring."

"Well, I think you are. I just wish you'd tell me your secrets."

"Like I said, no secrets."

Brody made an indiscernible sound before crawling in bed next to her. Before he got completely comfortable, he lifted the covers off her legs. "What did I tell you about covering up those legs?"

"I did cover them. With my comforter."

"Those are legs men dream about, Raven."

Karen shook her head and grabbed her book off the nightstand. "I'm nothing special, Brody Cooper. The sooner you figure that out, the better."

"Hmmmm," was all the response she got.

"Why can't you still be the annoying ass I met in the grocery store?" she asked with a huff.

"I told you I'm endearing once you get to know me. Why would you want me to be an ass?"

"Because it makes it easier to dislike you."

"I think that might be your way of saying you like me," he said with a grin.

Karen shrugged her shoulders. "I guess."

"I'll take that."

They sat in companionable silence, Karen rotating between her crossword puzzle and reading while Brody chuckled at videos he was watching on his phone. Before Karen knew it, it was time to get out of bed and get ready to go to her friend's house.

"Are Kelda and Burt going to be there?" she asked.

Brody shrugged his shoulders. "They are family."

Karen groaned. "I'm not sure I can handle them two days in a row."

Brody brushed the hair out of her eyes, a habit she was growing quite fond of the more he did it. "Stick with me, Raven. I'll keep you out of harm's way."

Karen didn't respond but in her heart she had the slightest hope fluttering in her chest at the thought she didn't have to be alone.

CHAPTER 12

*B*rody pulled next to the curb in front of his sister's house and killed Karen's car's engine. He shuddered at the sound it made when he put it in park. She really needed another car.

For the first time in his life Brody had woken up next to a woman and didn't have the urge to run for the door as fast as he could. And he hadn't even had sex. Raven had cast a spell over him that only grew stronger the more he was around her. She was smart and gentle and complex all wrapped up in a stunning package. He just hoped she didn't run when she realized she had opened herself up to him that morning.

"Looks like we're the last ones here," she said softly. "They'll see us walking in together."

"No problem. We can just tell them what happened. Besides, I'm sure they have questions. I left my truck here last night."

Brody walked to Karen's side of the car and opened her door. He reached for her arm but she pulled it back.

"I can get out of the car myself," she said.

"I don't doubt that. But I'm not willing to let you slip and fall again. One concussion is bad enough."

Snow had fallen during the night, covering the ground in a blanket of white. It wasn't snow he got in New York, but it was pretty nonetheless. He couldn't remember it ever snowing this much in his hometown. Opening the front door, Brody was met with the faces of Susan, his dad, his sister, Griff, Kelda, and Burt staring their way.

"I told ya!" Kelda said, slapping Burt on the arm. "I told ya they went home together and did the nasty! No woman could resist those buns."

If looks could kill, Brody would be dead the way his sister was boring holes in his forehead. "Why are you walking in together?" she asked heatedly.

"Because Karen slipped on the ice last night and hit her head on the ground. I was pretty sure she got a concussion and knew she shouldn't be by herself, so I stayed the night at her house to make sure she was okay."

Breckin's glare turned to concern. "Oh, my gosh! Kare, are you okay?" she asked.

Karen nodded. "I'm okay. I just didn't want to bother you."

"Bother me? You wouldn't be bothering me! You should've stayed here!"

"And had you keep her up all night with your baby's crying and you cooking at the crack of dawn? She did better in the quiet of her own house."

Breckin pointed a finger in his face. "You better have been a gentleman."

Brody held up his hands. "I was nothing but. Ask Karen if you don't believe me."

At his words, Brody couldn't help but remember the kiss he and the breathtaking woman standing next to his sister had shared in her bedroom. The feel of her skin, the scent of citrus wafting under his nose. He knew he promised Sadie he'd be good…but *damn*. And Karen had told him to keep his distance. But how could he resist? No man would have been able.

"He was good, Breck," Karen said softly. "He took care of me and made sure I was okay."

"Panty dropper indeed," Burt said loudly. "I don't care what those two tell *us*. Look at them googly-eyes they're makin' at each other. They *totally* did it."

Karen's face turned red as she turned around to head to the front door. Without thinking, Brody wrapped his arm around her waist and pulled her to him.

"What are you doing?" she whispered.

"Not letting you escape," he replied.

"They're all watching us. They think we had sex!"

Brody turned Karen to face the rest of his makeshift family. "Karen and I did *not* have sex. I checked her head, gave her medicine, and made sure she didn't throw up. I also drove her home. Just because *you two—*" Brody pointed at Kelda and Burt, "have dirty minds doesn't mean everyone that goes home together has sex. Karen needed help. I offered. End of story. Now, can we eat? I'm starving."

Kelda and Burt stared at Brody. "Well, I don't remember him having that big of balls when he was in high school," Kelda said. "He must've grown a pair in New York."

Karen dropped her head to hide her smile but not before Brody caught her grinning.

"You think that's funny, do you?" he asked.

"Kinda."

"Now you see why I didn't come home much? That's pretty much how the whole town thought of me. In New York, I fit. Here, I didn't."

"I do. But I don't think anyone sees you that way anymore."

"Good to know. Hey, Raven?"

"Yeah?"

"We're standing under the mistletoe again. Wanna kiss? What's the harm? They already thought we did it last night."

"Nice try."

"It was worth a shot."

"I believe you've already gotten a kiss from me this morning, Brody Cooper."

Brody leaned in and whispered in her ear. "And it was a lot hotter than that chaste peck on the lips from last night, too."

He loved the blush that crept up her neck and grinned when she walked off to join his sister in the dining room to put the food on the table. Yep. He was definitely getting under her skin.

"So, you know I can keep a secret."

Brody jumped at the sound of Kelda's voice next to him. He didn't know how but the old woman had snuck up on him. It must have been when he was watching Karen's shapely backside follow his sister into the kitchen.

Brody looked down at the woman and choked back a laugh. She was wearing a Grumpy Cat t-shirt. Grumpy Cat was wearing a Santa hat and the words—*I have a present for you. It's in the litter box*—was printed below the cat's face.

"Nice shirt, Kelda."

"Don't go changin' the subject. I'm a woman on a mission."

"What's your mission?"

"Did you really have sex last night? Like I said, I *can* keep a secret." Kelda pretended to zip her lips and place the key in her Christmas-tree green hair. "I just wanna know. For my own curiosity."

Brody shook his head. "No sex, Kelda."

The old woman gave her head a shake, the tiny bells

placed haphazardly on her head jingling with the motion. "I don't know what it is with young 'uns nowadays. I think *I* have more sex than the entire population of this town!"

Brody walked off before he had to answer any more questions Kelda wanted to throw his way. He also wanted to get away from her as soon as possible in order to forget the image her words were threatening to put in his head.

Brody plopped down on the couch next to his dad. "So what's with Breckin becoming such a good cook, huh? She was awful, if I remember correctly. Almost burned the house a couple of times, in fact."

His dad grinned. "She's comin' around. My Susan is teaching her how to be a really good cook."

His dad put his arm around his new wife and kissed her on the forehead. "The first time Breckin went to Griff's family's Thanksgiving, she burned her stuffing to a crisp. Susan offered to give her lessons and surprisingly, a lot of her stuff is edible now."

Susan playfully slapped his dad on the chest. "It's better than edible. She's actually turned into a good cook."

"But there's no dessert that can compare to your pecan praline bread pudding."

Susan leaned up and whispered in his dad's ear. "That's why I brought it. As a surprise."

Brody's dad kissed her on the forehead. "I knew I married you for a reason."

Brody hated to admit it, but his dad and Griff's mom were actually a little sweet. At least as far as old people went. Brody felt the couch cushion lean to the right. He bit back a groan when he turned as saw Burt sitting next to him.

"Don't say nothin' about my shirt, sonny boy," Burt said, shaking his finger in Brody's face. "Kelda *made* me wear it."

Brody hadn't even noticed Burt's shirt when he walked in. He was too preoccupied defending Karen. But once he caught a glimpse, he couldn't keep the laugh contained. Burt's sweater was bright green. On it was a Christmas tree made of cats with the words *Meowy Catmas* emblazoned on the front.

"I *said* don't laugh!" Burt said.

"No, you said don't say anything. Have I said anything?"

Burt waved his hand. "Fine, fine. That's not why I came over here anyway. I really came over here to get the skivvy about what *really* went down last night. Did you do it with the hottie schoolteacher? You secret will be safe with me. I won't even tell Kelda. Scout's honor."

Brody rolled his eyes. "No! We didn't have sex! Just because you and your...*woman*...do whatever it is you do all the time doesn't mean everyone else does. I can keep it in my pants, Burt."

"I gotta get it when I can, sonny. Never know when I'm gonna kick the bucket. It's my goal to go out with a stiffy. Can't think of a better way."

Luckily, Brody didn't have to answer. His sister came into the living room and announced lunch was ready. Brody hopped up from the couch as fast as he could and made his way into the dining room. Before he could get there to make sure he had a place next to Karen, his sister stopped him.

"One question, and I want the *truth*."

"No! We didn't have sex. I was a gentleman through and through. I took care of her. That's. It."

Breckin grinned before wrapping her arms around him in a hug. She was such a tiny thing. She barely came up to his chest. "Thanks, Brode. That was really nice of you."

"I've always been nice, Punky Breckster."

She looked up at him. "The longer you're in town the more you act like your old self. Think you could just stay for good? I've missed you."

Brody wasn't about to tell her he might not have another option. "I'm thinking about it."

Breckin let out a squeal. "Best. Christmas. Ever!"

Brody finally made his way into the dining room and pulled out the seat next to Karen. "Is this seat taken?"

"Now it is."

Brody grinned. "Somebody is feeling better."

"It wasn't as bad walking in together as I thought it would be. I haven't really gotten hassled by anyone."

Brody didn't want to burst her bubble and tell her he was approached by not just Kelda and Burt, but also his own sister about what happened. Let her think they all believed their initial words. "See? I told you if you stuck with me I'd keep you safe."

"Something tells me when I'm with you, Brody Cooper, I'm the very opposite of safe."

"Now why would you say something like that?" he asked, trying to portray the picture of innocence. He was pretty sure he was failing. Because Karen was right. She was so far from safe with him it wasn't even funny.

"Because of the way you're looking at me right now."

"How am I looking at you?"

"Like I'm the last piece of whatever your favorite food is and you haven't had any in a *really, really* long time."

Brody put his arm on the back of Karen's chair and leaned in until his lips were just a breath away from her ear. "It's this five thousand dollar sushi I ate in Las Vegas. And it's the most delicious food I've ever put in my mouth."

Brody grinned when Karen shivered. "So, whaddya say, Raven? Wanna try it out?"

"I don't like sushi," she whispered.

Brody chuckled and pushed her hair behind her ear. "That's just because you haven't had *this* sushi. Trust me,

Raven, once you get a taste of *this* sushi you'll never go back to subpar sushi ever again."

"I don't think we're talking about sushi anymore."

Brody pulled back from her and grinned. "What gave it away?"

Karen didn't answer. "Like I said before...definitely not safe with you."

Brody couldn't wipe the smile off his face. Because those words meant he was busting through the huge wall Raven had built up around her. And that made him happier than it probably should.

"HOT DIGGITY! Look at this kitty blanket!" Since she was the oldest, it was decided Kelda would be first to open her Christmas presents. Although, if she were being honest, Karen thought it was because everyone was afraid of the fit Kelda would throw if she *wasn't* the first to open.

Kelda had gone through all the presents in her stack in record time, saving Karen's for last.

"How'd you know I like kittens, Teach?" Kelda said, holding up the blanket for everyone to see. "Have you been spying on me?"

"You wear a cat shirt every day," Karen said, trying to keep the sarcasm from her voice. "You have two cats. Yours was the easiest present I bought."

Kelda stared at Karen. She was pretty sure a hole was being burned in her forehead. Finally, the old lady smiled at Karen. "Okay. I can believe that. And I like it. So thank you."

Karen tried not to cough. Kelda was being...nice. What in the world? "You're...you're welcome, Kelda," she stuttered.

"I think my sister put some pot in Kelda's food." Brody leaned over and whispered in Karen's ear. "She's actually being...*nice*. In fact, it is the most chill I've ever seen the woman. What's up with that?"

Karen grinned at Brody having been thinking the same thing. She didn't know what was happening but she would take it. A nice Kelda was better than a normal one. At least in her opinion.

"A nice Kelda is better than a naughty one," she replied.

Brody laughed out loud, causing all eyes to laser beam toward them. Karen tried not to sigh. As much as she tried to stay *off* people's radars, Brody seemed determined to put them *on* people's radars. He thought he had been secretive with all his little touches, smiles and whispers to her throughout the night but she knew *everyone* had noticed. Everyone meaning Kelda. And that was one radar she wanted to stay *completely* off...forever. Too bad the old lady was staring daggers at them...again.

"What's so funny over there, you two? Are you making fun of the crazy cat lady?"

"What? *No!* Why would you think that, Kelda?" Brody asked, flashing Kelda the smile Karen was sure had women all over New York dropping panties for years. "We were just talking about how that blanket...brings out the color of your eyes."

Kelda squinted her eyes at them while Karen tried not to squirm in her seat. To squirm was to show weakness. And you couldn't show weakness with Kelda...not if you wanted to survive.

Just when she was about to let out the breath she had been holding, Kelda quit staring. "I do look pretty in white," Kelda replied.

"You look pretty in everything, Kelda," Brody said with a smile.

"Watch yourself, mister," Kelda said, shaking her finger at

Brody. "I'm a taken woman. Even though my fiancé blows up the bathroom, I still love him. And I'm no cheat."

"I would never insinuate you were, Kelda."

"And anyway, you couldn't keep up with me...in the sack," Kelda said with a wink. "I may be old, but I'm a tiger."

Karen tried not to laugh. She had never met anyone in her entire life like the old woman.

"You better not laugh," Brody said under his breath.

"I wasn't laughing," Karen replied.

"Your eyes were."

Karen rolled her eyes at him deliberately. "There. Now they're *rolling*...at you."

Brody laughed and scooted closer to Karen on the fireplace.

"I thought you were going to leave me alone tonight to keep all rumors at bay."

"I've tried, Raven...and failed miserably. You just smell so damn good. I can't help myself."

Karen didn't trust herself to reply. If she opened her mouth, she might do something incredibly stupid...like say how wonderfully *he* smelled as well and how she had thought about licking his body from head to toe ever since he backed her up into her dresser that morning.

So instead, she watched as everyone in Breckin's family opened their presents. She thought it would give her a sense of melancholy because of what she lost. Instead, it made her surprisingly happy to see people opening presents she got them and smiling in pleasure. It had been too long. All of a sudden, it was glaringly apparent how much she had been missing in her life.

Brody was currently opening his presents, purposefully saving Karen's present for last. When he unwrapped the mug, he smiled broadly, that dimple in his cheek cratering in response.

"How'd you know I liked Iron Man?" he asked. "He's my favorite. The first comic I ever read was an Iron Man one. Always held a special place in my heart after that."

"I didn't know he was your favorite," she replied. "But a little birdie told me you like coffee and comic books, so I thought this was perfect."

"Me!" Breckin called from her perch by her fiancé. "I'm the birdie."

Brody leaned over and planted a soft kiss on her forehead. "Thanks, Raven. This is the only mug I'm going to use from now on. Thanks for thinking of me."

Karen's eyes met his and she stopped breathing. She hadn't seen that look on a man's face since…well…since her former life. And damn if it didn't do funny things to her insides.

"Kare, it's your turn," Karen heard Breckin say softly. Breaking eye contact, Karen turned toward the pile of presents in front of her…and saw everyone in the room staring. Right. At. Her.

Kelda had a cat-that-ate-the-canary look on her face and Burt was smirking away. Everyone else's eyes were wide. All except Breckin's. Karen knew the look on her friend's face. It was a look Breckin got when she had ideas with endless possibilities running through her head.

Just as she leaned down to pick a present off the floor, Karen felt a warm hand on the small of her back. "Open mine first," Brody whispered in her ear.

Karen loved the way his hand lingered in place…almost as if it was made to be there. All of a sudden, she didn't really care what in the hell everyone else in the room was thinking. All she could think about was the beautiful man sitting next to her who was the exact opposite of what she thought of him when they first met.

Karen swallowed down the emotions she was suddenly

feeling. It was just the holiday. The damn holiday was getting to her. "Which one is yours?" she asked, her voice cracking.

Brody leaned over and picked up the black and white polka-dot bag stuffed with red tissue paper.

"Nice wrapping, New York," she said.

"I'm not taking credit for that," he said. "It was all Jerica at Cure All. That girl knows how to wrap a package."

Karen took a deep breath before taking the tissue paper out of the bag. She didn't have any idea why she was so nervous. It was just a present. But Jeremy was so good at buying her presents. He knew how she was always cold no matter where she went. So every year, he would always buy her...

Karen gulped and her heart started beating a frantic rhythm in her chest when she pulled out the present Brody had picked for her. Inside the bag was the most beautiful red cashmere blanket she had ever seen.

"They did *not* have this at Cure All," she whispered.

Brody smiled softly. "I didn't say I *bought* it there. I just said Jerica wrapped it for me. If I was left to my own wrapping devices all my presents would have come in Swanson's plastic sacks."

"Where did you *get* this?" she asked. "I know it was expensive. Way more expensive than that coffee mug I got you."

"You think I care about what it costs?" Brody asked. "I haven't been gone from New York *that* long. There's a specialty blanket store there just around the corner from my favorite coffee shop. I had a friend stop by one day and Face-Time me so I could pick out the perfect one."

"How did you know red is my favorite color?"

"A little birdie told me," he said with a smile.

"Me! I'm the birdie again!" Breckin called. "Man, I sure do make a good birdie. Everyone is getting damn good presents!"

"Thanks, New York," she said. "I love it."

Brody tucked a strand of her hair behind her ear and smiled. "You know what I love, Raven? The way you've given me a nickname. I think I know what that means."

"Oh, yeah? And what is that?"

"That I've finally won you over."

CHAPTER 13

*B*rody cracked one eye open and stared at his dad's alarm clock. Ten a.m. He didn't think he had ever slept past seven since leaving Parker after high school. Too much to do and see. Too much to learn and discover. Tossing the covers back, he sat up and stretched before squinting his eyes at the light filtering through his dad's dusty blinds. By the looks of them, they probably hadn't been dusted since Brody was six years old.

After everyone had opened their presents the night before, Brody had taken Karen home where she *insisted* on staying…alone. He tried to argue with her about her head and further monitoring but she wasn't having any of it. So he had been a gentleman and driven across town to his dad's empty house to try and forget the woman who had consumed his thoughts since running into her at the grocery store just a short month ago.

Walking to the window, Brody blew on the dust, scattering motes of it into the rays of light. He pulled down one of the blinds and looked out the window, surprised to see a thick blanket of snow covering the ground. It had started snowing when they left his sister's but it must have snowed at least four or five inches in the middle of the night. In Parker, that was considered a blizzard. If school wasn't already out for Christmas break, the kids would definitely be jumping in glee for the snow day. He couldn't remember it snowing this much in his hometown in years.

With a yawn, Brody grabbed a pair of flannel pants off the top of his dad's dresser and walked into the kitchen. One by one, he opened every kitchen cabinet that held food. In every one, he turned up empty handed. On the final attempt, Brody found a jar of peanut butter and package of stale tortillas.

"Maybe there are frozen waffles in the freezer," he muttered. His dad didn't have any syrup but with any luck, they'd be chocolate chip and syrup wouldn't be needed. Fingers crossed, Brody opened the freezer and grinned. Bingo—chocolate chip waffles. His grin quickly faded, however, when he took one out of the package and realized they were probably the most freezer-burned waffles known to all of mankind.

"Well, guess I'm making a trip to Swanson's," Brody said with a groan. He knew the little grocery store would be mad chaos. Any time there was inclement weather in the area the entire town ran in and cleared the shelves of whatever they could get their hands on. Nothing was off limits. Brody remembered one time in high school Marty Samson even grabbing a can of dog food off the shelf when Kelda got the last can of Dinty Moore.

Throwing his NYU sweatshirt over his head, Brody put on his dad's pair of black rain boots by the front door and headed to his black Chevy pickup truck his dad had indeed saved for the time Brody came back home. He wasn't making much of a fashion statement, but considering he was just in Parker he didn't really care all that much.

Mentally thanking his dad for not only buying Brody a truck equipped with four wheel drive but also keeping it in pristine condition, Brody cautiously pointed his truck in the direction of Swanson's. He wasn't worried about *his* driving but with people like Kelda on the road driving illegally, a person never knew what could happen.

As soon as Brody pulled into the parking lot, he realized it was just as he expected. The lot was full of cars, trucks, vans, and SUVs with people rushing in and out of the store. Brody saw Kelda with yellow flags directing Burt's shopping cart. Even with his windows rolled up, Brody heard the curse words spew forth from Netty Delphino's mouth when Burt's cart ran into hers. Kelda answered with a very unladylike gesture in return. All Brody could say was his dad must adore Susan for having to put up with her mother.

Brody was exiting his vehicle when his eyes honed in on a very familiar bluish-green, rundown Mini Cooper. He smiled widely when he saw its owner crouched in front of the car trying to peer under it. What she was looking for, Brody didn't know. But he was going to find out.

"Hey, Raven. Whatcha looking for? Lose your keys?"

At the sound of his voice, Karen jumped and lost her balance. She landed on her bottom flat in the snow in front of her car, completely soaking her black leggings. With a roll of her eyes, she sighed. "Just great. As if my day could get any worse."

Brody held his chest. "I'm hoping that remark was because your ass is now soaked and not because I came to say hi," he said. "After all, I did nurse you back to health after your life-threatening concussion. How is your day *bad* after that?"

"I wouldn't say *life-threatening*," she muttered, her face turning red. If her blush was any indication, she was remembering their kiss just like he was.

"What seems to be the problem, Karen?" he asked. "Because I'm assuming you have a problem other than your wet pants."

"I came to Swanson's to get some food because I basically have nothing, and with this weather I figured it would be smart to get some stuff in case I'm stuck in my house."

"Just like the rest of Parker's population," he said with a smile. "If you had just let me stay the night we could have come together. You know, go green and all that."

Karen rolled her eyes. "Go green?"

"Yeah. Saving the environment and all that shit."

He chuckled when she completely ignored his statement.

"Anyway, on the way here, Sea Breeze started making this awful clanging sound. When I pulled into the parking lot, she shuddered and then went *kerplunk*."

"Kerplunk?"

"That's the only way I know how to describe it!"

"So after going kerplunk she…"

"Won't start," Karen said with a sigh. "I think she's given up the fight."

"Well, I'm sure it was a valiant effort on her part."

"But *now* what am I supposed to do? I can't afford to buy a new car right now. It's too cold to walk everywhere. How am I going to get my groceries home now?" she asked..

Brody tapped his chin in thought. "It seems you are in quite a pickle."

"A *pickle?*"

"You said your car went *kerplunk*. I think you can give me pickle."

He was rewarded with the tiniest hint of a smile. "Okay."

"I guess there's only one thing to do."

"What's that?"

"Ride with me everywhere."

Karen's eyes widened. "No. No, no, no, no, no. That is *not* a good idea."

"Why not? You *need* transportation. I *have* transportation," he said, pointing to his truck. "Not only is it four wheel drive, but my dad kept it in pristine condition. It can even still play my Ninety-Eight Degrees CD."

"You had a Ninety-Eight Degrees CD? Why didn't you play it for me when we went to the pond?" she asked incredulously. "I *loved* Ninety-Eight Degrees!"

"And have you tell me how much you loved Jessica Simpson's husband? No, thanks."

Karen giggled. "I can't believe you owned their CD."

"And why is that?"

"Because it doesn't seem like music you would listen to."

"Told you there was a reason I didn't exactly fit in with the rest of the male population of Parker."

"*The Hardest Thing* was my favorite song by them."

"I sang the one about being the invisible man," Brody said.. "That one was mine." He sang a few lines of the song.

Karen laughed. "That was awful."

"I never claimed to be a good singer. That song got me through some hard times."

"Oh, really?"

"I was in love with Tracy Dixon. She was in love with Tony Harper, star point guard of the Parker High Wildcats. It was very apropos to my sixteen-year-old self."

"I can see that."

"So what do you say, Raven?"

Karen sighed. "I guess I don't have much of a choice, do I?"

"I'm going to pretend that's your way of jumping in jubilation from my generous offer."

Karen rolled her eyes at his comment.

"You know, Raven, most women would be very grateful

for what I've done for you. I've nursed you back to health—which, considering the rate at which you've been rolling your eyes, I'm thinking you're completely healed. I stayed with you and made sure you didn't die, all without taking advantage of you. And trust me," he said, leaning down to whisper in her ear. "You have no idea how hard it was not to touch those bare legs that go on for miles. Now I'm offering you a free ride around town."

Karen pushed him away from her. "You sure do think highly of yourself, don't you, Brody Cooper?"

"It's not that *I* think highly of myself. It's that a *lot* of women in New York speak so highly of me."

"I forgot you were a man whore."

"I'm going to be a gentleman and ignore the mean name you just called me. Now, come on. If I'm taking you all around town, you have to help me shop for groceries. You're used to eating alone. I'm used to ordering takeout."

"*Now* who's not being nice?"

"Am I wrong?"

Karen sighed. "You're not wrong. But people are going to see us together."

"Raven, I'm pretty sure Kelda has told the entire town we kissed. Those high school cheerleaders saw us at school the other day. The rumors are already flying about us. There are probably bets going around about if we're going to beat my sister and Kelda to the altar."

"Let's just get this over with then."

Brody knew an opportunity when he saw one. Linking her arm in his, he walked into the automatic grocery store doors that opened with a whoosh. As soon as he grabbed a cart and pulled Karen next to him, he felt a hush fall over the crowded store. Looking up, Brody notice the eyes of every person on him and Karen.

"See?" she whispered fiercely. "Everyone. Is. Staring. At. Us."

"They're not staring at *us.* They're staring because I wore flannel pajama pants tucked into my dad's rain boots. Well, that and how incredibly attractive I am. Don't worry—I get this all the time."

Brody smiled when that elicited a small smile. Brody's smile quickly faded, however, when he saw Sadie marching toward them, a frown on her face. She was definitely one unhappy café owner.

"Brody Cooper, can I have you help me with something?" she asked through gritted teeth.

"What is it, Sade?" he asked innocently.

"I need help reaching an item on the top shelf. Be a dear and *help me. Now.*"

Sadie ripped his arm away from Karen's and pulled him down the first aisle she saw. "Grab that can. Now," she huffed.

"Which can?"

"I don't know! *Any* can!"

Brody grabbed the first one he saw and cringed when Sadie glared at him.

"Tripe? You had to grab *tripe?*"

"I don't even know what that is!"

Sadie slapped him on the back of his head. "It's the lining of a cow's stomach!"

"Ew! Why would Mr. Swanson even *carry* that?"

"I don't know but I'm stuck with it now. I can't make you put it back. Everyone in the grocery store is staring holes in our heads."

Brody looked around. Sure enough, the store was still dead silent, the customers' eyes rotating between Karen at the front of the store and Brody and Sadie at the beginning of the aisle.

"What are you doing with her, Brody Cooper? I specifically told you to leave her alone."

"No, you told me to be nice to the girls in town. You never said anything specific about Karen."

"I remember specifically talking about Karen!"

"I beg to differ. But despite what you think, I *am* being nice," he said, holding his hands up in the air. "Promise. Just ask her. I nursed her back to health after she got a concussion."

"Karen got a concussion? How?" Sadie asked before shaking her head. "Never mind. I can ask her all about that. But I'm warning you, Brody. You break her heart and I'm coming after you with my rolling pin. She's delicate, that one. And she doesn't need your New York wayward ways to break her."

Brody frowned at Sadie's insinuation. Was that what people in town really thought of him? "You have my word, Sade. I'll be nice...like I've been the entire time I've known her."

Sadie stared at him for what felt like an eternity before finally nodding her head. "Okay. But just know I'm watching you. And apparently, so is the rest of the town."

Brody nodded before walking back to Karen and their empty cart.

"Did you get Sadie what she needed?"

"Yep."

"What was it?" Karen asked.

"What was what?"

"What she needed."

"Oh...tripe."

"What in the world is tripe?"

"Apparently the lining of a cow's stomach."

Karen crinkled her nose and stuck out her tongue, an act

Brody found incredibly adorable. "Why would she want to buy something like *that?*"

"She told me it was Clyde's favorite food," he said. Sadie's poor husband. He already caught flack for so many other things. What was one more thing like tripe?

"I can't believe Mr. Swanson stocks it."

"I heard he keeps it just for Clyde. I can't imagine anyone else eating it, that's for sure. Unless you want to cook up some tripe tonight, Raven."

"Pass," she said.

"Then how about we fill this cart up with some edible food?"

"Anything to get all these eyes off me," she said. "I'm not used to being in the spotlight."

Brody didn't tell her, but he was pretty sure all eyes of the town were on the beautiful, mysterious schoolteacher long before he came back to town.

"Soooo...thanks for the ride." Karen and Brody had just pulled into her driveway, Brody turning the key to kill the engine of his truck. "I can take it from here."

Brody cocked one eyebrow her way. "Take it from here? That sounds like you're dismissing me," he said with a grin. "We both know I'm not leaving until I help you carry all your groceries inside."

"Seriously, that isn't necessary," she replied. "I'm no longer concussed. I'm perfectly capable of carrying my own groceries."

"Concussed? Okay, Meredith Grey."

"What? It's a perfectly acceptable word."

"Whatever you say, Meredith Grey. M.G. Maybe I'll call you that from now on."

"Why can't you just call me Karen? My *name?*" she asked with a huff.

"Because," Brody said, his eyes smoldering as he took a lock of her hair and twirled it around his finger. "Your hair is as black as a raven's feather. Your vocabulary is medically sound like Meredith Grey. But I like the initials best. M.G."

"M.G.?" Karen whispered. He was so close she could smell the watermelon bubble gum he had bought at Swanson's on his breath. It mingled with his cologne, causing all sorts of heat to pool in her belly. Who knew they could be such a heady combination?

"My girl. It has a nice ring to it, doesn't it?" Brody placed his hand behind her head and pulled her face to his until their lips were barely touching. "Whaddya say, Raven? Wanna be my girl?"

Karen's eyes widened. She started to respond but Brody didn't let her. Instead, he pressed his lips against hers. He hadn't shaved that morning, his scruff deliciously burning her cheek as he deepened the kiss. He opened her mouth wider with his tongue, exploring her mouth languidly. Karen moaned at the contact, her tongue intertwining with his. He tasted as sweet as the gum he was chewing.

Brody pulled her closer and wrapped his arms around her waist. He scooted to the middle of the bench seat of his truck and pulled her onto his lap. Lips still locked, he took her legs and placed them on either side of his body until she was straddling his lap. His hands squeezed her ass, Karen's body flush against his. Chest to chest, face to face. Karen could feel his hard erection pressing against her belly. As he ran his hands down her back and up her sides, Karen moaned again.

"Brody…" she whimpered into his mouth.

"Karen, Karen, Karen…what are you doing to me?" he said, pulling away from her and staring into her eyes. "I promised I'd be good but when you look at me like that the only thing I want to do is carry you inside and kiss every inch of your body."

"Promised who? Your sister?"

Brody leaned his forehead against hers. "Sadie. She said you were a nice girl and I should be good and leave you alone. I guess since I've been gone I've gotten a reputation of a man of ill repute."

"I think your reputation is just fine," she whispered.

"Is that so?"

Karen couldn't find her voice so she just nodded.

"What if I told you I've probably been with half the models who've walked the runways of New York? Celebrities, too. I've been a little bit rakish in my New York life. Living the sophisticated dream and all. I didn't date good girls. I didn't date. I wasn't good. So what do you say to that, Karen?"

"I don't want you to be good," she said, surprising even herself. But when she said the words, she realized she meant them. She had been living in the past long enough. Brody was here, in the present. Wanting her. Kissing her senseless every time they were together. Causing her to feel more alive than she had in years. Why not take advantage of the time she had with him? She didn't need a future. She just needed a *now*. "I just want you to be here. Now."

"M.G...Raven...Karen...whatever the hell I decide to call you," he said, kissing her neck and collarbone. "You have no idea how happy those six words make me."

"I think I said way more than six words."

Brody smiled that half-cocked grin of his. "Do you want to be a Meredith Grey or know-it-all?"

He grabbed and strand of her hair again. Running it through his fingers, he lifted it to his nose and inhaled. "Even your hair smells good, Raven."

Karen started to reply but was interrupted by a rap on the

truck window. Startled, she jumped off Brody's lap and tried in vain to right her hair and clothes before whomever was at the door decided to open it. Despite her effort, the steam fogging up the windows and her kiss-swollen lips were a pretty good indication that the two of them hadn't been playing an innocent game of *Truth or Dare.*

With a sigh, Brody looked at her with a grin before fixing her shirt sleeve. "Ready to see who's on the other side?"

"Do we have to?"

"You know whoever it is isn't going to leave until we do."

It was Karen's turn to sigh. "Fine."

Brody rolled down the window. At first, Karen was happy Kelda and Burt weren't on the other side. She had to hold back a groan, however, when she saw the face peering at them. It was none other than Marty Samson, Burt's best friend. There was no way she and Brody were keeping this a secret.

"I was wonderin' what was the matter with your truck," Marty said with a shit-eating grin. "Figured you musta left it runnin' or somethin'. Just a friendly neighbor makin' sure things are all right."

Karen knew Marty knew perfectly well that Brody's truck wasn't running. She also knew he wasn't her neighbor.

"I didn't know you lived around here," Brody said. "I thought you lived over on Elm Street, Marty. Did you move since I've been gone?"

Marty frowned. "Maybe I was just out for a friendly stroll."

"With all this snow? You better be careful. You'll fall and break your hip."

At Brody's words, Marty leaned into Karen's window and pointed an arthritic finger Brody's way. "Listen here, sonny. I mighta had the herpes on my ass a few months ago but there's no way in *hell* I'm gonna fall and break my hip."

Brody leaned over and whispered in Karen's ear, sending shivers down her spine. Her skin was still tingling with the feel of his hands on her body. "Do you know what he's talking about?"

Karen shook her head. "No clue."

"Well...I'm sorry about the...uh...*herpes* problem you had," Brody replied with a stutter. "And I'm sorry for insinuating you might break a hip. You look pretty spry for an ol—"

Brody stopped himself before he called Marty an old man. "You just look pretty healthy. I was mistaken," he finished.

Karen hid a smile behind her hand. Marty Samson did *not* look like the picture of health. In fact, with his hunched shoulders and gnarled hands he looked like he should be walking with a cane. But there was no way Karen was going to point that out.

Marty stared at them for so long Karen began to squirm in her seat. Lord only knows what ideas were coming to life behind the ancient man's watery blue eyes. Finally, he nodded.

"Don't think I don't know what you two were doing," he said. "But I'll let it slide. *This* time."

At his words, Mary continued walking down the sidewalk.

"What is he, the make out police?" Brody asked. "Saving the streets, one kiss at a time?"

Karen giggled. "We might as well go inside. Before he can call Burt, let him know, and have Kelda drive over here and take pictures of us getting out of the car together."

"Too late."

"What does that mean?" she asked.

Brody pointed out the windshield. "See Marty down there? At the stop sign?"

"Yeah."

"See that car stopping beside him?"

"Yes. So?"

"So I'm pretty sure that's Kelda's old Cadillac. I'm pretty sure she's driving illegally since she lost her license when *I* was in high school. I'm pretty sure that's Burt in the seat next to her. And I'm pretty *damn* sure Marty is hopping in the backseat."

Karen squinted her eyes. Sure enough. It was exactly as Brody said. "That little sneak. I wouldn't put it past Kelda to have dropped him off at the curb just to spy on us."

"You think she'd stoop so low?"

Karen raised one eyebrow and looked at him. "Have you ever met an old woman more nosey than Kelda Vanderburgh?"

Brody shook his head. "I guess not."

"Then why do you act surprised?"

"I shouldn't be. After all, some things never change. Especially in Parker, Oklahoma."

CHAPTER 14

*B*rody grabbed Karen's shopping bags out of the back of his truck and followed the pretty school-teacher into her house. Glancing a look around before heading into the kitchen with the sacks hung on his arms, Brody noticed the presents she had received for Christmas at his sister's house sitting on the couch. The lotion set she'd won in *Dirty Santa* on the table. The red scarf his sister had gotten her thrown on the back of the couch. But what brought the biggest smile to his face was the beautiful, red cashmere blanket he had purchased for her sitting in a ball on the couch. She had *definitely* used that blanket last night when she got home.

"You haven't put anything up yet," he said, grinning at her as he noticed her watching him looking around her living room.

"Yes, I have," she said. "I used the blanket last night watching *House Hunters.* I also rubbed the lotion on my legs and feet while watching my show."

Visions of her beautiful hands running up and down her

toned legs as she rubbed the sweet-smelling lotion onto them ran through his head, sending a shiver down his spine. He'd seen those legs bare. He could only imagine what they felt like, both to touch and wrapped around his body.

"I also put up some of the picture frames kids in my classes got me, ate some of their homemade snacks, and read part of the book Susan bought for me."

Karen walked over to the wall leading into the kitchen. "I even hung the sign Kelda got for me, as much as it pained me to do so."

Brody couldn't help but laugh when he saw the sign Kelda had purchased. Front and center was the infamous Grumpy Cat with the words—*You say teach. I say preach*—typed in a perfect symmetrical font.

"Do you ever plan on letting her in your house?" he asked, one eyebrow cocked.

"Not really," she said with a shrug.

"Then I'd chunk that thing," he replied, his smile widening as she giggled. "If she ever gets in, feign ignorance as to where it went."

"It's not like I have a lot of decorations on the walls. I can't say I didn't have room for it."

"Then tell her you hate cats and teaching is hard."

Karen's eyes widened. "She might kill me."

Brody dropped his bags on her couch and walked toward her. "I think I have a solution."

Karen backed up until her back was against the wall. Her head knocked against the tin sign, sending Grumpy Cat crashing to the ground. "What's that?" she asked breathlessly.

"I'll take some pictures of myself...some pictures of *us*...and hang them all over the walls. That way you have a legitimate reason to not hang the awful thing *anywhere*."

Karen rolled her eyes. "Does your ego know any bounds?"

"Why don't you ask the latest Victoria's Secret model? She'd probably have the answer for you."

The light he'd seen so rarely dimmed in Karen's eyes. While trying to keep it light so as not to scare her, he managed to make her feel bad. He *was* an ass. "Hey," he said, cupping her face in both his hands. "I was joking."

"You mean you didn't sleep with her?"

Brody stroked her cheeks with his thumb. They felt like the petals of a rose. "I did. But she doesn't hold a candle to you, Raven."

Karen looked at him, green eyes sparkling under thick, dark lashes. "Whatever."

"I don't ever say something I don't mean. Remember me telling you to ask my sister about that? I was always honest with Breckin. I had a black eye for a week in high school when I told her a skirt she was wearing made her ass look big."

"You didn't."

"I did. She was going on a date. I didn't want her to be upset I *didn't* tell her."

"Your plan backfired, apparently."

Brody nodded. "It did. But I still told the truth from then on. I just did it more tactfully. I mean what I say. And you, Karen Sue Posey, are the most beautiful woman I've ever seen."

His heart skipped a beat as she leaned her face into his touch and sighed. This woman…she was as sweet as she was mysterious. Frail as she was private. What he wouldn't give to see beyond the mask.

"So? You never answered my question in the truck," he said, pulling away from her.

"We were sorta interrupted."

"Well…we're not interrupted now. So? What's it gonna be? Wanna be my girl?"

He could see the hesitation on her face.

"Here's what I'm thinking," he said, not giving her a chance to tell him no. "I don't know how long I'm going to be in town. If I'm here to stay or if I'm going back to New York. I'm assuming you're here to stay. Why don't we take advantage of the time I'm here? We obviously have chemistry. I took care of you when you were concussed. I've never done that for any model in New York. So? Wanna just have fun?"

It was Karen's turn to raise her eyebrows. "Fun?"

"Fun. You know…carefree things that make you smile and not think too hard. Fun. I'm sure you've had fun a time or two in your life. Think back to when you were a kid. That might have been the last time it happened."

She stuck her tongue out at him. "I know what fun is."

"You *do* know what fun is. You know how I know?"

"I'm sure you're going to tell me whether I want to know or not."

"Because you had fun with me at the pond the other day. Admit it."

He grinned when Karen rolled her eyes. "I had fun," she grudgingly admitted.

"Then let me assure you I'm *loads* of fun in other ways. Both in bed and out," he replied, loving the blush that crept up her neck.

"So your *fun plans* were just a ruse to get me into bed?"

Brody stalked toward her again. Placing his hands on either side of her head, he left a trail of kisses along her collarbone and up her neck. He nipped at her earlobe, eliciting a gasp from between her lips, before whispering in her ear, "It wasn't a ruse at all. But rest assured, Raven, you'll have *lots* of fun with me. Fun that will leave you panting before screaming my name."

"Okay, then," she said breathlessly. "Let's have fun."

Brody didn't need another invitation. His lips crushed

against hers and he took both of her hands in one of his and locked her arms above his head. His other hand trailed down her neck and collarbone before cupping one of her ample breasts and kneading slightly. She moaned into his mouth and he deepened the kiss, his tongue tangled with hers. His hand moved from her breast to her hip. Gently, he lifted her leg and wrapped it around his waist.

"Do you feel what you do to me, Raven?" he asked, pressing his erection against her. "Just one look at you and I feel like I'm going to combust into flames."

Letting go of her hands, he grabbed the hem of her shirt and lifted it over her head before dropping it to the floor. This time, it was his turn to gasp. Her beautiful breasts were barely contained in a bright red lace bra. "These," he said, taking one breast in his mouth and sucking gently, feeling it pebble through the lace, "are the most beautiful breasts I've ever seen. Hands. Down."

"I'm assuming you've seen a lot," she replied.

Brody locked eyes with her. "My fair share," he said. One thing he was not going to do was lie to her. "But these put them all to shame. I might not remember another pair of breasts ever again."

He moved his thumb in circles over her other breast, feeling that nipple pebble under his touch as well. He lifted her higher against the wall with his arms and wrapped her other leg around his waist. He pressed his erection at the center of her thighs, grinning as she whispered his name.

"What's that, Raven? Are you by chance having fun?" he asked impishly. He knew he was being a rogue. That was the point. He knew anything serious would send his fragile beauty running as far from him as she could go. So he kept it light. Fun. Carefree. Let her think he was an ass. Better than reveal what he was truly feeling.

Eyes closed, she nodded. "So...much...fun," she said breathlessly.

Grinning, he kissed her collarbone. "Just you wait."

Brody gently placed her legs on the floor and chuckled as she frowned.

"What are you doing? Why are you stopping?" she asked.

"Because as much as I want you, I'm not taking advantage of you. I told Sadie I'd be good."

"And I told you I don't want you to be good! We're just having fun, remember?"

"I remember."

"Then what's the problem?" she huffed.

"If Sadie found out I slept with you before taking you out on a regular date, I wouldn't live to see tomorrow."

Karen groaned. "But you *took* me on a date. To the pond. Remember?"

Brody grinned wickedly. "I do. But it wasn't technically a date."

"Then what was it?"

"An outing. Because it was pretty private. A date is for all to see. So what do you say? Wanna go on a *public* date with me? For show? Then we can come home and ravish each other."

"Do we *have to?*"

"I feel like that's an insult," Brody said. "Seriously. I plan good dates. Promise. And it's all part of the fun."

Karen rolled her eyes. "I was having plenty of fun just now," she grumbled.

"As was I. Make no mistake, Raven. I want to kiss every inch of this gorgeous body. Make you moan. Worship you in every way possible. But I won't do it unless we go on a *public* date."

She sighed. "Fine. It's not like I'm already part of the town's rumor mill now, anyway."

Brody grinned. "Fine. I'll make it fun. I promise."

"One question."

"What is it?" he asked.

"Can we go now?"

Brody laughed. He really was getting to her. Playfully he kissed her on the nose. "Now what would be the fun in that?"

CHAPTER 15

*K*aren wanted to stomp her foot like a petulant child. Just when she decided to let go for the first time in seven years and do something *reckless*, Romeo decided they needed to go on a date. All she wanted was a fun sex session that would leave her sore in places that hadn't been sore in ages.

She shook her head at her thoughts. Fun, casual sex wasn't like her. At. All. Even when she was dating Jeremy it took her almost six months to go to bed with him. But with Brody...he was right. The chemistry was there and so hot Karen felt like she was burning from the inside out. She'd never felt anything like this. Pure, unadulterated lust. With Jeremy, she got butterflies. With Brody...she felt...pterodactyls.

A spark of shame ran through her body at the thought. She almost felt like she was...well, betraying Jeremy's memory. Betraying the love they shared. Even though he was never coming back. Would never hold her again. Jeremy's body was buried in a plot purchased by someone else in a cemetery she'd never set foot in. He wouldn't want her to be miserable.

"Live," he had always told her. "If something happens to me, I want you to live."

She had always shushed him with a kiss, thinking the unthinkable would never happen to them. But it had. And she was tired of not living. Tired of being caught in the nightmare of her past. She deserved this. Deserved fun.

Pushing her memories down deep where no one else would ever touch them, she managed to smile. "So? Can we go now?"

Brody laughed. "No."

"Why?" she said, this time really stomping her foot.

"Because I have to plan this date. And I'm starving and you just bought groceries. Will you feed me?" His stomach rumbled after his words, a testament that he was telling the truth.

"I guess so. We did buy all this food," she said, looking at the grocery sacks in both their hands. "Well, *you* bought all this food."

Brody had chosen to place their grocery items on the conveyor belt while Karen placed the sacks of bagged groceries in the cart. She was really perturbed when she realized Brody had paid for *everything* she had placed in the cart.

"I still can't believe you paid for all my food," she muttered. "I'm a teacher but I'm not dirt poor."

"I didn't do it because I think you're poor," he said.

"Then why did you?"

"Because I plan on eating this food, too. And probably more of it, by the looks of your tiny frame."

"I eat!" she replied indignantly.

"Not saying you don't. Just saying I eat more. Now, shall we go put these groceries away and cook something or are you going to let me faint on your floor from hunger?"

"So dramatic."

Brody grinned. "I *was* in the school play my senior year."

Without replying, Karen turned around, marched into the kitchen, and placed her sacks on the counter. Not sparing him a look, she started unpacking the items and placing them in the large pantry cabinet to the left of the stove.

"You didn't buy much to *cook* cook," he said, taking out a box of Ramen noodles, a couple of cans of Dinty Moore beef stew, and lots of packages of microwavable macaroni and cheese.

"I didn't know *you* were going to be eating my food, too," she said with a huff. "It's usually just me, so I rarely cook. When I do want something not processed I just go to Sadie's or Griff's."

"Make sense."

Karen took one of the cans of beef stew and opened the lid. Grabbing a can of stewed tomatoes and corn, she also opened those, grabbed a pot out of one of the cabinets and dumped all the canned items into it. She then grabbed a shaker of chili powder out of the pantry cabinet and shook some of it into the pot.

"It's Dinty Moore fancied up," she said.

Brody laughed. "Smart."

"I learned how to do it on Food Network's *Guy's Grocery Games*. Well, not to Dinty Moore, exactly, but how to make canned stuff taste better. Guy is always making them play a game called Meals from the Middle where they can only use cans of food to make their dish."

"Sounds interesting."

"You've never seen it?"

"I don't watch much TV," he said with a shrug.

"Well, you should. It's a fun show. My TV is usually always tuned to HGTV or Food Network."

"To compensate for what you *don't* do at home?" he said impishly.

"What's that supposed to mean?"

"Face it, Raven. Decorating isn't your strong suit. All except your bedroom, for whatever odd reason. You just told me cooking isn't, either. Looks like you're living vicariously through television shows."

Karen started to reply that decorating and cooking were things she used to *love* to do but stopped herself in time. Revealing that would only lead to more questions and she had already lied to him about her past too many times. "Grab the box of Jiffy cornbread," she said instead, motioning to one of the sacks. "It should be in there somewhere."

Brody did as requested, also handing her the milk and eggs required to make the batter.

"You know how to make cornbread?" she asked. "I figured you'd be used to all that fancy food New York has to offer."

"I've eaten at my fair share of fancy restaurants. But I grew up in small town Oklahoma. We don't have five star restaurants. At least none that have won any awards. Although I would put Sadie's up against anything in New York."

"Agreed," Karen said.

"One of the few things my dad taught me in the kitchen," he continued. "We mainly ate at Sadie's, but sometimes we would eat a can of Dinty Moore, unfancied of course, and cornbread."

Karen grabbed a bowl out of another cabinet and started mixing all the ingredients for the cornbread. Brody sat down in one of the rickety chairs at the chipped, wooden dining table Mason had included in the house.

"Don't sit in that one—" she started to say. Before she could finish her sentence, however, one of the back legs of the chair buckled under Brody's weight. He went crashing to the floor with a resounding thud. Karen couldn't help it. At the sight of the sophisticated, sexy New York man sprawled out on the floor, she started snorting with laughter.

"Are you *snorting?*" he asked.

"No!" Karen said, covering her mouth.

"I think you were, you big meanie. I could have a concussion now, just so you know."

"You didn't even hit your head."

"I see how it is. No sympathy for the guy who nursed you back to health."

"Don't be a baby," she said, holding back another laugh. "It was just a little fall."

"Tell my ass that fell on the spindles of the back of the chair. I think one lodged in my ass crack."

Tears started streaming down Karen's face. What just happened was too funny.

"You think it's funny? Me falling? You didn't even *warn* me."

Karen nodded her head. "I don't ever sit in here. I forgot."

"You're such a meanie," he said again with a chuckle. "I think you specifically didn't tell me just so you could watch me fall."

"Again with the meanie? What are we, in junior high?"

"I know you are, but what am I?" he said, continuing to chant phrases she said countless times as a kid.

She just rolled her eyes and turned toward the stove. Within twenty minutes, the stew was bubbling and the cornbread was cooked and steaming. Karen grabbed two bowls and filled both of them with stew. She took two pieces of cornbread and crumbled it directly into the stew before slathering one more with butter.

Brody leaned against the counter and watched her.

"What?" she finally said.

"Nothing. It's just that's exactly what I do. Cornbread *in* the stew, one piece slathered in butter."

"It's not like we're the only people to ever eat it that way," she said with a shrug of her shoulders. "Nothing to read into. Besides, you said we're just having fun. Right?"

Brody shook his head as if to clear his thoughts. "Right."

"So let's go in the living room and eat. I think I even have an episode of *Guy's Grocery Games* recorded on my DVR."

KAREN AND BRODY sat on both ends of her couch in companionable silence. It reminded him of the time not too long ago in her bed, Karen reading a book while he played on his phone. He was right that first night he brought her home. Her couch was *really* uncomfortable. He was glad he had made the decision to sleep in her room. For more reasons than an uncomfortable couch, if he was being honest with himself.

They were currently watching the grocery store show on Food Network Karen was telling him about. Sure enough, this episode featured one round where the chefs had to cook nothing but items from the center aisles of the grocery store. Brody crinkled his nose when one of the contestants started slicing and sautéing Spam.

"You don't like Spam?" she asked. He turned to see her watching him, a slight smile on her face.

"Nope. My dad used to take it out of the can and make us eat it. Raw. For breakfast."

She laughed. "It's already cooked, you know."

"Still disgusting."

"Why breakfast?"

"I guess he thought it tasted like bacon. Since he didn't know how to cook bacon, he offered the next best thing."

Brody shrugged and took another bite of his stew. "Which it didn't, by the way."

"It's not so bad if you fry it in a pan like this guy is doing," Karen said.

"I'll take your word for it. As soon as I left home I swore to never eat another bite of Spam again."

Karen grinned and took another bite of her stew. "I bet the Spam fryer wins," she said.

"What do you want to wager?"

"Huh?"

"You just said you would bet me. I asked what you wanted to wager. I'm a great gambler."

"You did have to kind of gamble with your job, didn't you?"

Brody frowned at the memory her comment elicited. "I guess so."

"Oh, I'm sorry. I didn't mean to upset you."

He shook his head. "You didn't upset me. So? The bet?"

"What do you want to bet?" she asked. "It was just a phrase to me. You're the one saying we have to wager something."

"You don't gamble?"

A wrinkle formed between Karen's eyes. "I don't. I've lost too many times."

Brody sensed there was more to the story behind her words but chose not to push it. "Fine. How about another date?"

She laughed. "We haven't even gone on our first official, in public one."

"Deal or no deal, Raven?"

He could tell she was weighing the pros and cons of his offer by the way she looked at the ceiling and bit the corner of her lower lip. It was adorable.

"Since I think I'm going to win," she said, taking his hand and shaking it, "I'll take your bet."

Brody grinned and took her hand in his. "Deal."

"By the way, I eat Spam on a regular basis," she said with a grin.

"Let me know on the days you do."

"Why?" she asked.

"Because those are the days I'll avoid kissing you."

Karen laughed. "You hate it that much?"

"Bacon Spam scarred me for life."

Karen scraped her bowl clean and placed it on the chipped coffee table in front of her.

"How do you stay so skinny eating all of this processed food?" he asked. "If I did that I would blow up fifty pounds."

"Good metabolism, I guess."

"I know a million women in New York who would kill for your metabolism," he replied.

She just shrugged her shoulders. "Be quiet! They're about to announce the Spam fryer is the winner!"

Brody turned to the TV just in time for the host with the bleached blond hair and tattoos, who looked like he should be riding a Harley instead of hosting a cooking show, announce the winner. It was most definitely *not* the Spam guy. He grinned at her triumphantly.

"Told ya," he said with a grin.

Karen groaned. "How could they think that dish was too salty?! It looked good to me!"

"Spam is the devil in canned food form. It curses everyone. He should've gone with the canned bacon and crab meat like the other guy. Then it would have been a fair fight."

She sighed. "Foiled by the Spam."

"Foiled by the Spam," he agreed.

"So? Date now?"

Brody grinned before grabbing her bowl off the coffee table. "Not a chance, Raven. I'm gonna make you wait for it."

"How long will I have to wait?"

Brody grinned at her. "I just thought of the perfect public date for us."

"What?" Karen asked. She couldn't get the feeling of Brody's hands roaming all over her body out of her mind. The sooner they could get the public date out of the way the sooner they could get down to having all the fun he promised her.

"Kelda's New Year's Eve party. It's public and in a couple of days. There will be dancing. You get to wear a pretty dress. Whaddya say, Raven? Wanna go dancing with me?"

Karen felt herself nodding. The thought of dancing with Brody Cooper sent a shiver of desire down her spine. The way he was *looking* at her sent a shiver of desire straight to her lady bits.

"I have one request," he said, staring directly into her eyes.

"What's that?" she asked breathlessly.

"Will you wear red? You look breathtaking in red."

Karen felt her face flush. "It *is* my favorite color."

Brody leaned down and kissed her deeply, his tongue probing her mouth. She moaned at the contact. "I didn't like it much before I saw you in it," he said. "Now I think it's becoming one of my favorite colors, too."

At his words, he walked to the kitchen with their empty bowls. Karen let out the breath she was holding. Saturday night couldn't come soon enough.

CHAPTER 16

*B*rody pulled up to Karen's house and walked onto her front porch. Tapping lightly on the door, he opened it and called, "Raven? You ready?"

It felt like forever since he had seen Karen, when in reality it had only been two days. He was getting used to her being in his daily life. And if he were honest with himself, he found himself counting the hours until he could take her to this damn party more than he'd like to admit. Maybe Kelda's theory about Karen being a witch was right, because he was obviously bewitched.

"Hello?" he called again. Karen's house sounded empty. He knew his sister had convinced Karen to go with her to Lakeview to shop for dresses for the party but surely they didn't mean the day *of.* Especially when it was time to *leave* for the damn thing. He just hoped she didn't freak out at the thought of people *officially* seeing them together in public and decide to run away.

Just as he headed up the stairs to search for her, Karen turned the corner. What he saw took his breath away. She was wearing a scarlet red dress that hugged her perfect curves in all the right ways. It wrapped around her neck in a halter top and fit her snugly all the way to her hip bones before flaring out into some flowy red fabric that stopped mid-thigh. He just thought she had long legs in regular clothes. The dress, coupled with the red satin stilettos she wore on her feet, had her long, smooth legs going for miles and miles and miles.

Brody gulped. He didn't know how he was going to keep his hands off her.

"Breckin *made* me buy it," she said, running her hand down her side self-consciously. "She said it made me look hot and if I refused to buy it she was going to buy it for me, drug me, put me in the dress herself, and drag me to the party. I figured it was easier not to fight her. Your sister can be stubborn. And you asked me to wear red. So this is me... wearing red."

"If that's code for my sister being bitchy, then you are exactly right," Brody said with a laugh. "Raven, you look...stunning."

A blush crept up her face at his words. "Are you sure it's not too...too..."

Brody rushed up the stairs and ran his hand down her face. "What it is is too perfect. Now let's get to this party. I want to see what shenanigans Kelda is causing."

Taking her hand, Brody grabbed her coat off the rack by the front door and carefully helped her into it before leading her down her front porch steps. Unlikely most snowy days in Oklahoma, the snow this time had stayed, some of it causing slick patches of ice to form since the temperatures hadn't gotten above freezing in a couple of weeks. He opened the passenger door of his truck and helped her in before running around to the other side and hopping in his seat.

"You kept the truck running," she said with a smile.

"I did. I didn't want you to get cold."

"It *is* cold outside. I think this might be the coldest it has been since I've been living in Oklahoma," she replied.

"How long *have* you been here?"

She paused before answering. "Going on seven years," she said.

"Seriously, Raven. I know you didn't just wind up in a tiny town like Parker. I think you know by now you can trust me. Wanna tell me what led you here?"

Karen sighed and looked out the window. Just when Brody thought she was going to ignore his question, he heard her voice.

"Something bad happened and I needed to get away," she said. "So I had some...friends...and they looked for a place for me. I lived in a couple of different places before here but never for very long. When I got to Parker...I don't know. I guess it just worked. The first person I met was your sister."

"Oh, lord. I'm sorry."

Karen turned back from the window. "The math teacher before me had quit mid-semester. Something about meeting a man online and going backpacking through Europe. I had seen the opening on the school's website and decided to apply. Your sister was working in her classroom the day I moved all my things in."

"I bet she was very quiet and respectful of you and your newness," he said with a grin.

"Something like that," Karen replied with a grin of her own. "She made me stop unpacking and took me to lunch at Sadie's. Said she was going to call dibs on me as a friend before bitchy Tamara Franks tried to win me over with her fake charm and even faker accent."

Brody grimaced. "I remember Tamara Franks. She was Tamara Tinley when we were in school. And my sister is right. She *is* fake."

"She doesn't teach anymore. Married some rich oilfield guy and now they live in a huge mansion outside of town."

"If she's anything like she was in high school, I feel sorry for the man who married her."

"I think his name is Blakely Wilson."

"Scratch that. Don't feel sorry for him at all. He was a douche who made my high school life a living hell."

Karen laughed. "Well, he's probably gained sixty pounds since you last saw him so I'm sure you could give him a run for his money."

"So anyway, you met my sister and decided to stay in the thriving metropolis that is Parker, Oklahoma?"

"Something like that."

"So?" he asked.

"So what?"

"Are you finally going to tell me where you're from originally?"

Karen stared out the window again. "You were close when you said New York. I grew up in Jersey."

Brody pumped his fist in celebration. "I *knew* it! Why didn't you just tell me?"

"No one here knows I'm from there. Not even your sister. I don't know…too many bad memories I want to escape."

"I understand that. But you know what, Raven?"

"What?"

"Your secrets are safe with me."

Karen smiled a soft smile. "Thanks, Brody."

"Anytime, Karen. And if you ever decide you need to tell someone your story, I'm here."

"I'll keep that in mind."

～

KAREN AND BRODY pulled up to the senior citizens' center just as Breckin and Griffin were pulling into a spot near the front door. Without waiting for Brody, Karen opened her door and walked over to her friend. She didn't like the way Brody's questions unnerved her. She didn't like her willingness to answer them even more. The man had an uncanny habit of weaseling her secrets out of her.

"*Told you* that you'd look like a hottie in that dress!" Breckin, just as small as she was before she got pregnant, hopped out of her husband's Bronco and smiled Karen's way. "I *love* it!"

"I think it's a bit much myself," Karen muttered. "But thanks."

"I bet my *brother* doesn't think it is too much," Breckin said with a wink. "If the way he's looking at you is any indication, he'd rather see you without that dress on."

Karen could feel the blush creeping up her neck. Breckin had a big mouth.

"Sister, I am forever in your debt for convincing her to purchase this dress," Brody said, pulling his sister in for a hug. "She's breathtaking."

"Look at this smooth talker." Griffin walked up to the group with a smile on his face. "No offense, Karen. You look beautiful, but everyone pales in comparison to my *fiancée*," he said, bending down to press a kiss to the side of Breckin's head.

"Hey, now! Don't be getting all romantic and messing up my hair. This is the first time I've dressed fancy since I had Emma and I want to look *good*," Breckin said, jumping out of her husband's arms.

"All I did was kiss your temple!"

Breckin patted her hair, which hadn't moved an inch. "A kiss to my temple leads to you putting your hands in my hair and pretty soon I'll look a hot mess!"

Griff rolled his eyes. "Not even married and already telling me I can't kiss her. The romance is dead!"

Karen laughed when Breckin rolled her eyes right back at her fiancé before leaning up on her tiptoes and kissing him on the cheek. "You can kiss me as much as you want...*after* the ball drops and we ring in the New Year."

Brody took Karen's hand in his and led her toward the door. "What do you think we're going to see in here? Cats? Mandatory hair dyeing stations?"

"You never know with Kelda," Karen said with a shrug of her shoulders.

"Please let it be somewhat normal," Griff muttered under his breath.

Breckin laughed. "Oh, honey. When is *anything* with your grandma *ever* normal?"

"My mom is the lucky one," Griff said, taking a deep breath and opening the doors for everyone. "She and your dad have an excuse to stay home. The excuse we could've used, since *their* excuse is *our* daughter."

"And I told you...I want to *dance!*" Breckin exclaimed, stretching on her tiptoes to kiss her fiancé's cheek.

To Karen's surprise, everything in the senior citizens' center looked...well...like a New Year's Eve party. Three tables filled with food, drink, and black and gold New Year's Eve party favors were to their immediate left. A multitude of chairs lined the other three walls of the large room. Black and gold streamers and balloons hung from the ceiling and a disco ball was circling slowly in the middle of the room. Karen was pleasantly surprised at the normalcy of it all. Could this be a time Kelda actually behaved like a normal human being?

"Oh. My. God. What are they *doing?*"

Karen turned to the sound of horror in Griffin's voice. When she saw what had him so disturbed, she couldn't help but laugh...and praise baby Jesus that Kelda Vanderburgh was *not* her grandma.

"That would be called *twerking*, dear," Breckin said, patting her fiancé on the back. "Your grandmother and her....uh...boyfr...well, I guess fiancé now...are twerking."

"What does that even *mean?!*" Griffin asked, covering his eyes with his face.

"It means she's shakin' dat ass," Brody said with a smile. "Or definitely giving it the ol' college try. She gets an A for effort from me."

"Make it stop," Griffin said, his eyes still solidly shut. "Babe, please make it stop!"

"Why can't *you* make it stop? She's *your* grandmother!"

"Because I will be blinded for all eternity if I have to open my eyes, walk over to her, and make her stop...twer...whatever the hell she's doing!"

Breckin sighed. "I'll try but I don't think she'll listen to me."

Before Karen knew it, Breckin had grabbed her hand and pulled her toward the center of the room.

"What are you doing, Breckin?" Karen asked, trying to take her arm out of her friend's vicelike grip. "She's not *my* grandma!"

"But you're *my* friend. And the closest proximity friend at the most inopportune time. Sorry for you, I really am. But not sorry enough to let you go and try to get my fiancé's ninety-two-year-old grandmother to *stop twerking* in front of everyone by myself. Let that sink in, Karen Posey. Fiancé. Ninety-two-year-old grandmother. Twerking. These words need never be uttered again. Understand?"

The longer Breckin spoke, the more agitated she became. The more agitated she became, the tighter Breckin's grip on Karen's arm. She wouldn't be surprised to see a bruise form later that night.

"Okay, okay! Fine! I'll help...but I don't know what I'll even say."

"You don't have to say anything. You're just there for moral support."

"I kinda think that should be something your fiancé does for you," Karen muttered.

Breckin stopped in her tracks and turned Karen toward where Brody and Griffin were still standing. Brody was patting Griffin on the back and saying something to him. Griffin's eyes were still covered by his hands.

"Does he look like he is going to be good moral support?" she squeaked. "He might break off Burt's boner with his bare hands! I can't have a broken boner on my conscience going into the New Year! It will ruin my marriage mojo! I already have to get married alongside these crazy old people!"

Karen sighed. "Fine. I'll be there for moral support. But you owe me."

Breckin nodded. She grabbed Karen's arm again, this time less tightly, and marched the duo to the center of the dance floor and the two nonagenarians attempting to twerk in the worst possible way ever imagined.

"Kelda. Kelda. Kelda!" Breckin's voice got progressively louder as she tried to get Kelda's attention over the rap music blasting from the speakers.

"Maybe you should tap her," Karen whisper-shouted in Breckin's ear. "She looks pretty caught up in the moment."

Kelda had dyed her hair jet black since Christmas. She wore a gaudy, gold rhinestone headband and flowy, gold flapper-style dress. She looked like a walking advertisement for the decorations filling the room. The dress was getting a good workout, seeing as Kelda's ass thrusts were...while not in *rhythm* with the music...fervent and frenzied. What she lacked in style Kelda definitely made up for in effort. Appar- ently what she was doing was working, at least for her fiancé, because Burt Gallagher was standing behind Kelda, eyes fixating on her gyrations, sporting a major boner.

"Kelda!" Breckin tapped the old woman on the shoulder. Kelda stopped dancing and glared at Breckin.

"What do you think you're doing, Breckin? Other than ruining my twerking action, that is! Do you know how many YouTube videos I had to watch before I mastered this move? It's not easy to do with arthritic hips, ya know!"

Karen wanted to tell Kelda ninety-nine percent of professional twerkers worldwide would not call what Kelda was doing *mastering* their craft but then remembered Breckin told her she didn't have to say a word.

"You're *embarrassing* your grandson!" Breckin said, slapping Burt's hand away that was headed straight for Kelda's derriere. "Ever since we walked in and saw what you two were doing he refuses to take his hands off his face. You're going to cause him to have a heart attack! If you want to....twerk...or whatever...in your *home,* by all means...go ahead. But can you control yourself for just one night... please? I'd like to dance with my fiancé."

Kelda harrumphed at Breckin. "My grandson is a fuddy dud. Always trying to kill my vibe."

"Kelda? Please?" Breckin said. "Just this once."

"Fine," she sighed. "No more twerking. Burty, you're gonna have to go to the bathroom to take care of that boner you're sportin'. I'm sure if I walked off the dance floor with you to *help* Griffin would pitch a fit about that, too."

Burt grumbled something incoherent before toddling off the dance floor and heading toward the bathroom.

"Thank you," Breckin said, giving Kelda a quick hug. "This is going to help make my New Year start out great."

"You think *your* New Year is starting out great? Just wait until you see what I've got up *my* sleeve," Kelda said with a wink.

"Anything having to do with anything sexual on the dance floor?" Breckin asked.

"Nope. Girl Scout's honor," Kelda said, before kissing her pointer and middle fingers and holding them up in the air. "This is the Girl Scouts symbol, right? Or is it the Katniss Everdeen sign for kicking some Capitol ass? I can't ever remember the difference between the two."

Breckin didn't even answer. Instead, she led Karen back to where Brody and Griffin were still standing. "You can open your eyes now, you big baby," Breckin said, punching her fiancé on the arm. "She's no longer twerking and said she wouldn't do it for the rest of the night."

"And Burt's friggin' boner? Yes, I saw it before my eyes were blinded."

"He's taking care of it himself."

"Thank god," Griffin said with a sigh. "Have I told you that you're the most amazing woman I've ever met?"

"Hold that thought. I'm not finished telling you everything."

"What is that supposed to mean?"

"Your grandma told me she wouldn't twerk...but she did tell me her New Year was going to be better than mine because she had something up her sleeve."

"Oh shit," Griffin said. "Somehow that makes me even more scared than the twerking."

Brody raised his eyebrows Karen's way. "Is that how it all went down?"

Karen laughed. "All I can say is I am incredibly thankful she's not my grandma."

"You and me both."

CHAPTER 17

*B*rody hadn't been able to keep his eyes off Karen the entire night. She danced as if she had rhythm in her soul. If he didn't know better, he would swear she was some sort of professional dancer before moving to Parker.

He had swung her around the dance floor, two-stepping to a popular country song. He had grabbed her hips as she swayed to the rhythm to one of the latest dance hits on pop stations nationwide. But his favorite by far was the times he got to hold her close in a slow dance. Smelling the citrus and honey fragrance that was entirely *her.* Feeling her silken hair brush across his arms. It was something he could get used to very quickly.

She and his sister were currently at the table that held a variety of bottled water, liquor, and punches. Karen ran a bottle of water down her neck and brushed her hair off her forehead. Brody's breath caught in his chest. She was stunning.

"She's a beauty, isn't she?" Griff walked up to Brody and grinned. "Not as pretty as your sister, but a looker for sure."

Brody cleared his throat. "She really is," he replied, trying to sound nonchalant.

Griffin put a massive hand on Brody's shoulder. "Nothing wrong with coming back home and putting down some roots, Brody. You sister has told me you didn't always have it easy here. I get it. Parker sure as hell isn't New York City. But we are a tight-knit little community with a lot to offer. Something tells me it would be different for you coming back, especially if you had a woman like Karen by your side."

Brody shrugged his shoulders. "I don't know, Griff. I barely even know her. Seems like a stretch to me."

Griffin smiled again. "I knew the moment I saw your sister get drunk on margaritas in my bar during one of her girl's nights that she was the one for me. I tried to deny it for a while, but I couldn't. Sometimes it just hits you. It doesn't matter if it's a week or three years. When you know, you know."

"Well, I don't *know* anything. Not about Karen. Not about my life. Not even when I'm going back to New York."

"I'm not buying what you're selling, Brody. Maybe you thought she'd just be another notch on your belt, but somewhere down the line that changed."

"Why does everyone think I'm a man whore?"

Griffin quirked one eyebrow. "Seriously? I've seen all the pictures, man. Your sister makes sure to show them to me when she's complaining about you never coming home. I believe one caption called you *New York's Playboy*."

Brody rolled his eyes. "I hate tabloids. I'm not even famous. I just happened to date a lot of…"

"Models? Actresses? Women with an infinite number of digits in their bank accounts?"

"Fine! I might have dated some women who are quite…"

"Popular."

Brody shrugged. "What can I say? I like pretty women.

Maybe it's the inner nerd in me still trying to prove I'm not that nerd anymore."

"Everyone can see you're not that nerd anymore. Even more importantly, everyone sees how you look at *her*," Griff said, nodding his head Karen's way.

"How the hell do I *look* at her, exactly?"

"To quote the great F. Scott Fitzgerald, 'You look at her the way all women want to be looked at by a man.'"

"I didn't take you for a reader, Griff."

"That's because I'm full of surprises."

Brody laughed. At that moment, his eyes caught Karen's from across the room. She had one hand holding her hair off her neck and her cheeks were still flushed with heat from dancing all night. Biting her lower lip, she stared at him and smiled softly. It was in that moment Brody understood what Griff had been talking about just moments ago. Because if Karen asked him to stay in Parker, he wouldn't even hesitate before saying yes. And that scared the hell out of him.

KAREN'S EYES caught Brody's from across the room and she found herself holding her breath. He made her feel alive. Invigorated. Carefree.

They had danced together all night. When other men had asked her to dance, Brody had put his arm around her waist protectively and told them she was with him. It was something she hadn't had in almost ten years. She didn't know if she should be scared, worried, or happy about the way it made her feel.

"I see the way you look at him." Breckin bumped Karen's hip with her hip and grinned. "He is pretty cute, even if he *is* my brother."

"I don't think I look at him any particular way," Karen said evasively.

Breckin laughed. "Oh, honey. You totally do, whether you know it or not."

"Is that so?"

Breckin nodded.

"Well, how do I look at him then?"

"Like he's the last piece of chocolate on earth and you can't decide if you want to rip the packaging off with your teeth and devour it in one bite or take little bits and savor it forever."

Karen could feel herself blush and was thankful her cheeks were still heated from dancing almost the entire time they had been at the party. "I don't look at him like that."

"Bullshit," Breckin said. "You totally do. And it's okay. Just because you haven't told me your story doesn't mean I don't know there's been a lot of heartache in your life, Kare. You of all people deserve all the happiness in the world. Just promise not to move back to New York with him. You have to convince him to stay here. I couldn't deal with Mr. Hammond by myself. You know this. I wouldn't survive."

Karen laughed. "You definitely have a love-hate relationship with our dear principal."

"Ninety-nine percent being the hate side of the equation," Breckin muttered.

"He's not *that* bad."

"That's because he wasn't *your* high school principal."

"Hello? Attention. Attention! That means shut up! Don't you know when to respect your elders?"

Karen and Breckin both turned toward the sound of Kelda's voice booming out of a microphone on the stage in the corner of the room. Instead of her gold flapper dress, Kelda had changed into a lacy white dress that looked more like a lingerie piece than an actual dress. On her feet were a pair of what looked like glass slippers. She must have purchased one hell of a push up bra because the knockers that were usually around her belly button were perky and at attention. Kelda took a few teetering steps toward the edge of the stage. Karen could hear the people in the room collectively holding their breaths, praying Kelda wouldn't fall off and break her hip.

"Burty and I just want to thank everyone for coming to our party," Kelda said. "We sure know how to throw a New Year's celebration, am I right?"

Karen could help but laugh as hoots and hollers came from the geriatric section of the room.

"Now, I told my soon to be granddaughter-in-law I had a surprise for tonight. I want to do it before the ball drops and we usher in 2019. And let me tell ya, it's a doozie."

"What is she going to do?" Karen asked Breckin.

"I have no idea. But I'm kind of scared."

"I don't blame you. I think everyone in the room is."

"So without further ado, I want my hot stud muffin to come up here with me on stage."

Burt emerged from the kitchen area dressed in a black tuxedo, a shit-eating grin on his face.

"Oh, my lord," Breckin whispered. "They're going to get married."

"What? No! Seriously? You think?"

"Why else would she be in white and Burt be in a tux?"

Karen giggled. She bet her friend was dead on with her guess.

"Marty?" Burt called, a hand over his eyes as he searched the crowd. "Get your old ass up here. I didn't pay for you to get ordained online for you to puss out now."

Griffin rushed over to where Breckin and Karen were standing. "Please tell me my meemaw isn't getting married right now."

Breckin chuckled. "Oh, honey. That's exactly what she's doing."

"I can't believe this!"

"Why? It just means we won't have to have a double wedding with them. I'm ecstatic!"

Griff scratched his chin before a smile lit up his face. "You know what? You're right. Get after it, Meemaw!" he yelled loudly.

Karen saw two people rushing over to their small group out of the corner of her eye. She turned and watched Susan and Donnie hurriedly walking toward them, concern written on their faces.

"Mom! What are you doing?" Griffin asked. "Where's Emma?"

"I left her with Gretchen from next door," his mom replied breathlessly. "Mom texted me to get over here as soon as possible for an emergency. I'm freaking out. Is she okay?"

Breckin pointed to the stage. "She's more than okay. I'm pretty sure she and Burt are getting hitched."

"What?" Susan squeaked. "*Now?*"

"I'm not complaining," Breckin replied. "It means no double wedding."

"You know she probably planned this to beat you two to the punch," Breckin's dad said.

"Ask me if I care," Breckin said with a smile. "We're cheering them on."

"Some of you might be thinking, Why is Kelda getting married *tonight?* I'll tell ya why. Burty might kick the bucket at any time. His bowels aren't what they used to be."

"Kelda! You said you wouldn't say anything!" Burty said, trying to grab the microphone from his soon-to-be bride.

The room gasped as Kelda moved even closer to the edge of the stage to get away from her fiancé. Luckily, she realized how close she was just in time and retreated to the safety of the middle of the stage, narrowly missing tripping on the microphone cord.

"Lord, everyone here has heard you blowing it up during our weekly Canasta games," she said into the microphone. "But I promised I wouldn't say anything about your hemorrhoids so I won't."

Kelda turned back to the crowd. "Another reason I wanted to get hitched before the ball drops is because I want to be the last one to get married in 2018. My Instagram followers will love it and I might get a write up in some big fancy magazine like *US Weekly*. They love this sort of shit, especially when it's with old people. Reminds everybody of *The Notebook*."

"You're wasting time, woman. If you want to get married before midnight you better shut your trap and get over here!" Burt yelled.

"Lastly," Kelda said, completely ignoring her man. "Everyone knows by now Breckin and Griff are getting married. My daughter already married Breckin's dad in secret...oops. I don't think I was supposed to tell that. Oh, well."

Donnie and Susan just shook their heads. Karen didn't know if they didn't want people to know or what, but the cat was definitely out of the bag now.

"Anyway, I feel like since *she* already beat me to the punch I deserve to at least get married before my grandson. I've earned the right as the matriarch of the family."

"We whole-heartedly agree, Meemaw," Griffin called. "You get yourself hitched. I'll call *US Weekly* myself."

"I knew you were my favorite grandson for a reason!"

"Kelda, the clock is winding down!" Burt said. "You're gonna miss it!"

"Madge! Hurry up out here with my babies!" Kelda said. "I'm counting on you!"

Madge Perkins, usually Kelda's arch-nemesis because of what Kelda claimed were copycat hair dyes, came out of the kitchen carrying two animal carriers. The room was filled with hisses and yowls of what could only be Kelda's two devil cats, Diablo and Harley Quinn.

"I couldn't get married without my babies," Kelda said. "They're carrying the rings in their little paws and ecstatic to get a new daddy."

"What about the cover charge to get in here?" One of the old ladies in the crowd shouted.

"Easy. That's our honeymoon money...to Bermuda," Kelda said. "I've never been out of the country. I bought Burty a Speedo and me a thong bikini. We'll be the talk of the island!"

Karen shook her head. She was pretty sure this wedding was going to be one that would go down in history as the most memorable wedding in Parker...and the most trauma-tized crowd of people who happened to be on the beach the day Kelda and Burt decided to go for a swim in their new suits.

Placing the microphone back in its stand, Kelda walked over to Burt, smacked him on his butt and smiled. "Ready to get hitched?"

"Ready as I'll ever be."

"Can you believe this?" Karen felt the whisper of Brody's breath on the back of her neck and a shiver ran up her spine. "I shouldn't be surprised that Kelda tricked everyone into coming to her wedding."

"Nothing about Kelda surprises me anymore."

"I guess you're right about that," he said, sending a shot of electricity through Karen's body as he wrapped his arm around her waist and pulled her close. "Let the shenanigans begin."

"Do you, Kelda, take Burt to be your lawfully wedded husband?" Marty, Burt's best friend, asked.

"I plan to love you until my va-jay-jay clunks out and the Viagra don't work for you no more," Kelda replied. "Even then, I'll probably still love you as long as you keep rubbing my feet."

"I guess that means I do," Marty grumped. "You should really stick with the script, Kelda."

"My wedding, my rules, you old coot. Now hurry up."

"Do you, Burt, take Kelda to be your lawfully wedded wife?"

"I love you Kelda, even when you make me dress up in those damn cat shirts, live with your devil cats, and make me drink decaf coffee. I'll rub your feet, even with all the bunions, and I promise to always find illegal Viagra on the internet until your va-jay-jay quits working."

"Then by the power vested in me by Get Ordained Fast dot com, I now pronounce you man and wife. You can kiss your bride."

Burt proceeded to lay a cringe-worthy, open-mouthed, messy, full of tongue kiss on Kelda, much to the dismay of the crowd.

"Yuck," Brody said.

"Agreed," Karen said with a smile.

Everyone in the room began counting down from ten along with some woman Karen didn't know who was hosting *Rocking New Year's Eve* on the television in the corner. At one, the ball dropped and everyone in the room cheered.

"I don't care what you say about it, Raven," Brody said, turning Karen around until they were a hair's breadth away from each other. "I'm going to kiss you now whether you like it or not. Even with the entire room watching."

"Go ahead, Brody Cooper," she breathed. "I already told you I don't want to be good."

At her words, Brody's lips met hers in a toe-curling kiss that Karen was sure to bring her good luck for the New Year.

CHAPTER 18

*K*aren stood in front of her closet and sighed. Brody was scheduled to arrive at her house in less than thirty minutes and she had no idea what to wear. A week had passed since Kelda's New Year's Eve surprise wedding.

She had thought for sure after the New Year's Eve party Brody would have sealed the deal and she would have gotten the long overdue orgasm she deserved. But just as he was walking her to her door, Breckin had called him about Burt and Kelda. Unbeknownst to everyone in her family, Kelda and Burt had decided to leave right after their wedding to head for a hotel in Oklahoma City to catch their flight to Bermuda the next day. They had gotten caught in the snow on the way and were sitting on the side of the interstate waiting for help.

Karen knew neither one of them wanted to call the highway patrol since she didn't think either of them had a license. But Griffin needed someone to go with him to fetch them out of the snow before taking them to the airport and returning their car to its rightful place in Kelda's garage. Reluctantly, Karen had told him not to worry about her and go help out his sister and Griff.

Since then, she had only seen him in the mornings. True to his word, he had been picking her up and taking her to school since Sea Breeze went kaput. She managed to convince him to let Breckin take her home. But that had been the extent of their time together. She had started back to school and he, according to Breckin, had been staying busy helping his dad cut and haul firewood off Annie's property. Karen hadn't realized how much she had gotten used to seeing him on an almost daily basis. Shaking her head at her thoughts, she tried to convince herself it was a good thing. He would probably charm his way back into his boss's good graces soon and would head back to New York. Karen would stay in Parker and forget all about the *bad girl* roll in the sack she almost had. It was probably for the best, anyway. She had never been good at being bad.

One evening, she and Jeremy had been at their favorite karaoke bar. She had hopped up on the stage and belted Carly Simon's *You're So Vain.* Karen smiled to think about the carefree person she had once been. Imagine her surprise when a talent agent who happened to be at the bar for his friend's bachelor party had walked up to her after her performance to ask if she had ever performed professionally. After that, things had become a blur.

Singing in bars all across New York City. Wearing fancy dresses. Being wooed by bands and producers alike. She had caught her big break. A dream she hadn't ever tried to pursue for fear of the unknown. She had been on the brink of stardom when tragedy had struck. In the blink of an eye, her family was ripped from her. Her dream shattered. Reeling from her loss, Karen had holed up in a hotel room with a stranger keeping her safe day in and day out until one day, the powers that be told her they had a way to keep her safe forever as long as she followed their rules. Which Karen had done for almost ten years.

It was a stroke of luck that Karen had chosen her dependable math degree. Instead of banks and financial institutions, however, her protectors had decided math teacher was better suited for a life of quiet solitude. They had pulled some strings to get her a national certification so she could teach wherever she happened to land. Many towns and cities had been Karen's home for short periods of time but nothing had stuck until Parker. She might not have the life she always imagined, always dreamed of, but she was safe. And that was what mattered.

Shaking her head to rid herself of the memories, she stared at herself in the mirror. Karen had let her hair hang free, curling it into soft spirals that fell down her back. What minimal makeup she wore was put on in less than five minutes. Her only frill was the bright red lipstick she had donned. It made her feel sexy.

Staring into her closet, she mentally declared the majority of her clothing too...*something*. Too tight. Too casual. Too simple. Too fancy. Finally, her gaze settled on a simple, kelly green cashmere sweater. Paired with her new favorite camel ankle boots and a pair of dark skinny jeans, she decided it would have to do. As soon as she threw on the jeans and sweater, a knock sounded at her door. He was early.

Grabbing her boots out of the closet, she ran down her stairs and opened the door. As usual, Brody Cooper was looking delicious in a pair of dark wash jeans and a dark grey sweater that had Karen drooling. It was a crime for a man to look as good as he did.

"Hey," she said breathlessly.

"Hey," he replied, smiling that half-smile that had Karen's toes curling in appreciation. "You look...well...wow."

Karen grinned. "I could say the same thing about you."

"Are you ready to go?"

"It depends on where we're going."

"Well...I figured I would take you to eat. Either Griff's or Sadie's, whichever you prefer. Then...well, it's a surprise."

"I told you I don't like surprises."

Brody leaned down and kissed her softly on the cheek. "You'll learn to like them. They're all good surprises. Promise."

Karen rolled her eyes. *"Fine."*

Brody took her hand, led her down the porch and helped her into his truck. "So what will it be? Griff's or Sadie's?"

"I guess we should support your family," she said with a grin.

"To Griff's we go then," Brody said, reaching across his seat to grab her hand. They sat in comfortable silence on the way to the bar, Brody's thumb rubbing a soothing rhythm on the top of Karen's hand.

Opening the door for her, Brody and Karen walked into a bar. Karen swore everyone in the room went silent as all eyes zeroed in on them. Luckily, Megan, the assistant manager, came up to them rather quickly.

"Hey, guys," she said with a smile. "Want a booth in the back?"

"We most certainly would like a booth in the back," Brody replied.

Megan led them through the bar. Karen and Brody walked by a table where Burt and Marty were eating gigantic plates of nachos.

"Well, Jesus, Mary, and Joseph," Marty said, looking over his bifocals at the couple. "I guess you *were* right. She ain't a lesbian."

"I told you!" Burt said, holding out a hand. Marty grumbled before taking a five dollar bill out of his wallet and slapping it in Burt's hand. "Just cuz she hasn't dated since she moved here don't mean she likes the lady bits. I just figured she was an ice queen...or a hermit."

"I for sure thought she was one of them hot lady lovers," Marty grumbled.

"Didn't you see her at my wedding, grinding on that boy she's with right now? That's not something any lesbian I've ever met does!"

"What lesbians do you know?" Marty asked. "I bet you can't name one."

"Well, I just know it ain't that teacher," Burty said, taking a bite of his fries. "Anyone can see how she's got the hots for Donnie Cooper's boy. And I do know a lesbian. That Ellen DeGeneres on TV. She's a *big* ol' lesbian!"

"That don't count! You don't *know* her!"

As Brody and Karen walked away from the old men's table, Brody tried not to laugh...and failed miserably.

"It's not funny!" Karen said through her teeth. "Hot lady lover? The hots for you? *Really?*"

"Hey, look on the bright side. At least he thinks you're hot."

Karen rolled her eyes. "Great."

"Here you go," Megan said, motioning to the booth in the back corner where the lighting was dim. "I wish I could put up a partition for you but this is the best I can do."

"Thanks, Megan," Karen said. "This is fine."

Megan handed both of them menus before walking off with a wave.

"So what's good?" Brody asked.

"You haven't eaten here yet?"

He shook his head. "I've only been here a couple of times, and it wasn't when Breckin and Griff were together. The menu has changed a lot since Megan started working here and Griff let her start adding things."

"What a bad brother you are."

"Yep," he said, a hint of sadness in his voice. "I should've come home more."

Karen took his hand from across the table. "Well, you're here now. That's what matters to them I'm sure."

"I hope so."

Megan came back and took their order, Karen ordering a margarita on the rocks and the grilled chicken sandwich with fries. Brody ordered a double cheeseburger with fries and a Corona with lime.

"I'm glad you eat," he said with a smile.

"Of course I eat. It *is* essential to staying alive."

Brody rolled his eyes. "I know that. But most women in New York...well...they don't eat."

"Well, I'm from *Jersey*, not New York. And we Jersey girls have healthy appetites."

"I like that," he said. "It's a welcome change."

Their food was brought to the table quickly. The food at Griff's was simple but delicious. They engaged in casual conversation, Karen laughing at several things Brody told her. Not only was he handsome, but Brody Cooper was quite the conversationalist. He was smart and witty and engaging. Karen could see why he was such a successful stock broker in New York. He could charm the pants off...well, anything. Probably even a goat. If goats wore pants.

Brody pushed back his plate and sighed in contentment. "Are you ready for our next adventure?"

"Ready as I'll ever be without knowing where we're going," she said.

"Then let's go. We will be there in just a few minutes."

"I can't wait...hopefully."

~

BRODY PUT his truck in park in front of the senior citizens' center. He ventured a glance at Karen, who was staring at the building, a small smile on her face.

"You brought me to Bingo?"

"I hear it's all the rage when the high school is playing out of town during all the sports seasons," he said. "I asked my sister—basketball is on the road tonight."

Karen was still staring out the window. All of a sudden, Brody was rethinking his idea. "Is this okay with you, Raven?"

She turned to him, a huge smile on her face. "I used to go to Bingo with...well, with someone. Good memories."

Brody let out a breath he didn't know he had been holding. He loved seeing the smile his surprise brought to her face. He wanted to make her smile more often. It made the sadness always shadowing her face disappear.

"Since Burt was at the bar, I guess that means Kelda is back from her honeymoon. I bet she's here," Karen said.

"I bet you're right."

"Let's sit as far away from her as we can."

"My thought exactly."

When Brody and Karen entered the building they were met with the noise of the Bingo balls spinning in the metal sphere on the table placed in the middle of the stage. Brody's dad, Donnie, was the man in charge of spinning. He'd pull out a ball, call the number, and hand the ball to Susan, who wrote down the number before placing the ball in a basket.

"I didn't know your dad worked the Bingo table," she said.

"I didn't, either," Brody said with a grin.

"B forty-two," his dad called. "B forty-two."

"What was that?" Netty Delphino called from the back of

the room. "You're gonna hafta speak up, Donnie Cooper! We don't all got elephant ears like Marty Samson! And *someone* took my chair up front!"

Brody's eyes searched the front of the room. He wasn't surprised to see Kelda front and center. Her skin was a hideous orange that could only come from a bottle. Her hair was dyed ocean blue and she was wearing a tank top that said, *I got bagged in Bermuda,* under a red and black flannel button down and black yoga pants.

"I don't see no sign on this back of this chair that says *Netty Delphino!*" Kelda called back to the other woman. "I can't help it you came in late!"

"I sit in that chair *every* Bingo night, Kelda Vanderburgh! You just want everyone to see your tan from your honeymoon!"

Brody snorted. That tan was *not* from a beach. He could see the streaks between Kelda's fingers from where he was standing.

"That's Kelda *Gallagher* to you, Netty!" Kelda said. "I'm a married woman now."

"About time he made an honest woman out of you!" Netty yelled back. "Living in sin for so long I'm surprised God didn't smite you down like he did Sodom and Gomorrah!"

"Those were cities, not people! And besides, God don't care that we do it like bunnies. He wants us to get as much enjoyment out of life as we can before He calls us home. You're just jealous because you don't get any."

"Ladies! If you can't get along you'll have to leave," Brody's dad said into the microphone. "Let's try to keep it civil, okay?"

Netty stuck her tongue out at Kelda, who returned Netty's insult with her middle finger. Brody shook his head. The old people in Parker were nuts.

"Brody! Over here!" Brody looked in the direction of the voice calling his name and smiled. One of his sister's best friends, Colleen "CC" Chandler, was sitting beside a man Brody didn't know. He assumed it was the nurse practitioner who took on the monster job of running the town's clinic.

"Y'all can sit by us!" CC said with a grin. "I was wondering when I was going to see you."

CC looked exactly the same as she did the day Brody left town. Her hair was dyed a bright cherry red and she had a look of happiness on her face that could only come from being in love. "Hey, Cees," he said. "I've been meaning to come by."

"It's okay, Brode. I've heard you've been...preoccupied," she said with a smile directed Karen's way.

Karen's face flushed in embarrassment, so Brody wrapped his arm around her waist and pulled her to his chest. "Something like that," he replied.

"Hi, Karen," CC said.

"Hey," Karen waved. "Hi, Brant. How are things at the clinic?"

"They were quiet while Kelda was on her honeymoon," Brant said. Brody had guessed correctly. He was the nurse practitioner. "Now that she's back...well...Patty has been busy fielding Kelda's and Burt's phone calls. At first, they were convinced they had West Nile before saying it was Avian flu. Now they're stuck on some sort of leprosy or plague."

Brody quirked an eyebrow. "We saw Burt in the bar when we ate. He looked fine and Kelda seems to be holding her own."

Brant rolled his eyes. "Exactly. But it doesn't stop them from finding any ailment they can on Web MD to say they have. I'm Brant, by the way."

"Brody Cooper," he replied, holding out his hand for Brant to shake. "I'm Breckin's brother."

"I've heard about you from your sister and this one," Brant said, nodding toward CC. "It's nice to finally meet you."

"All good things, I'm sure."

CC nodded. "Of course! You were a good big brother. You'd always take us places without complaint."

"Only because Breckin threatened death in my sleep if I didn't."

CC giggled. "Well, whatever. It worked."

"How long have you guys been here?" Brody asked, taking two Bingo cards from the tray on the table, handing one to Karen.

"Oh, I don't know. Long enough for Kelda to call Netty and Madge cheaters," CC said with a waggle of her eyebrows.

"We heard that's what happened last week, too. How can you cheat in Bingo?"

Brant shrugged his shoulders. "Beats the hell out of me. You just dot the numbers."

"O thirty-six," Brody's dad called. "O thirty-six."

"Bingo!" Brody heard Kelda call from her place in the front row.

"Mother!" Susan said, grabbing the microphone from her husband and staring at Kelda. "There's no way you can already have a Bingo! Donnie hasn't even called enough numbers!"

"Come look at it if you don't believe me!" Kelda said. "If it ain't a Bingo I'm a monkey's uncle."

Brody watched in amusement as several people gathered around Kelda's table to see who would win the argument—mother or daughter. Brody thought Susan was nice and all, but his bet was on Kelda.

"I guess you're going to figure out if someone can cheat in Bingo or not," Karen whispered in his ear. He tried not to shiver in response.

"I guess you're right," he said, suddenly not interested at the commotion at the front of the room at all. "Did I tell you how pretty you look tonight?"

Karen smiled softly. "No, you actually didn't."

"Well, that's because I guess I just take it for granted that you know I always think you look gorgeous."

He was rewarded with a blush that crept up her neck and onto her face.

"Want to know my favorite look on you?"

Karen rolled her eyes. "I can pretty much guess which one."

"Oh, really? What would you guess then?"

"The red dress from the wedding."

Brody shook his head. "Wrong."

Karen's brow crinkled. "Really?"

"Really. The dress was amazing, don't get me wrong. But my favorite look I've seen on you was when I had you backed up against your dresser the morning after your concussion. You...clothed in nothing but an old t-shirt, showing all. That. Leg. I'm tellin' ya, Raven, those legs of yours..."

Brody grinned at the heat that danced in Karen's eyes. He was definitely getting under her skin. Which was a good thing since he planned on seeing a lot of her skin before the night was over. He'd been a gentleman long enough. Time to let her loosen up and not be good like she wanted.

"See! I told ya! I wasn't lyin'! Now, give me my card back! I wanna go cash out."

Brody heard Kelda yelling triumphantly at the front of the room. His eyes wandered from Karen's face to Kelda's table.

"I don't know what happened," he heard Susan say to his dad. She must not have been aware she was standing so close the microphone. "I can't find the G twenty-one ball anywhere but she has a Bingo. It must not have fallen in the basket."

"Wait just one cotton pickin' minute!"

"Who's that talking?" Karen asked. "I can't see anything now."

Sure enough, the entire room was now up and gathered around Kelda's table. All but their foursome at the back.

"I *knew* it!"

To Brody's amusement, Madge Perkins, Kelda's arch nemesis, toddled onto the stage holding Kelda's winning card. Where Kelda's hair was ocean blue, Madge's hair was dyed the color of baby poop green.

"What is wrong with her *hair?*" Brody asked.

CC rolled her eyes. "I told her if she wanted to mix blue into the mustard yellow she had dyed her hair last month it would look like baby poop," she sighed. "She wouldn't listen. I dyed it but I take no responsibility for the color."

"What is wrong with the old people in this town?" he asked incredulously.

"I think it's the water," Brant said. "Maybe some sort of metal in the treatment plant isn't getting flushed and is inter-acting negatively with their meds. It's the only thing I can come up with."

"I don't know but I plan on retiring to Mexico before I grow old and get crazy," CC replied.

Madge crinkled her eyes and pointed an accusing finger Kelda's way. "I *knew* one day I would catch you, Kelda Vanderburgh!"

"It's Kelda *frickin'* Gallagher! Get. It. Right." Kelda replied through gritted teeth. "And quit telling CC to make your hair look like baby shit while you're at it!"

Madge's face turned the color of a tomato. "I've been biding my time, waiting for *months* to catch you in the act! And today all my hard work paid off. I *know* you've been cheating and I have *proof!*"

Kelda harrumphed Madge's way. "All that hair dye has gone to your brain," she said. "You can't prove anything."

Donnie rubbed his temples. "What sort of proof do you have?" he asked Madge. "And it better be concrete."

"I always saw Kelda staying after Bingo was over," Madge said, grabbing the microphone from Brody's dad and talking into it. "Before you started working the table, Donnie, Miles Handy worked it. We all knew he had the hots for Kelda."

"Who wouldn't?" Kelda called. "I'm a dime piece!"

"We all knew she was flirting with him relentlessly because he was senile, had one foot in the grave and desperate for a woman. She was working him shamelessly!"

"Who's we, Madge? You and the little birdie who told you all this malarkey?"

"Me," Netty said, having another person in the audience help her onto the stage. "We've been planning it for months. Once Miles got put in the nursing home by his daughter, we saw our chance. All we had to do was ply him with a little extra red Jell-O and some boob action."

Brody saw the smile fall off Kelda's face. Her eyes narrowed, the bad fake tanner settling into the wrinkles on her forehead. "What did you do?"

"We got him to admit he gave you all the old Bingo cards that are supposed to be destroyed after every game!" Madge said gleefully. "I betcha she has a stack of 'em in her purse!"

"No one is gonna look in my purse!" Kelda cried. "Susan, as my daughter, I *demand* you put a stop to this nonsense!"

"How do you know this is an old card, Madge?" Susan asked, the pained expression on her face matching her husband's.

"Because I always marked my cards with a teeny, tiny M in the top left corner, just in case I forgot where I was sitting if I went to the bathroom or something. This old brain isn't as sharp as it once was."

"Sharp enough to foil Kelda's master scheme, apparently," Karen said softly.

Brody let out a laugh.

"I knew nobody could be so lucky all the time. When she called Bingo and I looked at her card, you know what I saw?"

"I bet you saw your little M in the corner!" Netty said triumphantly, pushing her bifocals back up on her face.

"I *did!*" Madge said. "And if you look, Mr. Bingo Official…"

"That's not my name," Brody's dad said. "Donnie's fine."

"If you look, then, Donnie," Madge continued. "You'll see that tiny little M right where I said it would be."

Donnie took the card from Madge's hands and looked in the corner. He handed the card to his wife and shook his head. "She's right. There's an M there."

"I object!" Kelda cried. "This is unconstitutional! I want the evidence thrown out on the basis of illegal entry!"

"Mother, this is Bingo night, not Judge Judy," Susan said with a sigh. "And this is evidence that proves you've been cheating. You obviously won't be able to get your winnings tonight."

"Does that mean she can't play no more? Cuz I vote guilty and say that should be the verdict!" Madge said, giving Kelda the two-fisted bump like Ross on *Friends.*

"I second that verdict!" Netty said. "Give 'er the old heave ho! No more Bingo. Say it with me, everyone. No more Bingo! No more Bingo!"

The rest of the senior citizens in the room started chanting softly at first, growing more vigorous with every emphasis on Bingo.

"Order! Order in the court!" his dad yelled into the microphone.

"This isn't Judge Judy," Susan yelled at her husband over the roar of the crowd. "Stop feeding into the frenzy!"

"Everyone, shut up!" his dad finally yelled into the microphone at a volume Brody was pretty sure woke up everyone in town.

The crowd went silent. Even Kelda didn't have anything to say.

"This is getting out of hand," he continued, this time at a softer volume. "I'm not making this decision myself and neither is Susan...or any of you, for that matter. We'll take it up with the board of the building and see what they have to say. For now, I think it would be best if we wrap up tonight's Bingo a little early and all go home to cool down."

The crowd began groaning. One stern look from Donnie, however, had everyone quieting down quickly.

"Man, your dad can put on a scary *I mean business* face," Karen said.

"No joke. I saw that face a time or two in my youth. I may or may not have wet my pants each time he brought it out."

Karen laughed. "I bet."

"So everyone go home and drink some tea," his dad continued. "Eat some ice cream. Calm down."

Brody laughed when he saw Susan raise her eyebrows at his dad. His dad just shrugged in return. Brody couldn't blame him. He didn't know the right answer to calm the crazies, either.

"Who knew Bingo night would be so entertaining?" CC said, reaching for her purse and her date's hand. "I should say I'm surprised at her behavior, but Kelda's antics stopped surprising me a long time ago. Poor Griffin. Poor Susan. Poor any member of that crazy lady's family."

"Don't forget poor nurse practitioner who has to doctor

that crazy lady," Brant said, kissing CC on her forehead tenderly. "Don't forget to feel sorry for me."

CC returned the kiss to Brant's lips. "My poor, pitiful medical man. I wouldn't trade positions with you for anything."

"I wouldn't trade positions with *you*," Karen said to CC. "You're the one responsible for dyeing their hair all colors of the rainbow…and making sure they like it."

"You're right about that, Karen." CC turned to Brant. "I think it's your turn to feel sorry for *me*."

"Let's be equally sorry for each other and find comfort together," Brant said with a smile. "Deal?"

CC grinned, her entire face lighting up in happiness. "Deal. See you guys."

Brody and Karen waved goodbye to the couple as they walked out the door. "I'm happy for her," Brody said. "CC had a hard childhood. Her parents were pretty kooky."

"Brant was raised in the foster care system and wasn't adopted until he was almost a teenager," Karen said. "I'm glad they found each other."

"Do you hang out with them a lot?"

Karen shook her head. "Sometimes your sister will invite me out with CC and Annie but I've only gone a handful of times."

"Why?"

She shrugged her shoulders. "Scared, I guess."

"Of opening up to people?"

"Something like that."

Brody grabbed her hand. "You ready to get out of here? It looks like the drama is resolving itself. I saw Kelda stomp out of here already."

Karen nodded. "Yep."

"Oh, Raven?"

"Yeah?"

"Don't think our date is over."

"It isn't?"

"Nope."

"What else are we going to do?" she asked.

Brody grinned wickedly. "Something that lets me see you in my favorite outfit."

CHAPTER 19

*K*aren could feel her palms sweating. She tried to wipe them inconspicuously on her pants leg. After they had been interrupted so many times, Karen figured sleeping with Brody Cooper would always be a fantasy rather than a reality. Good thing she decided to shave that morning.

Within what felt like moments, Brody pulled into her driveway and killed the engine. He walked around to her side of the car and opened her door. Grabbing her hand, he led her up to the front porch, grabbed her keys out of her hand, and unlocked it.

He tossed the keys on the table by the door before shutting the door behind them and faced Karen, his face inches from hers.

"So…" he said.

"So…" she echoed.

"Are you sure this is what you want?" he asked, tucking a strand of her hair behind her ear. "I don't want to pressure you, Raven. I want you, I do. But I want you to want me as much as I want you."

"I do," she said breathlessly. "I want you, Brody. So much."

"Then I only have one question."

"What is that?"

"What are we waiting for?" At his words, Brody backed Karen against her front door and brushed his lips against hers. "I think you have the softest lips I've ever kissed, Raven. So, so soft."

He deepened the kiss, opening her lips with his tongue. His tongue languidly explored her mouth, tangling with hers, causing Karen to sigh in pleasure. He was such a good kisser.

"What do you say we take this somewhere more comfortable?" he said, ridding her of her coat before tossing it on the couch. "Your bedroom, let's say."

Karen could only nod in response. His touch rendered her speechless.

Brody grabbed the bottom of her sweater and pulled it over her head, tossing it on the couch with her coat. He growled low in his throat. "I know your breasts are gorgeous, but good lord, Raven."

His eyes met hers, his heavy-lidded with lust. "What are you doing to me?"

Brody grabbed her hips and crushed her to him. His hands traced the outline of her lace bra in lazy circles, eliciting sighs and quiet moans from Karen's lips. He lingered at the underwire before flicking his thumb over her right nipple. Karen gasped. She hadn't been touched there since he last touched her. And that was far too long ago.

"Do you like that, Raven?" he asked. "Does that do it for you?"

Karen moaned again as he repeated the motion, her nipple pebbling at his touch. She nodded.

"I want you to tell me what you want, Karen. Tell me what you like. Let me make it good for you."

"Bedroom," she managed to utter, his lips still touching hers. "I want to go to my bedroom."

Brody leaned back from her and smiled. "Then let's go."

To her surprise, he picked her up and wrapped her legs around his waist. "I knew all that working out would come in handy one day," he said. "I don't want your skin away from mine, so I believe I'll just carry you."

Once in her bedroom, he gently placed her on the edge of the bed. Unsnapping her bra, he dropped it to the floor and just stared. "You are breathtaking. You know that?"

"I haven't had someone touch me in a long time," she said softly, suddenly feeling vulnerable. What if he didn't like what he saw? What if she had forgotten how to do *anything*? It would be beyond mortifying.

Brody uncrossed her arms from her chest where they had settled after he removed her bra. "Then let me make up for all the lost time."

Brody took her left breast in his mouth, flicking the nipple with his tongue. As if they had a will of their own, Karen's hands found Brody's hair. She ran her fingers through the strands, amazed at its softness. He quickly paid attention to her other breast. Karen swore her eyes rolled back in her head and she purred. Backing her onto the bed, Brody quickly rid Karen of her pants, socks, and underwear. She sent up a prayer of thanks that she didn't don a pair of granny panties and chose a pair of slinky lace ones that matched her bra instead.

"Breathtaking," Brody said again. "I can't get enough of you."

At his words, Brody rid himself of his clothes and settled on top of her. Skin to skin, Karen could feel the pounding of his heart against her chest, could feel his erection poking into her stomach. His tongue ran a trail from her earlobe to her collarbone, periodically nipping her skin softly with his teeth.

"You taste so good, Raven," he said against her skin. "So freaking good."

His hand ran up her side, taking her breast and kneading gently. His tongue traced the spots where his hands had been, leaving Karen quaking with need. His tongue was magic. His fingers, pleasure times five. He gently kissed and nipped the skin on her inner thigh before running his tongue up her center. Karen cried out in pleasure. His fingers followed quickly, easing into her as he licked and sucked and did amazing things that had her writhing in pleasure.

Her body coiled tighter and tighter, his tongue and fingers moving in time with Karen's hips. Suddenly, lights exploded behind Karen's eyes as waves of pleasure danced over her skin. What. An. Orgasm.

"Holy hell," she said softly when her body stopped shaking. "Wow."

Brody's eyes met hers and he grinned devilishly. "You taste as sweet as the honey of your perfume. But we're not finished."

He reached into the back pocket of his jeans he'd thrown on the edge of the bed and opened the condom packet with his teeth. Covering himself, he looked down at her and grinned.

"Was that good, Raven?"

Locking eyes with him, she shook her head. "It was."

"Just you wait," he said.

"Seriously?" she asked. "I don't know if…"

Before she could finish her sentence, Brody thrust himself inside her. "I told you we weren't finished yet. Not even close, Raven. Not. Even. Close."

"Brody," she whispered, her body reacting to the feeling of him inside her. He felt so…so…*right.*

"I'm right here, Raven. Just tell me what you want. I'm listening."

"You," she replied. "I want you."

"I'm yours," he replied. "Yours, Raven."

Their bodies fell in a frenzied rhythm, Karen reveling in the feeling of his skin on hers, the pressure building inside her again. His hands roaming over her skin, gently tugging her hair, holding her wrists over her head. His mouth kissing hers, then moving to her shoulder, her collarbone, her breasts.

"Raven," Brody breathed her name into her neck, his body tightening as the orgasm gripped his body. Karen quickly followed, waves of pleasure crashing over her. Brody dropped his chest against hers, his breathing hot against the crevice of her neck.

It was that exact moment that Karen knew she was in big trouble. Brody Cooper had woven a magic around her so tightly she didn't know if she would ever recover.

BRODY COOPER HAD plenty of orgasms in his adult life, but he could honestly say nothing came even close to the one he had just experienced with Karen. She took his breath away. Her touch, the feel of her skin, the noises she made. It was mesmerizing. She just felt...*right*.

"Do you need something to drink?" he asked, his face still pressed into her skin as he breathed her in. "I can go get us some water."

Karen's eyes were still closed. "Mmmhmmm," she muttered. "Water sounds good."

Gently raising himself off her body, he kissed her stomach before grabbing the glass off her nightstand and heading to her bathroom. Dumping the water in the glass in the sink, he filled it with fresh water and took a deep drink. Removing the condom, he threw it in the trashcan and walked back into the bedroom.

Karen was sitting up in bed, the sheet pulled over her breasts while her head rested on several pillows stacked behind her. A sated look of relaxation was on her face.

"You look comfy," he said, handing her the glass of water. She took a long drink before handing it back to him.

"I am," she said with a smile.

"You look happy," he said, grinning back at her.

"You know what? I think I am."

"You know, you'd look a lot comfier and happier if you didn't have that heavy sheet covering up your wonderful breasts," he said with a mischievous smile, pulling the sheet off her chest and looking inside. "Yep, they definitely need to breathe."

"Do they now? And why is that?"

"Haven't you heard? The secret of firm, perky breasts forever is to let them air out whenever possible. Fresh air is good for the perkiness. Or so I'm told."

Karen threw her head back and laughed, a sound so carefree it had Brody laughing as well. Karen's body was amazing. Her intelligence and charm dazzling. But that laugh? That laugh could bring a man to his knees.

"I like hearing you laugh, Raven," he said, his eyes searching hers. "I don't hear it enough."

"I like it when you call me Raven," she replied softly.

"I'm glad you like it," he said, tucking a strand of hair behind her ear. "It's what you remind me of. Beautiful, dark, mysterious."

Karen leaned her face into his hand, Brody cupping her cheek and rubbing it softly with his thumb. She sighed at his touch before yawning deeply.

"We've sure had some exciting dates, haven't we?" he

asked, kissing her on the top of the head. He couldn't manage to take his hands off her.

"We have," she said, snuggling into his chest. "I never thought playing Bingo would be so entertaining."

"You told me you used to play," he said. "Who'd you play with? Mom? Dad? Grandparents?"

Karen didn't say anything for what felt like an eternity. Finally, she whispered, so softly Brody almost missed it.

"No. My husband."

His hand that was rubbing soft circles on her bare back paused. Did she just say what he thought she said?

"You were married before?" he asked quietly.

Karen nodded into his chest. "A long time ago."

"I remember you telling me that the last time I was in your bed but I just thought it was the concussion talking."

"It wasn't. I was married. And unlike what I told you when I was concussed, it was a happy marriage."

"What happened?"

"He died."

Brody's eyes widened in shock. Of all the secrets he thought she would tell him, this was most decidedly *not* one of them. "Wanna talk about it?" he asked. He didn't want to push her. But she was finally opening up to him. He felt if she clammed up now he might not ever get the full story. And he wanted to. He wanted her to trust him.

"It was so long ago," she said. "I don't want to talk about it. Can we just sleep?"

"Sure we can, Raven. Just sleep," he replied. "I'll be right here."

Brody continued to rub soothing circles on Karen's back until he felt her breathing regulate and heard her snoring softly. *Married.* Huh. Maybe she was running from an abuser. It would make sense of why she ended up in a tiny town in Oklahoma. He was probably the Jeremy she yelled at in her sleep the first time he was at her house. But what about the Bella she mentioned? And she said it was a happy marriage. She could have been lying about that. Or meant it was happy in the beginning. He only hoped she would be open enough to tell him all about it when morning rolled around. Until then, he wouldn't worry.

Eyes heavy with sleep, Brody pulled Karen closer and drifted away.

～

FIRE. Heat. Screaming. Death.

Karen sat up in bed with tears running down her cheeks, gasping for breath. Where was she? Where was Jeremy? Oh, my god. Bella.

She hadn't had the dream in so long. Why tonight? Suddenly, a hand ran gently down her back and she realized where she was. Jeremy and Bella were gone. So was Olivia O'Connell. Karen was in Parker, Oklahoma, with Brody Cooper in her bed. Of all the nights for the dream that haunted her to come, tonight was *not* the night.

"Karen?" Brody asked. "Are you okay? You're crying. And you were yelling for Jeremy and Bella. Was that your husband? It's okay. He can't hurt you."

Karen knew she had a look of bewilderment on her face. "Hurt me? Why would you think Jeremy hurt me?"

Brody's eyes met hers. His were squinted in concern. Tenderly, he wiped a tear from her cheek. "I don't know," he said softly. "You said you were married before but didn't want to talk about it. You ran to Parker, Oklahoma from the east coast. I figured it was a case of running from an abusive husband. You said it was a happy marriage, but I thought that could have meant in the beginning or you could have been lying. Did I jump the gun?"

Karen took a deep breath and nodded. "You jumped the gun."

"Want to talk about it then?"

Karen didn't say anything for a few minutes. She had done so well hiding her past from everyone for so long that she had forgotten what it felt like to truly be *her*. Being with Brody for just a short time, Karen had finally felt *alive* again. Happy, even. Taking another deep breath, Karen spoke softly.

"My real name is Olivia. Olivia O'Connell."

Brody gasped, a look of shock on his face. "Holy hell," he said breathlessly. "How on earth did I not recognize you?"

BRODY KNEW shock was written all over his face. He was trying to hold himself together but he knew he was failing miserably. He had completely forgotten about her telling him her last name was O'Connell in her concussed state at Christmas. Shit. He had just slept with Olivia O'Connell. Up and coming jazz singer from a decade ago who, one day, disappeared from the face of the planet. No one had seen or heard from her since. Some people said she was sold into sex slavery. Others thought she had been taken by aliens. No one knew the real truth. Several months after her disappearance with nothing being uncovered, the media moved on to another sensational story. Something told Brody he was going to be shocked by the story he was about to hear.

"So you know who I am?" she asked.

"Of course I know who you are," he said. "I saw you perform a couple of years after I moved to New York. You were mesmerizing. Definitely special. I just knew I was going to have all your albums. Your voice...my god. What *happened* to you? Why'd you disappear?"

Karen...well, *Olivia*...took a deep breath and let it out slowly. "I didn't even mean to become a jazz singer," she said with a small laugh.

"Raven, that's not a career you just fall into," he replied.

"But I did. My husband, Jeremy, and I were at our favorite karaoke bar one night. You should have known me back then. I was wild, carefree. Nothing like I am now."

Karen waved her hand. "Anyway, that's not important. So I got on stage to sing like I always did. When I was finished, a man came up to our table. He was actually an agent who happened to be at the bar at his friend's bachelor party. He asked what I did for a living."

"What did you do for a living?" he asked.

"I was a bank teller," she said with a smile. "I had just graduated with a mathematics degree."

"That explains the teaching," he said. "Sorry for interrupting. Go on."

"After that was a whirlwind. Singing in bars across New York. Going to glamorous parties. My life had changed in the blink of an eye."

"What about your husband? Was he okay with it?"

"Oh, yes. He was totally supportive. And so good with our daughter..."

"Daughter?" Wow. The surprises just kept coming.

Karen looked off in the distance. A smile graced her face but sadness dimmed her eyes. "Isabella. We called her Bella. She was just a year old when it happened."

"When you got discovered?"

Karen shook her head as a tear slipped down her cheek. "The fire."

A knot of dread coiled in the pit of Brody's stomach. He had a feeling what he was about to hear would have him crying as well.

"I thought he worked in finance," she said. "I had no clue."

"No clue about what?"

"My husband was an undercover FBI agent. While we were married, he had infiltrated the Caruso mob in New York. He was about to blow the cover on their entire operation—the sex trafficking, money laundering...all of it."

"Ho. Lee. Shit," Brody said softly.

"I don't know how they discovered who he really was. All I know is one evening I had a show and Bella was sick. We didn't want to leave her with a sitter with her having fever and all, so I went alone. Jeremy stayed home. He was such a good dad," she said, wiping more tears that were falling from her eyes off her cheeks. "When I pulled up to the house, it was nothing but a big ball of flames."

"Oh, Raven," Brody said. "I'm so sorry."

"All I remember is falling to the ground and screaming. I guess I passed out or something. I woke up later in a hotel room with three people I didn't know. They were FBI agents like my husband. They told me what had happened. The fire. The mob. Jeremy's real job."

Brody pulled her to him and kissed her on the forehead. He didn't know what he could say, what he could do to make it better. So he just held her and let her speak.

"To this day, I don't know how I didn't know anything. How could I have been so clueless? How could he have not told me? At least *something*. He owed me that much at least."

Karen pulled away from him and shook her head. "I didn't even get to go to their funerals. The agents said it was too risky. Said the mob definitely knew who I was now, especially since I was an up and coming singer in the city. They said I wasn't safe. Two days later, I met the WITSEC agents responsible for my safety."

"WITSEC?"

"Witness Protection Program," she said, smiling sadly. "From that day forward, I was no longer Olivia O'Connell. I was Karen Posey. I didn't even get to choose my new name. They cut my hair, dyed it auburn, and got me the hell out of Dodge. Luckily, I had a degree in math. They got me a national teaching certification so I could teach wherever I needed to move. It was convenient because teachers are always needed."

"Did you go to Parker first?"

"No. They first sent me to Chicago. Figured I would be comfortable in a large city like New York. Apparently the mob got wind I was there because I was moved in the middle of the night about a month after I arrived. Then I wound up in L.A. Again, another city to make me feel *at home*," Karen said, laughing sarcastically. "As if I would ever feel at home anywhere else."

"Someone apparently recognized me there as who I really was, Olivia O'Connell, so they moved me again. Dozens of different places. No roots anywhere. Somewhere down the line I saw the ad online for a math teacher needed in Parker. At that point, I figured I could find a better place to live than they could, so I told them I was moving to a small Oklahoma town in the middle of nowhere. They agreed."

Karen held her hands in the air. "And here I am."

"Here you are. Are you still part of WITSEC?" Brody asked.

"I don't know if you're ever *not* a part of WITSEC," she said. "But I haven't heard from any agents in at least five years. They would check on me every now and then but once no one heard anything, they stopped coming around. Stopped calling. I've been on my own ever since."

"What about other family?"

Karen sighed and rolled her eyes. "See? They told me I was *lucky*. I was an only child and both my parents had died in a car accident when I was a junior in college. It was just Jeremy and me."

"His parents?"

"He was raised by an aunt who died right after he graduated high school. So if tragedy was to strike anyone, we were the easiest, I guess. No one with any ties to us. No one to have to disappear from."

"Raven," he said softly. "I'm so damn sorry."

"They were my entire world. And then poof! Just like that…they were gone."

Karen wrapped her arms around his waist and cried. Brody just held on. Even when his arms went numb. Even when his back pinched at the awkward angle in which he was sitting. He wasn't going to move until she did. To hell with what his body was feeling.

Finally, she leaned back and wiped her eyes. "Look at you. I got tears and probably snot all over your chest."

"Do you think I give a shit?" he asked. "All I care about is you. Just you, Raven."

"See now why I like it when you call me Raven? It's not Olivia, my real name. But it's not a name given to me by some agent who didn't even give a shit. I always hated the name Karen. There was a girl in elementary school named Karen who used to pull my hair every day."

"Then Karen shall forever be banned from my vocabulary. Piss on mean elementary Karen and fake adult Karen. I will only call you Raven. Or maybe Babycakes? Perky breasts? Legs for days?"

He was rewarded with a small smile. "Maybe you could sometimes call me Olivia? I always loved my real name. I was named after my grandma."

"Absolutely, Olivia. That is something I would be more than happy to call you." And damn if that name didn't roll off his tongue even easier than Raven.

CHAPTER 20

"*Well*, someone is looking very happy this morning." Breckin was leaning against the doorway of Karen's classroom, a large, shit-eating-grin on her face.

"It's too early for your nonsense," Karen said with a wrinkle of her nose.

"What? You can't say that. Of all my friends you are the most morning person," Breckin said.

"That's before..." Karen didn't finish her sentence. If she told her friend the reason she quit being a morning person was because Breckin's brother had been keeping her up all hours of the night she'd never hear the end of it.

"That's funny, because a little birdie told me you've been losing a lot of sleep lately."

Karen could feel her face turning red. "I don't know what you are talking about."

Breckin raised her eyebrows. "Sure you don't. Just keep telling yourself that...Raven," she said with a snort of laughter.

Karen rolled her eyes. Her friend wasn't going to let this one go. "I am happy," she said softly. "Really happy."

It had been a month since Brody had discovered Karen's true identity. It was so refreshing not to hide herself from one person. She had been Karen so long she felt as if she was losing Olivia slowly, which made her sad. Olivia was the best part of her. The part that had been fading ever since she lost her real name and gained the one she hated.

But Brody had torn down her walls and started to mend her heart she thought was forever broken. And slowly but surely, she could see herself becoming the woman she once was.

"I'm so happy for you, Kare," Breckin said. "You've been alone for so long. I'm glad you have someone to put a smile on your face. Although if someone had told me my brother was going to be the one who put it there I would have laughed in their face."

"You and me both," Karen agreed. "I thought he was the biggest ass when I first met him."

Breckin laughed. "He had become kind of pompous. New York made his ego enormous. But since he's been with you, the old Brody has started to show himself again. I like it."

"I'm glad."

"So, has he given you a timeframe of how long he's going to be here? I'm in the dark," Breckin said. "He could pack and leave tomorrow and take you with him."

"Take me with him?" Karen said, trying to hide her nerves. "Why on earth would he do that? We've only been... well, I don't even know if we're *dating*...for a month or so."

"Because I see how he looks at you. And how you look at him. Besides, what is keeping you here?"

Karen tried not to panic. She could *never* go back to New York. But her friend didn't know that. And never could. "You. My job...you."

"You know they have these things called planes that I can hop on and come see you any break I have," Breckin said. "And since I work in a school, I have a lot of breaks."

"What about Griff?"

"He and Emma can come with me."

"What about the bar?"

"Megan can run it."

Her friend wasn't going to let it go. "Well, I don't know what to tell you, Breck. But I'm not going to New York. Heck, I don't even know if *Brody* is going to New York. For all I know he might be staying here."

"Hmmmm," Breckin said, rubbing her chin. "What would he do? He has to have a job."

Karen shook her head. "I have no clue."

"Well, leave it to me to find out. I'll have an answer in no time."

"Oh, really? And how do you plan to do that? What if he doesn't want to tell you what his plans are?"

The truth was, Karen *knew* what Brody's plan was. And the fact of the matter was he didn't have a plan. He was living off his savings and trying to keep his family from finding out there was a high likelihood he'd lost his lucrative job. Karen told him on several occasions he should just be honest with his family. He replied by saying Karen should just be honest with them, too. That always shut her up.

But Brody's secret wasn't hers to tell. Just like hers wasn't his. At least they had each other.

"I've always had a way of eliciting information from my brother he doesn't want to share," Breckin said with an evil grin. "It usually involved blackmail of some sort. Things he didn't want my dad to know."

"He's an adult now. I'm sure he doesn't really care what his dad knows about what he did in his youth."

"Yes, but he probably doesn't want *you* to know some of

the things he did in his youth. Just like he probably doesn't want you to see all the totally embarrassing pictures of him as a nerd before he became the hot stud muffin he is now."

Karen was sure her smile was just as evil as Breckin's. "Ooooh, these I need to see."

"Then leave it to me to find out all his dirty secrets."

At the sound of the bell, Breckin turned to go. "Hey, Breck?"

"Yeah?"

"Can I still see the pictures, even if you find out his secrets?"

Breckin wagged her eyebrows up and down. "Absolutely."

"I can't believe you've never seen *Mystery Men!*"

Brody had just pulled into Karen's driveway after eating at Griff's for Friday dinner. They had planned on going to the high school basketball game since they were playing at home but dinner had run late. Instead of showing up at half-time of the girl's game, they decided to head back to Karen's house to watch a movie.

"Nope," she replied. "Sorry."

"It's one of the greatest movies of all time!" Brody replied.

"Then how come I've never heard of it?"

Brody shrugged his shoulders. "You were incredibly sheltered? I don't know. But Ben Stiller is Captain Furious. Hank Azaria throws silverware. William H. Macy is The Shoveler. It even has Pee-wee Herman."

"All the more reason for me *not* to watch it," she replied.

"I'm telling you, Liv, you're in for a treat," he said, totally ignoring her insult.

"Liv?" she asked.

"Thought I'd try it out," Brody said with a grin. "I like the way it rolls off the tongue."

Karen grinned. "I like it, too."

"Better than Raven?"

Karen pretended to think about it. "I don't care. Whatever you want. Surprise me."

"So, can I also surprise you with the amazing movie that is *Mystery Men? Please?*"

Karen sighed. "Fine. But after we have to watch a movie of *my* choice."

Ben groaned. "Will it be girly?"

"Possibly."

"That means absolutely."

She grinned. "Hey, I'm watching a movie where a guy throws spoons."

"And Pee-wee Herman farts."

Karen groaned. "Sounds *so* like my kind of movie."

"I hear some smartass in that tone."

It was her turn to shrug her shoulders. "Maybe."

Brody scooted over in his seat until their thighs were touching. "I can show you what I do to smartasses, Liv. But you're probably going to like it."

"Does it mean we don't have to watch that ridiculous movie?"

Brody's lips paused inches away from hers. "Absolutely...not."

Right before his lips touched hers, Brody pulled back and grinned. "Now, let's go inside."

He loved the way her breath hitched and he could see the pulse beating a frantic rhythm in her throat. Of all the things he thought he'd find when he returned home, a woman like the one sitting next to him was the last thing he would have pictured. But he had, and the longer he stayed in town the more New York faded into the background. All he could picture when he closed his eyes was the way Olivia's hair fanned across the pillow as she was sleeping. All he could smell was the scent that was so...*her*...he couldn't get it out of his nostrils. All he could hear was the way his name sounded as she whispered it while they were making love. He was in over his head but there was nowhere else he'd rather be.

"You're a punk ass," she whispered.

"Absolutely," he said with a wink. Grabbing her hand, he pulled her over to his side of the truck and out the door. "When are we going to go get you another car?"

"Why? Are you getting tired of hauling me around?" she asked.

"Never. I just know you might want to go to the store at night and I might not be there."

"I can't go to the store at night," she replied. "Everything closes at eight in this town."

Brody laughed. "Isn't that the truth? You know what I miss most about New York?"

"The women?"

Brody rolled his eyes. "No. Being able to get greasy Chinese or a slice of pizza at all hours of the night. I could literally walk out of my apartment at two in the morning, go down to Tony's on the corner and get two slices of the tastiest, cheesiest, greasiest pepperoni pizza in the city."

Karen groaned. "Yum. I really *miss* New York pizza. It's the best."

"Isn't it?"

"Yes," she said with a sigh.

"Do you ever think you'll go back? To New York?"

Karen shook her head. "How could I? Just because...well, just because my family is dead doesn't mean they'll stop looking for me. Who knows what information I could have that would incriminate them?"

"But you don't. Do you?"

"No. But they don't know that. They killed my husband and baby. If they knew where I was...who knows what would happen?"

Brody pulled her to him and kissed the top of her head. "Hey...maybe we can have Tony's delivered."

"To Oklahoma?" she asked, wiping a tear that had rolled down her cheek.

"Why not?" Brody asked, planting a kiss on her forehead, then her eyelids and her cheeks. "Or I could go get it and bring some back."

"You'd do that for me?"

Brody looked her in the eyes and ran his fingers down her cheek. "I'd do anything for you, Raven. Don't you know that?"

And the scary thing was...he would. Being with her made Brody forget all about New York and the things he should be doing with his life. All he could focus on, all that suddenly mattered...was her.

"The scary thing is..." she said with hesitation, "I think I do."

"Well, good. Because I mean it. Now let's go inside before you forget all about watching my favorite movie of all time."

Karen let out a loud groan before walking up her porch steps. "You owe me, mister."

Karen unlocked the door and opened it wide. Before either she or Brody could enter the house, however, a *huge* behemoth of a dog raced up her stairs and ran into her house, the door slamming behind him with a loud *thunk.*

"What the hell?" she said. "Did you just see a huge dog run into my house and slam the door or am I imagining things? Please tell me I'm imagining things."

Brody started laughing. "You're not imagining things. There's a big ass dog in your house. And apparently he wants to be alone."

"Where the hell did he *come* from?" she asked incredulously. "I didn't think any of my neighbors even *had* a dog."

"You talk to your neighbors?" he asked skeptically.

"Well...I've never heard a dog barking, anyway."

"I guess we should go inside and see what the poor fella wants," Brody said with another laugh.

Karen reached for her doorknob and turned the handle but the door didn't budge. "What in the world?" she said under her breath. "Did the damn dog *lock* my friggin' door?"

"How the hell could he possibly do that?" Brody asked. "Maybe the knob is just stuck or something."

Brody reached for the knob himself. It turned, but the door itself didn't open. "I think he threw the deadbolt," he said.

"Please explain to me how on earth a dog could throw a deadbolt?" she shrieked. "He doesn't have opposable thumbs. He doesn't know how to lock things!"

"I don't know! Maybe he hit it with his tail or something. Or jumped up and accidentally turned it with his paw. Did you see the size of his paws? And I've locked your deadbolt before. It turns really easily."

"Unbelievable," Karen replied. "You do know this is something that could only happen to me."

"It's okay. Just unlock the door again and we can go inside and shoo him out."

"Uh...slight problem with that," she replied.

"The problem being?"

"He knocked the keys out of my hand when he barreled past me."

"Still not seeing the problem."

"The keys went sliding on the living room floor and landed behind the couch. At least I think that's where they landed. I couldn't exactly see because his big ass was in the way."

"Are you serious?"

"As a heart attack."

Brody started laughing. "I can't believe this."

"Well, believe it because it's true. My keys are in the house. The door is locked. We're outside."

"Maybe we can tempt him to come outside with some bacon."

"What, do you think I carry bacon around in my pockets?"

"I don't know. Maybe he'll realize his mistake and unlock the door on his own. He's probably waiting by the door right now, just trying to figure out a way to leave."

At his words, the dog inside her house began howling one of the deepest, longest, saddest howls Brody had ever heard. Then Brody heard crashing. Lots and lots of crashing.

"What the *hell* is he doing to my house?!" Karen's voice had risen another octave.

"At least look on the bright side," Brody said.

"There's a bright side to this?"

"Absolutely. There's not much in your house to destroy."

Brody narrowly evaded Karen's fist connecting with his arm. "What? I'm being honest."

Karen rolled her eyes. "You're probably right. But what are we going to do?"

"We'll just get your hide-a-key and open the door."

"I don't have a hide-a-key."

"Who doesn't have a hide-a-key? *Everyone* has a hide-a-key in a gray, plastic rock sitting on their front porch, not fooling anyone."

"I don't."

"Well, why not?" Brody asked.

"Because, like you said, they don't fool *anyone*!"

"No key in a potted plant?"

"Do you see any potted plants?"

"Hiding in the bushes?"

"I. Don't. Have. A. Freaking. *Hide-a-key!!!*"

Brody sighed. "Okay, okay. What about an open window?"

The howling in the house got louder and they heard another crash.

"No open window. Witness protection, remember? I keep everything like a fortress!"

Another crash and more howling came from inside the house. "Brody!" Karen shrieked. "We have to do something! He's going to eat everything inside!"

"I'm thinking!" Brody said. He didn't want to tell her, but it looked like they were up shit creek with no paddle in sight. At least not for a while. He was sure Mason, Karen's landlord, had a spare key. Since he owned the marina at the lake, however, it was going to be at least half an hour before he could get to the house. A half hour they didn't have, not if the howling and crashing from inside the house was any indication.

"Hey, love birds! Did either of you see a big ass, goofy looking dog run this way?"

Brody groaned at the sound of the voice behind them. He turned and saw Kelda standing at the curb, her hands on her hips. Half her hair was candy apple red, the other half was cotton candy pink, no doubt tribute to Valentine's Day.

"As a matter of fact, we have," Karen said. "He's destroying my house as we speak."

"Well, why'd you let him in?" Kelda asked. "That mutt is bad news."

"Why do you have a dog, Kelda?" Brody asked. "I thought you were a cat person."

"Oh, I *am*," she said with an eye roll. "But ever since I called Burt out on his...well, bowel problems...he's been pouting and withholding the sex. He's a dog person so I figured I would get him a dog from Sophie's Haven to make up with him."

"And you chose *that* thing?" Karen asked. "He's the size of a small horse!"

"I figured the bigger he was the less scared of Harley Quinn and Diablo he'd be," Kelda replied. "My cats have been known to be a little temperamental."

"More like the spawns of Satan," Karen muttered.

"No, this *dog* is the spawn of Satan," Kelda said indignantly. "He took one look at my Harley Quinn, who did nothing but let out a friendly little hiss, mind you, and ran out the door. I was holding onto the leash. He damn near tore my shoulder out of socket."

"And he ran all the way *here*?" Brody asked incredulously. "That's like two miles."

"Why do you think I'm so out of breath?" Kelda asked. "I've been chasing him this entire time!"

"How on earth have you managed to keep up with him? That's a long way for someone your age—"

Kelda's eyes narrowed into slits. "You best not say what I think you're gonna say, Brody Cooper. I may be old, but I'm not dead. Besides, I keep in tip top shape by conducting all my Kama Sutra classes at CC's gym."

Brody tried not to shudder. That was an image he never wanted in his mind.

"Well? What the hell are you two standing like idiots for on the porch? Open the door so I can get the damn dog and take him either home or back to Sophie's Haven. Didn't know I'd be adopting a pussy dog. I just don't know if he's gonna work out. I'll bribe Burty for sex in a different way. I'm not a dog person, anyway."

"We can't," Karen replied.

"What do you mean, you can't?"

"Well, when he came barreling up my steps he knocked

the keys out of my hands and then slammed the door in our faces. Then, somehow, he locked the deadbolt. We're locked out."

Kelda stared at them for a few seconds. "You've got to be shitting me."

Karen shook her head. "I'm not."

Kelda let out a loud guffaw and slapped her knee. "That's some funny shit, right there."

"Not really," Karen replied.

"Why not? All you gotta do is get your hide-a-key and unlock it."

"She doesn't have a hide-a-key," Brody said.

Kelda looked at Karen. "You don't have a hide-a-key? Who *doesn't* have a hide-a-key?"

Karen rolled her eyes. "Me. Apparently the only person in Parker."

"I can't believe that. All you gotta do is buy one of them natural looking plastic rocks at Nailed It and hide it in your bushes. Works like a charm."

"Well, I haven't done that yet and I don't have another key," Karen huffed. "So on to plan two."

"I'm sure Mason has a spare but it'll take him at least half an hour to get here from the lake."

Another crash and an even louder howl sounded inside.

"I can't wait that long, Kelda! There's no telling what damage he's caused!"

"At least you didn't have much in the place," Kelda replied. Brody hid his laugh with a cough. Laughing would probably be a mistake right about now.

"Hold on just a second!" Kelda said. "I think I know just how to solve this little problem."

Kelda reached into her hair and pulled out a hot pink bobby pin. "This should do the trick."

"What are you going to do with a bobby pin?" Brody

asked.

"Easy. I'm gonna pick the lock."

"I think that only works in the movies, Kelda," he said. "Not in real life."

"That's why you should leave the thinking to us sexy, older ladies," Kelda said, patting Brody on the cheek as she passed him. "Prepare to be amazed."

Kelda walked up the stairs and pushed Karen out of the way. With a sigh, Karen walked down the stairs and stood next to Brody.

"Do you think she's as full of shit as I do?" she muttered.

"Absolutely. But what can it hurt to have her try? Like she said, it will be half an hour before Mason gets here."

Karen pulled her phone out of her back pocket. "I'm still going to text him now."

"Probably a good idea."

Brody watched as Kelda unbent the bobby pin and proceeded to stick one end of it into the deadbolt lock. To his utter amazement, after a few seconds he heard a click, Kelda turned the knob and the door swung open.

"Told ya," Kelda said, turning to them with a triumphant smile on her face. "Just like taking candy from a baby."

"I can't freakin' believe that," Karen whispered. "Kelda just picked my deadbolt with a hot pink bobby pin."

"Un-freaking-believable," Brody replied.

"She is one scary ass old lady," Karen said. "She's a witch. She has to be. It's the only answer that makes sense."

Brody laughed. "I wouldn't be surprised in the least."

Karen groaned. "I guess we should go survey the damage."

"You know you'll never be able to repay her, right? She's going to want something from you for the rest of her life. And she's probably going to outlive us all."

"I think that terrifies me even more than what she just did with the bobby pin."

CHAPTER 21

*K*aren and Brody walked into her house, Kelda following closely behind. All she could do was stare. There was shit *everywhere*. In just a few minutes, Kelda's damn shelter dog had managed to destroy everything in the entire house.

One couch cushion had a big piece missing, the worn leather tattered and hanging in shreds, couch stuffing poking out the top. The table next to the front door was upended, the basket that held her mail and its contents scattered all over the floor. What few pictures she had on the walls were now in disarray on the floor. The picture she had gotten from Kelda for Christmas was broken into pieces and lying on the floor. It appeared that the only thing to come out unscathed was the red blanket Brody had gotten her for Christmas.

"What the *hell* is *this?*" Kelda pushed her way between Karen and Brody and stared at the broken Grumpy Cat picture on the floor. "That damn dog broke the picture I got you! I paid good money for that, too. Way more than I usually spend on people who aren't even members of our family."

"I'm sorry, Kelda. I hung it up and everything. I never would have guessed a demon dog would have barreled through the front door and destroyed my entire house in one fell swoop."

Kelda picked up a couple of pieces off the floor and fit them together. "Eh. Nothing a little hot or super glue can't fix. You'll have it back on your wall in no time. I'll even come over and help you put it together if you want."

"That won't be necessary!" Karen said a little too quickly. "I…uh…I'm a *master* at super glue. And I love jigsaw puzzles. It will be a fun activity for me to do one night."

Brody quirked his eyebrows her way. Yep. Her excuse was just as lame as she thought. His eyebrows proved it.

"Puzzles? Seriously? There's only one reason a woman who looks like you likes puzzles. And that's because her man has already stopped putting out. Is that the case?" Kelda asked, giving Brody the stink eye.

"If so, I'd kick him to the curb. Life's too short to live it without sex is what I say. Besides, I know a whole lotta men who would be lined up in front of your door if they knew you were single. Especially now that they for sure know you ain't a lesbo since you're dating Brody here. For a long time people wondered. I even had a poll about it on my social media."

"Kelda!"

"What? I gotta have new material to keep my followers interested. There's only so many crazy colored hair pics a gal can post before people start hitting that unfollow button. It's a social media person's worst nightmare!"

"Just curious…how many people thought she was a lesbian?" Brody asked, his eyes laughing as Karen shot daggers his way.

"I think somewhere along the lines of sixty percent or so."

"Sixty percent?" Karen shrieked. "That many people *really* thought I was a lesbian? Why?"

"Because you're beautiful and have gone without a man for such a long time. Things like that don't happen in Parker. We all figured you went to Lakeview for a little hanky panky with another lesbo. Things like that happen in a bigger town, ya know. Not that I have a problem with it. Love is love is what I say. All I know is I could never eat a va—"

Karen interrupted Kelda before she had to hear the words that were about to come out of the old woman's mouth. "Well, I'm not a lesbian!"

"And her boyfriend is definitely *still* putting out," Brody added with a wink.

"I *knew* you two were doin' the nasty!" Kelda said. "You're gonna make some damn pretty babies."

"No babies, Kelda!" Karen said. "We're not even boyfriend and girlfriend!"

"That's not what Mr. Hottie over here just said. He just said boy. Friend. You know the old song. First comes love. Then comes marriage. Then comes Brody pushing a baby carriage."

Karen put her head in her hands, took a deep breath and then graced Kelda with a smile. "Okay, well. Now that we got in the house you can take your dog and go, Kelda. I think we can handle it from here."

"Oh, I think I'm just gonna leave that dog with you two. Now that I think about it, me and dogs just don't mix. And Harley Quinn *may* have stuck her claws in the poor doggy's ass a time or two if I remember correctly. This ol' brain ain't what it once was."

"Oh, no, you're not! You are most definitely *not* leaving that beast of a dog in my house," Karen said.

Kelda shrugged her shoulders. "Why not? He *obviously*

likes it here or he wouldn't have locked you out of your own house."

The pound puppy took that moment to run around the corner. In his mouth was a loaf of bread that had been sitting on the counter that morning. One look at Kelda, however, and the dog's eyes went wide, he dropped the loaf of bread and barreled up the stairs.

"See? Look at him, already making himself at home," Kelda said, patting Karen on the shoulder. "They always say the animal chooses its owner, not the other way around."

"But you chose it, Kelda! *You!* At Sophie's Haven!"

"And his heart led him here. To you. His devoted owner. Besides, the way I see it, possession is nine-tenths of the law, anyway. Seeing as that dog is in your house, he's basically already yours. Consider me a good Samaritan for paying your adoption fee."

With a grin and another pat to Karen's back, Kelda called, "Toodle-oo, Love Birds!" and walked out Karen's front door. Minus one dog.

Karen turned to Brody. "What the hell am I supposed to do with that dog?"

She could tell Brody was trying not to laugh. "Keep him?"

"I can't *keep* him!" she screeched.

"Why not?"

Karen opened her mouth but no words came out.

"I mean, it's not like you don't have the space," Brody continued. "And you could use the company. He looks nice."

"He *looks* like the massive dog in *The Sandlot* that ate all the balls! What if he eats all my balls?"

"The only balls I've seen in your house since I first spent the night here have been my own," Brody said with a smirk. "And trust me, he's not coming nowhere near *my* balls."

Karen threw the piece of Kelda's broken picture she was

holding in her hand his way, which he easily dodged. "I'm serious."

"I'm serious, too. The poor dog was obviously trauma-tized by Kelda and her devil cats. Maybe fate brought him to you."

Karen sighed. She didn't want a dog. She didn't need a dog. But he did look terrified of returning with Kelda. And she didn't think she had the heart to return him to the shel-ter. Even though Sophie's Haven was an amazing place for animals of all kinds, it still wasn't a home.

"Fine. But if he eats anything else I'm returning him."

"Maybe you should buy him some balls. The kind from a store."

"Smartass."

Brody grinned the half-smirk of his that always made butterflies take flight in her belly. "Always," he replied.

Well, that was easy, Brody thought. He just knew when he suggested Karen keep the dog she would have laughed in his face. All it took was just a little nudge and she had agreed to keep the big oaf. Which told Brody one thing—how lonely she had really been for so long.

Brody actually thought her keeping the dog was a fantastic idea. He had a dog growing up. It had gotten him through a lot of dark times. And even though the beast had destroyed Karen's house in just a few minutes, Brody could understand the reason why. If Kelda had taken him home on a leash he'd be terrified, too.

"So what are you going to name him?" he asked.

"I think the more important question is, *Why don't we go up to your room and keep the dog from destroying the one room in your house that looks like you?*" she replied.

Brody motioned with his hand. "Lead the way."

Karen fled up the stairs and into her room, Brody following quickly behind. He let loose the breath he had been holding when he saw her room. It was perfect—not a thing disturbed. The only difference was the behemoth of a dog perched in the middle of Karen's bed.

"Well, it looks like he has made himself at home," Brody said with a laugh.

"Where am I supposed to sleep?" Karen asked.

"You know you can push him down."

"But he looks so comfortable."

Brody looked at the dog. He did indeed look comfortable. His front paws were tucked under his chin and his huge, floppy ears were hiding most of his face. He opened one eye to see who was watching him before letting out a huff and closing it. Guess since he didn't see Kelda he figured he had nothing to worry about.

"You know, he really doesn't look that much like The Beast now that I really see him," Brody said.

"Who?"

"You said he looked like the dog on *The Sandlot*. His name was The Beast. At least that's what the kids called him. Technically, his name was Hercules but the kids didn't know that until the end of the show."

Karen stared at the dog while Brody stared at her. Her hair had come out of its messy bun, silken strands falling in her eyes. The large, stretchy collar of her sweatshirt had fallen off her shoulder, highlighting her delicate collarbone. She really was breathtaking.

"You're right. He looks nothing like that dog."

"Except in size."

Karen nodded. "Except in size."

"So what are you going to name him?" he asked.

"Hershey."

"Hershey?"

"Yep. He's the color of a Hershey bar."

Brody frowned.

"What's wrong with Hershey?" she asked, throwing her hands in the air. "You're the one who told me to keep the damn dog!"

"I was thinking something more…big…bold. Like him."

"Does he look big and bold to you?" Karen asked.

The dog took that moment to roll over on his back, his front legs stretched up in the air, ears flopping to the side of his face and his tongue lolling out of his mouth.

"Definitely not big and bold," Brody said with a laugh. "He looks pretty damn goofy, if you ask me."

"That's it!" she said.

"What's it?"

"His name. Goofy. It fits, right?"

Brody looked at the dog. Ironically enough, it did fit. The dog looked just like Mickey's friend, Goofy. "It fits."

Karen smiled. "I think I'm in big trouble."

"Well, go on, then, Liv. Go introduce yourself."

Karen crawled up on the bed and sat down by the dog. "Hi, Goofy. I guess I'm your new…mom? Owner? I don't really know what to call myself to you. How about your human? That sounds nice."

Brody smiled. Karen with soft edges was someone he could get used to seeing every day of his life.

Goofy rolled over until his head was in Karen's lap. He looked up at her and Brody swore the dog smiled. Apparently Karen's effect on the male species didn't stop at humans.

"I think you are going to be very happy here. You just can't make any more messes," Karen continued. "Because I don't like cleaning."

Goofy licked her arm and Karen giggled. "I'm glad we've come to that understanding."

Brody smiled. "There's one other thing you forgot to tell him."

"What's that?"

"Who I am. And that I don't like sharing the bed."

Karen rolled her eyes. "Goofy, this is Brody. He's my—"

"Boyfriend," Brody supplied.

Karen's face turned red. "Really?"

"Why else do you think I follow you around like a little puppy dog, Liv? Of course I'm your boyfriend."

She smiled and Brody couldn't help but think making her smile was something he wouldn't mind doing for the rest of his life.

"Okay, then. Goofy, meet my boyfriend. Brody. P.S. He doesn't like to share the bed."

As if the dog could understand what she was saying, he hopped off the bed and onto the green chair in the corner.

"Well, would you look at that. I think he understood me," she said, a hint of amazement in her voice.

"I think you two will be perfect for each other," Brody replied with a smile.

"Me, too."

"Too bad he doesn't have opposable thumbs to help you clean up the mess he made downstairs."

Karen sighed. "Do we have to clean it up right now? It's a *big* mess."

"I can think of something else I'd much rather do."

Karen raised her eyebrows and leaned in for a kiss. "Oh, me, too."

"It's settled then. I'll grab my laptop and pull up *Mystery Men* from my queue."

Karen punched him in the arm. "That's not what I meant!"

"Oh, really? What else did you have in mind?"

Karen pulled him onto the bed with her and whispered in his ear. Brody couldn't keep the smile off his face.

"Now that, my dear, sounds much better than watching Hank Azaria throw silverware."

"You're so easy," she said with a grin.

"When it comes to you, always."

CHAPTER 22

"**Y**ou got a *dog?*"

Breckin, Karen, Annie, and CC were sitting in their usual booth at Sadie's sharing a banana split. Ever since Brody learned who she was, Karen found herself participating in things she'd usually shy away from. The girls met every Wednesday to gossip and catch up with each other. Karen had been invited ever since Breckin befriended her but she had only gone to a handful.

It was weird, but since Brody knew about who she really was, Karen found it easier to reach out to more people. She had no intention of ever telling anyone else her truth but she finally felt like she could start making connections with others.

"Well, technically *Kelda* got a dog and decided to leave it at my house," Karen said, taking a big bite of her chocolate ice cream with caramel topping. No, it wasn't a traditional part of a banana split but since Karen made four, she felt like she could come up with her own section. Sadie had no problem adding the extra scoop. Karen was pretty sure the café owner was thrilled Karen was finally participating in the girls' ice cream date on a regular basis and not eating a basic strawberry cone like she used to on the few occasions she would attend.

"Why the hell did Kelda want a dog?" Annie asked, taking a bite of her section. "She's got those crazy mean cats to keep her occupied."

"Shouldn't you know?" CC asked. "She adopted the dog from *your* shelter."

"Just because it's *my* shelter," Annie said, taking a bite of her part of the sundae, "Doesn't mean I'm up to date all the time on every adoption that goes on. Besides, Wyatt and I were out of town last week. There's no way I would have known about it."

"She said Burt was…uh…not putting out," Karen stuttered. It was so disturbing talking about ninety-year-old people having sex. "So she thought she'd get him a dog to make up and *get some.*"

Breckin put her head in her hands while the other two women laughed.

"You are willingly marrying into her family," Annie said, patting Breckin on the back. "Just remember that."

"Yeah. And she's going to be your *grandmother-in-law,*" CC added. "Just let that sink in."

"Guys! Don't tell me things like this," Breckin said with a grimace. "It will make me back out of the wedding."

"Liar," Annie said. "You would marry Griffin Stephens even if Kelda moved in with you."

"Knock on wood before that happens!" Breckin said, leaning over Karen where she was sitting on the inside of the booth to knock on the wooden windowsill next to their table. Karen saw her friend's features relax and a sweet smile form on her face. "But you're right. I would. I'd take a million Keldas if it meant I could have Griff for the rest of my life."

"Whoa! Let's not get ahead of ourselves!" CC said. "You may be able to handle it, but I don't think the rest of us would. The world would end in a Kelda Armageddon."

The other women nodded their agreement. "CC's right, Breck," Karen said. "Don't wish that on the rest of us."

"You might as well finish your story," Breckin said. "We all want to know what happened."

"What story? Is it juicy?" Sadie walked up to their table, a towel draped over her shoulder, her ever-present white apron tied around her waist. Today's eyeglasses were hot pink frames with turquoise stripes down the sides.

"Karen got a dog. Willed to her by Kelda, of all people," CC said, licking her ice cream spoon clean.

"Okay, so not juicy, but interesting nonetheless," Sadie said, grabbing a chair from the empty table next to their booth and sitting down in it. "Now that I am here you can spill."

"So Brody and I are walking up the porch of my house when this dog comes barreling up my stairs from seemingly nowhere," Karen began.

"How are things with you and Brody?" Sadie interrupted. "I told him to be nice to you."

"Sadie, no changing of the subject right now," Annie said. "We can hear all about it after the story about Kelda and the dog. Karen, please continue."

"So this dog comes barreling up my stairs, runs inside and slams the door with...his tail, I guess. My keys go flying in the house after him because he knocked them out of my hand. Somehow, the turd turns my deadbolt and locks us out of the house."

"How did *that* happen?" Breckin asked.

"I don't know. The only thing we can think of is he tried to get out and moved it with his paw on accident. My deadbolt turns crazy easy."

"So what happened next?" CC asked.

"Kelda comes huffing and puffing around the corner, asking if we've seen a dog. We tell her the story and she laughs."

"Of course she does," Breckin replied.

"In fairness, I would, too," Sadie said. "That's pretty crazy."

"That's not even the craziest thing that happened. We're trying to figure out how to unlock the door..."

"Couldn't you just use your hide-a-key?" Sadie asked.

Karen threw her hands in the air. "That settles it. I'm the only person in Parker who doesn't have one. I now know this."

"Who cares about the hide-a-key?" Annie asked, her part of the sundae melting. "Kelda. Dog. Story."

"So she proceeds to pull a hot pink bobby pin out of her half pink, half red hair..."

"She wanted it for Valentine's Day," CC interjected. "I couldn't talk her out of it."

"No one can talk Kelda out of anything," Breckin muttered. "Trust me, I've tried."

"And she picks. The. Damn. Lock. With a bobby pin," Karen finished before turning to Breckin. "She's the scariest lady I've ever met."

Breckin nodded. "Agreed."

"This doesn't explain how you came to keep the dog," Annie said.

"Well, the poor thing destroyed my house trying to find an escape route. And then he took one look at Kelda in my house, his eyes went wide, he dropped the bag of bread he was holding, and ran up my stairs."

"In all fairness, I would probably do that, too, if I was a dog and Kelda adopted me. I'm assuming she adopted him, right?" Sadie asked. "That's the only explanation."

Karen nodded.

"Damn it!" Annie said. "Why would Gretchen let her do that? She knows Kelda is a cat person."

"She can be pretty persuasive," Breckin said, patting Annie's hand. "I'm sure she could charm the devil himself."

"Either that or she stole him," CC said. "I wouldn't put it past her."

"So she tells me she got the dog to make Burt put out but Harley Quinn clawed the dog in the ass as soon as she saw him and the dog took off down the road. She followed him all the way to my house."

"It was fate. You were meant to have that dog," Sadie said. "That's all there is to it. What's another explanation that makes sense?"

"Kelda basically tells me the same thing and that she can't have a pussy dog for a pet. Said she'd get Burt to put out in other ways. And then left."

"Was the dog happy when Kelda left?"

"Brody and I went into my bedroom. I was worried it would be destroyed like the rest of house. But it wasn't. He was curled up on top of my bed, hiding his eyes with his floppy ears."

"Aw! The poor guy was terrified," Annie said.

"When I got on the bed with him, he just rolled over, put his head in my lap, and sighed."

All the women around the table sighed in happiness.

"That's such a happy ending," Breckin said. "I'm glad you have company now. My brother is fine, but dogs are great."

"So what did you name him?" Sadie asked.

"Goofy. With his floppy ears and crazy howl, it fit."

"What does my brother think?"

CC rolled her eyes. "Who cares what Brody thinks? Her house, her rules. He doesn't have to give his permission for

Karen to have a dog. If he doesn't like it, he doesn't have to go to her house."

Karen laughed. "Thanks, CC. I appreciate that. But he's actually the one who convinced me to keep him."

"So now back to Brody Cooper and sleeping in your bed," Sadie said with a sly smile.

"Who said he's sleeping in my bed?" Karen asked evasively.

"The *entire* town. That's who," CC added, throwing her spoon on the table after taking the last bite of her part of the sundae. "Trust me, I hear all the gossip in the shop. Now that people know you aren't a lesbian, they're taking bets on how long before Brody puts a ring on it."

Karen rolled her eyes. "We've only been dating since…"

"Christmas is what I heard," Annie said. "That's when he made out with you at Breckin's Christmas and you got a concussion from running away."

"You know, sometimes I hate living in a small town," Karen muttered. "People are always up in your business."

"Is it wrong?" Annie asked with a smile.

"Well, it's not…*wrong*…but the details are skewed," Karen said with a huff.

"Have you done it yet?" Sadie asked with an evil grin.

"Ew!" Breckin said, covering her eyes. "I don't want to hear about my brother having sex with one of my best friends! Please don't answer that question, Kare. If you love me, you will avoid answering that question at all costs."

"Well, I don't think it's fair to deny *all* of us the details," Sadie said, winking Karen's way. Karen smiled. She knew Sadie was just messing with her friend. "I'm old. I have to live vicariously through all you young 'uns."

Breckin uncovered her eyes. "If you guys are going to talk about this, I'm out. I can't handle it."

Breckin took one last bite of her part of the sundae before sliding out of the booth. "Besides, I have to go pick up Emma. She has a checkup with Brant today."

"Oh, no. Is she sick?" CC asked.

"No. Just a normal well baby visit. By the way, we really love Brant," Breckin said with a smile. "We've started going to him instead of the pediatrician's office in Lakeview. It just hasn't been the same since Dr. Kraig retired."

"Wow, that's saying a lot, Cees," Annie said. "You should tell Brant that. If they trust him with their precious baby then he must be good!"

"I'll let him know," CC said with a soft smile.

Breckin waved goodbye to her friends before heading out the door. This was a turn of events. Karen was always the first one to leave. And the fact she wasn't silently screaming in terror told her just how much she was changing. In a good way.

Sadie turned to Karen. "Okay, girl. Now that the buzzkill is gone we need details."

"I don't know, Sadie…" Karen started.

Sadie slid into the booth Breckin had just left, successfully trapping Karen inside. "Too bad. If you're going to be part of these sundae dates, you have to give details. Those are the rules. Isn't that right, girls?"

CC and Annie nodded, smiles plastered on their faces.

"Don't worry," Annie said. "What happens in sundae club stays in sundae club."

"So what's going on between you and the teacher you gave a concussion to?"

Brody and his dad were sitting in the back booth at

Griff's, sharing a plate of cheese fries and drinking a couple of beers.

Brody, not feeling like answering any of his dad's nosy questions, stuffed a bunch of fries in his mouth and raised his eyebrows in response instead.

"What?" his dad said. "Can't a father worry about his only son?"

Brody swallowed his fries before rolling his eyes. "You're not worried. You're being nosy. Probably because your even nosier daughter put you up to it. Tell Breckin to ask Karen herself if she wants to know what's going on in her friend's life. I'm not spilling the beans."

His dad chuckled. "Yep. You're definitely in a relationship."

"You got *that* from what I said?"

His dad nodded his head. "Sure did. You're worried about what your lady is going to think if you tell something she doesn't want you to tell. You're *definitely* in a relationship."

Brody rolled his eyes. "Whatever you say, Dad."

"Oh, I say," his dad responded, waggling his eyebrows. "What I'm wondering is how she's going to fit into that fancy New York job of yours. Something tells me Karen isn't much for the big city."

Brody couldn't tell his dad, but that thought had entered his mind more times than he'd like to count in the time he and Karen had been unofficially official. Ever since he learned Karen's truth he had been wracking his brain trying think of a way to be with Karen in New York. Every time, he'd come up short. And he hated the way it made him feel.

"We're just two people enjoying each other's company," he said evasively, hoping that would be enough to stave off his father's questioning. "She's a pretty girl, I'm a handsome guy. That's it."

This time his dad raised his eyebrows in disbelief. "That's right, son. Just keep telling yourself that."

"Keep telling yourself what?" Breckin walked over to their booth and plopped down next to Brody, stealing a fry off the plate.

"That he's not in love with that pretty schoolteacher friend of yours," their dad replied, taking a long pull of his beer.

"What? My brother, man of the New York hour, in *love?*"

Brody almost choked on the fries he was swallowing. "I never said *anything* about being in love. I don't know where he got that."

"The look on your face when you talk about her. The way your face lights up when you see her. *That's* where I got that," his dad said, a smug smile on his face.

"You can't fall in love with my friend and move her across the country," Breckin said, stealing a drink of his beer. "I told Karen I was okay with it but the more I think about it the less I'm okay with it. My friend belongs here with me. So just move your ass home already."

Brody rolled his eyes. "Yeah, because jobs are in abundance in Parker, Oklahoma, dear sister."

Breckin's hand hovered over the plate of fries. "You'd really think about it? Moving home?"

Brody grabbed a fry off the plate. "I didn't say that."

"Oh. My. God. You really *do* love her," Breckin said quietly.

"I'd forgotten how nosy you two are," Brody muttered, taking a final drink of his beer. "That's one thing I didn't miss about being home. Always up in my damn business."

Breckin leaned over in the booth and kissed his cheek. "Well, dearest brother, that's because we love you. And you successfully kicked us out of your life for almost twenty years. I feel like I'm entitled to be a bit nosy now that you're back in town."

"You really think that? That I kicked you out of my life?"

Breckin shrugged but he could read the hurt behind her eyes.

"Breck, that's not true. You of all people know how hard it was for me here. I had to get out."

"I know that," she said softly. "But would it have killed you to visit every once in a while?"

Brody felt tears well up behind his eyes. "No, you're right. It wouldn't have. I guess I was working so hard at forgetting my past I also let go of the people who loved me unconditionally."

Brody looked at his dad and sister and tried to squelch the tears threatening to spill. "I'm sorry, guys. I really am."

His dad wiped away tears that were falling from his eyes. "Losing your mom was hard on you," his dad said softly. "I know that. I probably didn't handle it in the best way. I was broken, too. I was just trying to survive. I don't know. I should've gotten you counseling or something."

Brody shook his head. "It's okay, Dad."

"I love you, Kid. You do what you need to do, but just know I'd love having you back home."

Brody was about to answer but his phone took that time to ring. Pulling it out of his pocket, his eyes widened. It was someone he was unsure he would ever hear from again. His boss, James.

"Hold that thought, Dad. I have to take this."

His dad nodded in response, his sister leaned over and kissed his cheek. Walking quickly out of the bar, Brody stepped outside into the crisp air and pressed the green button on his phone.

"This is Brody," he said, hoping his boss couldn't hear what he felt was a slight tremor in his voice.

"Brody, my boy," James's booming voice ripped through the line, "Where in god's name have you been?"

"Well, considering our last conversation back in November, I figured it was in my best interest to make myself scarce for a little while," Brody said. "Or have you forgotten the things you said to me?"

James chuckled. Brody could picture him behind his massive desk in his corner office, smoking a cigar and nursing a Scotch on the rocks. It didn't matter the time of day it was; James always seemed to have a Scotch in his hand. He didn't know how James's liver wasn't liquefied yet.

"Oh, come on now. Don't let that sensitive Southern head of yours get you all pussified. I'm sure I said some unkind things but you have to understand…it was in the heat of the moment," James said. "You lost quite a few clients large sums of money. My phone was ringing off the hook."

"A little birdie told me Sebastian lost even more money than me but he wasn't told to get his *hick ass* off your property," Brody said softly.

"Look, Sonny. Are you wanting an apology? Fine. I'm sorry. I flew off the handle, I did. But the truth is, we have people asking about you, missing your work. So I need to know when you're coming back. I feel like I've been very generous in your time off."

"Time off? James, I didn't even know if I *had* a job waiting for me!" Brody said exasperatedly. "I thought I was *fired* until Jax called me and told me everyone thought I quit."

James sighed. "I don't know what you want from me, Brody. A raise? Bonus? Name your price. I'll pay it. I have clients actually threatening to *leave* the firm if you're not back within the week. So tell me what it will take to make you come back. But let me warn you, Sonny. This is a limited time offer."

"So you'll give me whatever I want? Seriously?"

"Brody, I hired you fresh out of college, green as the day is long and a country bumpkin to boot. I gave you a job when no one else would give you the time of day and watched you grow into your profession. You've made me millions. Did I lose my temper when you lost all the money you did? Yes. Does that mean I think you're not worth saving? Not at all."

"So if I said I wanted a five hundred thousand dollar bonus?"

"Done," James said.

"And a five percent raise?"

"I'll have the paperwork on your desk when you get back."

Brody let out a slow breath. Of all the things he thought James would say, yes to both of his ridiculous requests wasn't one of them. "How much time do I have to think about it?"

"I'll give you three days."

Shit, Brody thought. Three days wasn't near enough time to do what needed to be done. "Does that include the weekend?"

"I'll give you *through* the weekend, just so you can remember how good of a guy I can be. That gives you a week. Plenty of time to get the hell out of wherever you've been hiding all this time and your ass back in your office where you belong. After that, good luck finding a job and money like I can help you get."

Brody dropped the phone back in his pocket, leaned against the side of the building, and let out a huge breath. Damn. Five hundred thousand dollars *and* a five percent raise. He honestly thought he was out of a job. Now look at him, back in the swing of things. Hell, the way things were headed he would probably be next in line to run the company once James retired.

All of a sudden, Brody felt light-headed. If his boss had called him in November, his decision would have been a no brainer. He would have left on the first plane out, no matter the time of day. But now...shit. Now he had a raven-haired beauty that complicated the hell out of things in a big way.

Brody had a big decision to make. The problem was he had no idea what he was going to do.

CHAPTER 23

*K*aren looked up when she heard the knock on her door. She grinned widely when she saw who it was on the end of the knock.

"To what do I owe this fun surprise?" she asked. Brody was leaning against the doorjamb of her classroom, looking too delicious for words.

"Fun? Might I remind you how just a few short months ago you didn't *want* me here? In fact, I think you *threatened* to kick me out if I ever came back," he said, walking up to her desk, perching on the edge, and kissing her sweetly on the forehead. "What has changed your mind, Ms. Posey, hmm?"

"Oh, I don't know," she said teasingly. "I guess you've won me over."

"Well, it's about damn time," he said with a soft smile. "It took you long enough."

"Maybe if you hadn't been such an ass in the grocery store those first few times we met it wouldn't have taken so long to win me over," she replied with a wink.

"I was being my usual charming self. I can't help it you had a stick up your ass in the worst way."

"Hey!" she said, punching him playfully in the arm. "I had no stick up my ass."

"You had a huge, gigantic stick up your ass, Raven. I'm surprised you could even walk."

Karen rolled her eyes. "Whatever. You never answered my question. To what do I owe this surprise?"

Brody looked at her, smiled softly, and tucked a stray strand of hair behind her ear. "Not much. Just went to lunch with Breckin and my dad and got an itch to see my girl. That's all."

"Then why do I sense some sadness behind your eyes?"

"There's sadness behind my eyes?"

Karen reached up and touched his cheeks. "I should know. I often see it when I look at my reflection in the mirror. I'm very in tune with sadness. So what's wrong? Your secret is safe with me, Brody."

Karen watched as Brody took a deep breath and let it out slowly. For some reason, her heart started beating a frantic rhythm in her chest. Whatever Brody was going to say, she had a bad feeling the news wasn't going to work out in her favor.

"I got a phone call while I was eating with Breckin and my dad," he said slowly.

"Yeah? What kind of phone call?"

"A phone call from work."

"As in, your firm in New York?"

"Yeah."

"Oh, no. Brody, did you lose your job?"

To Karen's surprise, Brody laughed softly. "You know, I almost wish I had. But no, I didn't. Quite the opposite, in fact."

A hard knot of dread settled in the pit of Karen's stomach. "What does that mean?"

"My boss called me and basically told me to name my price to come *back* to work."

"But I thought you lost a bunch of money for a lot of clients."

"I did."

"I thought your boss was *really* mad at you for that."

"He was."

"I thought he pretty much told you to get the eff off his property."

Brody raised his eyebrows. "Eff? Really, Raven?"

Karen shrugged her shoulders. "I can't drop the F bomb in my *classroom*. It feels so wrong."

Brody laughed. "You're such a teacher."

"So if you didn't get fired, what *did* he say?"

"He said a lot of my old clients have been asking about me. He told me to name my price to come back. He apologized even. And James Trammell does *not* apologize."

"What did you name?" she asked.

"Something absolutely ridiculous."

"Being?"

"A five hundred thousand dollar bonus and a five percent raise."

Karen nearly swallowed her teeth. She was a math teacher and would have a hard time doing the math on how many years' salaries of her teaching salary that *bonus* would be. "What did he say?"

"He said yes. To both," Brody said, shaking his head and laughing. "Like, what the hell, Raven? I thought he would laugh at me and then fire me for sure. But he said "Absolutely" without even thinking about it."

Brody ran his hand over his face and through his hair. "And the worst part? He's only giving me until the weekend to decide. After that, I guess I really am fired if I say no."

"But that's like a week," Karen said softly.

"At first he said I had to decide in three days," Brody said, locking eyes with her. In his eyes she saw pain she was sure was reflected in her own. "I asked him if I could have through the weekend. I'm honestly surprised he said yes."

"So what are you going to do?"

"I don't know. I mean, I *have* to take it…don't I?" he asked, grabbing her hand and holding it to his chest. "What other choice do I have?"

Karen wanted to tell him it wasn't the only choice he had. She wanted desperately to tell him he could stay in Parker and build a life with her. Move in with her and Goofy and life a happily ever after life just like in a Hallmark Christmas movie. That's what she wanted to say. Because somewhere between calling him an ass in Swanson's and him finding out her truth, she had fallen hopelessly in love with Brody Cooper. Which is why she uttered the words, "Sure. You should definitely take it," instead.

Because the last thing she wanted to do was keep Brody in a town he ran away from so many years ago.

BRODY FELT his heart beating a frantic rhythm as he waited for Karen to answer him. He knew it wasn't fair to spring his news on her like he did. He also knew it wasn't fair to ask her opinion in the way he phrased his question; it basically gave her no way to answer but the way he wanted her to. But he didn't know what else to do.

Part of him wanted her to tell him to stay with her in Parker. Part of him wanted her to give him permission to go. And part of him just wanted to take her to her house, pull her in his arms, and make love to her until he forgot all about any hard decisions he had to make. Because this was the hardest decision he'd ever had to make in his life.

He'd nearly choked on a fry when his dad accused him of loving the woman sitting at her desk in front of him but as he looked into her eyes, he realized it was true. He loved her for her strength. For her resilience. Her determination. And how he was going to walk away from that, he had no clue.

"Come with me," he heard himself say.

"What?"

"You heard me," he said, tucking a strand of hair behind her ear again. "Come with me. To New York. We can build a life there. Together."

"Why do you want me to come with you? You know I can't do that," she said, tears welling in her eyes. "My past… it's just too…"

"It's been so long, Raven," he said softly. "Maybe no one will even remember. You can find a small suburban school where you can teach under your name you have now. And then you can come home to me every night."

"I don't know, Brody. It's so…"

"I love you, Olivia…Karen…Raven. It doesn't matter to me what your name is. I love you so much. I love you for who you are and that beautiful soul that is so damn resilient it shines as bright as the stars at night. And I don't know how the hell I'm going to walk away from you. So come with me. Please."

Her beautiful green eyes widened at his words. "You love me?"

Brody smiled softly. "Yeah, I do. Even after you've severely mistreated me in every way. I'm crazy about your snarky ass. Try not to rub it in."

The woman he loved laughed softly. "I love you, too, Brody. God help me, I love you, even though you were the most vain man I think I've ever met when I first met you in Swanson's."

"Are you trying to tell me it was love at first sight?"

"I'm trying to tell you I had to really talk myself out of punching you in your smug face."

Brody laughed. "Man, you're mean. Tell me why I love you again."

"I don't know the answer to that. Why don't you tell me? All you declared is your love. That's the easy way out, if you ask me," she said with a shrug.

"Telling you all the reasons I love you is going to take a significantly long time," Brody said, kissing her softly on the forehead. "You think you're ready to hear all the ways?"

"Possibly," she said, sighing into his chest as he wrapped his arms around her.

"Well, let me just say I probably fell in love with you the second I saw how atrocious of a skater you are."

Not taking her head off his chest, she punched him playfully on the arm. "Rude."

"Or maybe it was when you graciously wiped out in front of your car at my family's Christmas. That was pretty memorable."

"You're not winning any brownie points here, mister."

"Raven, I love you because you're you. And I can't imagine my life without you in it. Simple as that."

Karen looked up at him, tears in her eyes. "I'll take it."

"So? Are you going to move to New York with me? You can even bring your new roommate."

Karen shrugged. "Why not?"

Brody let out a breath he had been holding. "Thank god."

"Did you think I was going to say no?"

"I did. And I had no clue what I would have done."

"I guess it's good you have me to make all the important decisions then."

Brody kissed the woman he loved gently on the lips. "You're damn right about that."

CHAPTER 24

"*I* can't believe you're leaving for good in a month and a half! What am I going to do when you're gone, huh? Leave it to my stupid brother to make one of my best friends fall in love with him and move across the country."

Breckin was sitting on Karen's bed, watching Karen pack her suitcase. It was the weekend before spring break, and Karen was packing for a trip to see Brody during the week she was off work. She was equal parts nervous and excited. As soon as Karen had agreed to move to New York with him, they had told his family he was going back to New York the following week, Karen to follow right after the school year. They had been understandably upset, but also happy for Karen and Brody.

"You'll be fine. Your actual best friends are still here in Parker, Breck," Karen said with a shrug, tossing a couple extra pair of underwear in her suitcase for good measure. "You probably won't even miss me."

"Don't you dare say that to me, Karen Posey!" Breckin said vehemently. "Yes, Annie and CC are my best friends and we grew up together. But that doesn't make them any more important than you in my life. I love you and consider you one of my very best friends right along with those two. It's not going to be the same without you here. Who am I going to talk to at school? I'm going to have to make other friends now. Ugh. Gross."

Karen pulled Breckin in for a hug. "I'm sorry. I didn't mean to make you feel bad. Of course I'm going to miss you, too. You'll just have to come see us in New York, is all."

Breckin wrinkled her nose. "I don't know about New York. There's an awful lot of people there."

"Oh, Breckin, you'll *love* New York. I've missed it so much," she said. "It's going to be surreal going back."

"I'd forgotten you let it slip a while back that's where you're from," Breckin said. "How in the hell did you wind up in a place like Parker from New York?"

Karen blanched. She couldn't believe she let it slip. Oh, well. It's not like her friend was going to put two and two together about who Karen really *was.* She doubted Breckin had ever heard of Olivia O'Connell, anyway. "Yeah, I did. I grew up there and traveled all over before seeing an ad on a teacher website advertising Parker needed a math teacher. I had traveled so much and so often I thought a quiet, little town was just what I needed."

That was close enough to the truth.

"Well, no wonder you seemed so much more sophisticated than the rest of us," Breckin said with a grin. Her grin suddenly turned into a sad smile as her eyes welled with tears. "God, Kare, I'm going to miss the shit out of you."

"Good thing I'm only a plane ride away," Karen said, pulling her closest friend in for a hug.

The two of them sat like that, wrapped up in a warm friendship hug, for a several seconds before Karen's phone back pocket started to buzz.

All packed, Raven? Karen saw on her screen. *My bed is ready for you.*

Karen smiled.

"Well, I can tell by your smile that's my brother messaging you," Breckin said, wiping a tear away from her eye. "I haven't seen you smile this much since…well…ever."

"What can I say? I'm a happy girl," Karen said with a shrug.

"And my brother is a happy boy. And that's exactly why I'm okay with letting you go."

"Promise you'll take good care of Goofy while I'm gone? I've gotten attached to the idiot."

"Only if you promise to take him with you to New York when you leave for good."

～

BRODY WAS JUMPING up and down on the balls of his feet. He had been waiting for Raven's plane to land for what felt like *forever.* It had been almost a month since he had touched her skin, smelled her hair, seen her smile across the table from him. And a month was too damn long.

"Come on, come *on,*" he muttered under his breath. "Where *are* you?"

Finally, just when he was beginning to think she had gotten cold feet and decided not to come, he saw her walking around the corner, suitcase in hand.

"Raven," he yelled, waving her way. Her eyes met his, and suddenly all was right with the world. Running toward her, he wrapped her up in a huge bear hug and just breathed her in. "God, I've missed you. You have no idea."

Brody could feel her smiling into his sweater, but he wasn't quite ready to let her go yet. He simply held her in his arms, not saying a word. She was here. In his city. With him.

Finally breaking out of the hug, he looked down at her and smiled. Brushing a strand of hair out of her eyes, he simply breathed, "Hey."

Raven smiled softly. "Hey," she said back.

"You're here."

"I'm here."

"So what do you want to do? Where do you want to go?"

Karen shrugged her shoulders. "You know? I'd kinda just like to go back to your place, at least for now. It's a little overwhelming being back here after so many years, and I haven't even made it out of the airport."

Brody leaned down and kissed her forehead. "I can totally understand that and that is not a problem. I have great Chinese food right down the street from my apartment. We can order in and watch trash TV."

"That sounds fantastic," she replied with a smile. "Thanks for understanding."

"Always, Raven."

Taking the handle of her suitcase out of her hand, he placed his other hand in hers and headed for the exit. "I can't believe you're here."

"What? Did you think I wouldn't show?"

"You know, in the back of my mind part of me wondered if you'd get cold feet," he said with a sheepish smile. "I know how skittish you are about New York."

"I guess that really solidifies how much I love you, huh, New York?" she said with a wink.

"Raven, now that we're actually *in* New York, can you refrain from calling me that? It's a little ridiculous, now that we're actually *here* and not in Parker."

The woman he loved crinkled her nose before smiling wickedly. "Never. You'll be New York until the day I die."

Brody chuckled. "And *there's* the sass I have come to know and love so much. You had it the first day I met you in Swanson's, looking all cute as you were talking to yourself."

"And you were looking all asshole-y as you were trying to hit on me," she said, playfully punching him in the stomach. "I can't believe I fell in love with you. Good thing you stopped being such a total douchebag."

Brody let out a loud laugh. "Ouch, Raven. That one hurt."

"Liar."

He kissed her on the forehead again. "Absolutely. Because you and I *both* know I'm anything but douchey."

It was Karen's turn to laugh. "Whatever you say there, New York. Now, can we quit talking and start walking faster? I'm starving and some greasy lo mein is calling my name."

"Only if I can order sesame chicken and we can share."

"Deal."

KAREN LOOKED around Brody's apartment in awe. The views were stunning. The furniture looked too pristine to sit on, the décor straight out of a fashion magazine. When Breckin told her Brody made a lot of money, Karen's friend seriously underestimated how much he was worth. Hell, maybe Breckin didn't *know* how much Brody made. All Karen knew is she was afraid to sit on the sofa that probably cost more than three months' worth of her rent in Parker. Or more.

"The fridge and cabinets are stocked with all your favorite food and I had Claudia buy all your regular toiletries when she went to the store this week, so they're all in the shower and bathroom cabinet," Brody said, walking back into the living room after putting her suitcase in his bedroom. A place Karen had yet to venture. She was still staring in shock at the view of the Manhattan skyline from Brody's floor to ceiling apartment windows.

"Claudia?"

"My housekeeper," Brody said sheepishly.

Of course he would have a housekeeper. "I thought you said you're afraid of heights," Karen said, choosing to ignore the fact he actually had hired help to do all his cooking and cleaning.

"I am," Brody said.

"Then why did you buy an apartment with floor to ceiling windows?" she asked.

"Have you *seen* that view? It was worth what I paid for the apartment. Plus, I don't have to get up close and personal with the windows. I can admire the view from the kitchen island, far away from the windows. And I sure as hell don't have to go out on the balcony," he said with a grin.

Karen didn't agree with him about the heights, but she sure could agree with him about the view. She was currently standing at the kitchen island. The apartment was open concept, offering the living, kitchen, dining, and office space the breathtaking view of the Manhattan skyline. The sliding glass doors next to the large dining table opened onto what appeared to be a large, private balcony. A place Brody apparently never ventured. Karen thought it looked like the perfect place for a morning cup of coffee.

"Does your bedroom have the same views?" she asked.

"Yeah, but I keep the curtains drawn."

"Why on earth would you do that?" she asked.

"A ridiculous fear of plummeting to my death?" he replied sheepishly.

"You don't know what you're missing out on," she said with a grin. "That view is stunning."

"It certainly is."

Karen's eyes met Brody's, and she realized he wasn't talking about the view outside anymore.

"Do you know how much I missed you, Raven?"

"How much?"

"Sometimes I woke up, smelling you, and thought you were in my bed with me," he said, walking toward her, lust and love and longing written all over his face. "But when I woke up, I was alone. And it was the most empty feeling in the world. I didn't realize how attached I had gotten to you."

"You, Playboy of Manhattan, attached to little ol' me?" she said, batting her eyes furiously.

"You, Raven, are larger than life," he said, wrapping her in his arms and kissing her forehead and cheek before planting a soft kiss on her lips. "And I never want to be away from you for that long ever again."

"Is that so?"

Brody deepened the kiss, curling Karen's toes and sending all sorts of heat to her lady bits. "It's so," he replied.

"But I have to go back after spring break. Who will finish out the year?"

"I'm sure they can find someone to fill in for you. Isn't school practically over after spring break, anyway?" he asked.

"No! There's state testing in April, and I'm a class sponsor, and have to help with prom and graduation and all that stuff," Karen replied.

"You can't go back if I kidnap you," he said with a wink.

"Brody, I have to go back. But I'll be back before you know it."

He rolled his eyes. "You're ruining my vibe. Besides, I need to show you something else now. Something I have a feeling you're going to get very familiar with."

"But I'm hungry."

"Chinese can wait. I promise. You'll want to see what I'm about to show you."

"What exactly are you about to show me, New York?"

"My bed," he said, giving her a wink.

Karen grinned mischievously. "You read my mind. I am feeling pretty sleepy after the flight."

"Oh, you can sleep, Raven. You can sleep all you want... after I have my way with you. I haven't had my hands and lips on your body for far...too...long. It's going to take me a while to get reacquainted, I think."

Brody kissed her again, parting her lips, entwining his tongue with hers, and Karen moaned in pleasure.

"I'm okay with that," she said breathlessly.

"What was that?" he whispered in her ear, sending chills down her spine.

"I said I'm okay with that," she said, louder this time. "In fact, I just decided I'm not really that sleepy or hungry at all."

CHAPTER 25

*K*aren couldn't believe she had been in New York for almost a week already. She and Brody had easily settled into a daily routine. He would be up and off to work before Karen even woke up. She would wake up to the smell of fresh coffee brewing in the kitchen (thanks, Claudia) and take a cup out on the balcony to read the New York Times, before going down to the private gym in Brody's building and running on the treadmill or doing some other workout on the fancy equipment. Brody said they even had a personal trainer on staff for residents in the building, but there was no way Karen was taking him up on that offer.

Brody would come home around noon, and they would go eat at one of his favorite places in his neighborhood. Karen worried about him getting in trouble for missing work to spend time with her, but he told her it was his business what he did on his lunch break, and if his company didn't like it, they could kiss his ass. She also worried about him coming home at five and six every night, because she was willing to bet those weren't his normal working hours, but he told her not to worry about that, either, so that's what she was trying not to do.

Karen hadn't had the nerve to venture out on her own yet. She was still worried about being seen or recognized by someone. Scared that someone from the mob would still be looking for her ten years later. So she would stay in Brody's oasis of an apartment, snacking on all the delicious goodies Claudia baked and reading novels she said she would read back home but never did, and wait for Brody to come home. Then they would either eat something delicious Claudia had cooked, or Brody would tell her to put on one of the fancy dresses he had bought for her and take her to dinner at a place Karen had always wanted to try but never could afford.

She saw the price tag of one of the dresses he had bought for her, a clingy little hunter green silk number that hugged her curves in all the right places and made her feel breathtaking. She was slowly learning not to gawk at the prices of things Brody bought; she realized it was just his way of life. He must've seen the look on her face, because, again, Brody told her not to worry about anything. She didn't even mention the prices of the French restaurant he had taken her to that night. This was a lifestyle Karen had never known before. She didn't know if she would ever get used to it.

But today was her last day in New York before going back to Parker and finishing the school year. A month and a half until she was back for good with Goofy and the small amount of things she wanted to keep from her seven year life in the small Oklahoma town. So Karen decided to take the first brave step to making herself feel at home again in The Big Apple. She grabbed the book she was currently reading off the nightstand on her side of the bed, her thermos filled with water, and an apple out of the bowl on kitchen island

and headed to the elevator. She was going to sit on a bench in Central Park, read, and people watch.

Not too much longer, Karen was perched on a bench overlooking the The Pond, Karen's favorite body of water in Central Park. It was peaceful and serene, and the day was absolutely gorgeous. Brody had tried to get her to go ice skating the day after she arrived because it was still cold enough in March to do so, but she had vehemently denied his request. Skating on Sophie's pond in Parker with just Brody watching was one thing. Skating in New York City where anyone could watch how atrociously she sucked was another.

The day was unseasonably warm for March in New York. The sun was shining brilliantly, to the point Karen didn't even need the beanie she had donned before leaving the apartment. She placed it beside her on the bench and opened her book to the page she had stopped reading on the plane. Soon, Karen was lost in the fantasy world Pierce Brown created in his amazing series, *Red Rising*. She was currently reading the third book in the series and couldn't put it down. One of her students had suggested it to her, and she loved it.

"Excuse me, ma'am."

Karen looked up from the book she was reading and squinted her eyes at the sun shining through the trees at the voice above her head. She quickly glanced down at her watch. She couldn't believe the time. She had been sitting on the bench at the park for almost two hours.

"Ma'am."

"Me?" Karen asked, pointing to her chest.

"Yes. You."

"I'm sorry. Am I sitting in your place or something?"

The woman staring down and Karen smiled. "No, you're not sitting in my spot."

"Then is there an issue I can help you with?" Karen asked. "Missing dog? Need to find the nearest hot dog stand?"

"No, none of that," the woman laughed softly. "I'm a native New Yorker. But I do have a question for you."

"Okay," Karen said hesitantly.

"I know this sounds completely crazy, and my husband told me not to even ask you, but I had to know." The woman motioned to a man standing under a tree a few yards away, who waved sheepishly when he saw her staring.

"Know what?" Karen asked.

"Know if you're Olivia O'Connell."

Karen felt the blood drain from her face. Her heart started beating a frantic rhythm in her chest, and she felt like she couldn't breathe. Her worst nightmare was coming true. She heard the woman speaking, but she wasn't completely registering the words being said.

"She was our absolute favorite singer in the entire world. We went to all her shows when she first started her career, oh, I don't know, about ten years ago. Then she just disappeared without a trace. No one knew what happened to her. If you're *not* her, you are for sure her doppelganger. The resemblance is uncanny."

"No," Karen heard herself whisper.

"What? I couldn't hear you."

"I...I...I don't even know who that is," Karen said, louder this time. "I'm not that person. No. I'm sorry."

"Well, it was worth a shot," the woman said. "I thought the odds were slim, but I had to ask. Imagine, seeing my favorite singer after all these years without a trace, back in New York. It would be the weirdest thing!"

"Totally weird," Karen whispered. She stood up quickly. "I'm sorry. I have to go."

"Of course. I'm so sorry to have bothered you," the woman said.

"It's no problem," Karen heard herself say before hurrying as quickly as she could back to Brody's apartment. She had to get back and then...then she had to go home. She was a fool to think being in New York would be anything but disastrous.

∼

"Hey, Raven. You'll never guess what happened at work today."

Brody walked through his front door, tossed his keys in the basket by the front entry, and looked around.

"Raven? You here?"

He was met with silence.

"Raven?"

Brody walked through his apartment, his frown deepening the longer he was met with the deafening silence. None of Karen's toiletries were on his bathroom counter. Her clothes were no longer in any of the drawers he had designated as hers. It was obvious she had left. The question was, why? And where did she go. Brody felt a ball of dread knotting in his stomach. Something had sent Karen running. And that something had him terrified.

Brody walked back in the kitchen. Sitting on the island was a letter written in Karen's handwriting. Heart in his throat, he picked it up and read it.

Brody, I'm sorry. I had to go back. To Parker. Something happened, and I couldn't stay. I love you. Please forgive me. Raven.

Brody stared in shock at the letter the love of his life wrote in haste. She left New York. Without even a phone call. Or text. Nothing. Not a damn word. He called her phone, which went straight to voicemail.

Brody fell to the floor, the note falling from his hand, and to his surprise, felt a tear trickle down his face. Raven was gone and for the first time since his mom died, he felt completely and totally lost.

CHAPTER 26

"*K*aren, what in the world is going on? What did my stupid brother do?"

Breckin met Karen at the airport when Karen had called her in a panic, telling her she was leaving New York two days early and needed a ride home. Breckin told her she would be there. True to her word, Karen's best friend was waiting as soon as Karen's plane landed.

"No, nothing like that," Karen said. She knew she probably looked like a hot mess. As soon as she arrived back at Brody's apartment, she threw everything in her bag as fast as she could, scribbled a haphazard note to Brody, hailed a cab, and hauled ass to the airport, grabbing the first flight she found back to Oklahoma.

"Then what the hell happened? I didn't expect to get you for two more days," Breckin said, throwing Karen's bag in the trunk of Karen's car before hopping in the front seat.

"I just…I just had to leave," Karen said evasively.

"Nope." Breckin turned and looked at Karen.

"What do you mean, nope?"

"I mean exactly what nope means. That's bullshit. You're

hiding something and I'm tired of secrets between us. You never talk about your past. You're hiding a secret. And I want to know what it is. I've proven I'm a good friend to you. You're in love with my brother. *Something* made you turn tail and leave New York. If it wasn't Brody royally screwing everything up, I deserve to know what it is. So we're not leaving until you spill."

Breckin crossed her arms over her chest, turned in her seat, and stared at Karen. "So…spill."

Karen took a deep breath before letting it out slowly. Breckin was right. She had been hiding her past from her friend. What could be the harm in telling her?

"Ever heard the name Olivia O'Connell?" she asked.

Breckin shook her head. "Nope."

"Well, let me introduce you to her." Karen proceeded to tell her best friend her story, Breckin's eyes growing bigger and bigger the further along in the story Karen got. When she got to the part of the story where she told Brody, Breckin interrupted her.

"Are you kidding me? My brother knows?"

Karen nodded.

"Man, he couldn't keep a secret for shit when he was younger. Props to him," she said with a laugh. "Sorry, continue. What happened in New York that sent you running?"

Karen continued with her story, telling how the lady walked up to her in the park and recognized her. "I just freaked," she said. "It terrified me that lady recognized me. If she did, that means other people would, too. What if the mob is still a thing? What if they recognized me? Then what? Would they kill me? Torture me? Would I have to go into hiding again, with WITSEC? I didn't want that. So…I panicked, and I just left."

"Did you even tell my brother?"

"I wrote him a note," Karen said softly.

"A *note?*"

"What's wrong with a note?"

"What's wrong? What's *wrong?*" Breckin screeched. "Karen, to be so smart, you are some kind of dumb. Girl, my brother is butt crazy in love with you. You left him a note and left. Two days early. Did the note even say why you were leaving?"

"No," Karen replied softly.

"So all he knows is you left. Now he's probably thinking you left him. He has no way of knowing someone recognized you and sent you into a panic."

"Shit."

"Yeah. Shit," Breckin said. "Normally, I would think my brother was the one who screwed up, given his history with women, but girl, you did something real stupid."

"So what do I do?" Karen asked.

"You fix it! Call him! Maybe he hasn't gotten home yet to see what an idiot you are."

Karen grabbed her phone and punched Brody's number. It went straight to voicemail. "Hey, Brody," she said softly. "So it seems I did a really stupid thing in a panic and left without explaining exactly *why* I left. Some lady in Central Park recognized me. Like, the real me. Olivia. And I freaked out. Instead of waiting for you to get home and tell you about it, I packed all my things, caught a cab to the airport, and came back to Parker. I'm here with your sister now, and she's telling me how stupid I was for doing that. So...yeah. I'm really sorry. Would you please call me back? I want to fix this. Please."

Karen hit end on the phone, put her head back on the headrest, and sighed. "Boy, I messed up big, huh?"

"Yeah," Breckin said. "At least there's one good thing you have going for you."

"What's that?"

"My brother is butt crazy in love with you. Maybe that means he'll forgive you for being so dumb."

BRODY SIGHED and stretched his limbs. He was aching and sore, his muscles needing a good massage. As soon as he fell to the ground in his apartment, he had himself a good cry but quickly pulled himself together. Not much could be done about what happened. Karen had made her choice. Instead, he had gotten on the phone and started taking care of business. Within a few hours, he had everything settled. His life was back on track.

Brody walked up the steps to his destination and adjusted his shirt. He had one more piece of business to tend to before he could call it a day. Knocking on the door, he sat back and waited.

"Breckin, I told you I'm fine..." the love of his life stood in front of him, her hair pulled back in a messy bun. Her eyes were swollen from crying, her nose was red. She was holding a wadded up tissue in her hand, which dropped to the floor when she saw him.

"Brody? What are you doing here?" she said. "I tried calling you...several times...but you didn't answer."

"I know I didn't," he said softly, pushing a strand of hair that had fallen out of the disheveled bun on top of her head behind her ear. "I had some things I had to take care of first."

"Did you get my messages?"

He nodded. "I did."

"Then why didn't you answer any of them?" she asked.

"Well, for one, I was totally pissed at you," he said honestly. "How could you just leave like that? It freaked me out, Raven. To come home and see you gone? Then to see that weird note without a detailed explanation? It broke my damn heart."

A tear leaked out her eye and trailed down her cheek. Brody wiped it away with his thumb.

"Yeah, I had a few of those leak out of my eyes, too. Quite a few, in fact," he said softly. "I sobbed like a big pussy. Then I got your messages. Then I started thinking about everything. And I realized something."

Karen just stood there, looking at him.

"Well? Aren't you going to ask me what I realized?" he said.

"I didn't figure I had the right," she said with a small shrug.

"What I realized," he said, taking her hands in his and placing them on his chest, "Is that I had been incredibly selfish asking you to go back to New York with me, especially knowing what I know about your history there. You were terrified. The chances of you running into people who recognized you were there. I shouldn't have ever risked it."

"It's okay, Brody. I knew what—"

Brody put his fingers gently on her lips. "No, it wasn't okay. I shouldn't have asked you to do that. So I've been doing some things since you left. Do you want to know what I've been doing?"

"What?"

"Well, first off, I went and I resigned my job, effective immediately," Brody said. "Then, I called my realtor friend and put my apartment on the market. He already has someone interested in it, willing to pay way above the asking price. I won't even have to place it officially on the market. Finally, a little birdy told me that the bank president in Parker was looking to retire. I called and inquired about a job. You're looking at the newest president of First National Bank of Parker."

"What? Why would you do all that?" Karen asked.

"Because, you idiot, I love you. More than New York. More than my job. More than anything in the whole damn world. My world revolves around you, Karen, Olivia, Raven...whatever the hell you want me to call you, and it has since the first time I saw you in the grocery store. I would move to a cabin in the middle of nowhere if it meant I would get to spend forever with you and your snarky little ass. I don't need the big city to be happy. I just need you, giving me shit all the time and putting me in my place. So whaddya say? Wanna put me in my place forever and ever?"

Karen looked up at him, loving shining in her eyes. "Is that a proposal, New York? Because if it is, you're going to have to do better than that to get me to say yes."

All of a sudden, Goofy came running around the corner, barreling into Brody's legs, barking excitedly. Brody laughed. "It looks like your dog approves of my proposal, Raven. So let me ask again? How about you do your best to give me shit the rest of your life, huh?"

"I guess if Goofy approves, I can't say no," she said with a smile.

"Man, the best thing I ever did was convince you that you had a concussion on Christmas Day," he said with a wink.

"Brody Cooper! You lying sack of..." Brody pulled Karen in for a kiss before she could call him any more names. She agreed to be his, and that was all he needed to hear, because wherever Raven was, that was his home.

BEFORE YOU GO...

If you enjoyed my book please take a second to leave a short review. These reviews help me as an author be found by other amazing readers like you.

Thank you so much! :)

ABOUT THE AUTHOR

Olivia Sherwood writes romantic comedies with quirky characters meant to make people smile. She believes in happy ever afters, the power of chocolate to cure one's woes, and the idea that the ocean is a soothing balm for the soul. She loves working in her flower beds, walking her dog, or doing yoga in her living room. If you can't find her there, she's probably lounging in bed binge-watching Parks and Recreation or Schitt's Creek or reading a book in her comfy bed, her three animal children taking up the majority of the room.

Titles by Olivia Sherwood:
The Parker Lake Series
Unlikely in Love
Unlikely to Fit
Unlikely to Stay
Unlikely to Tell

The Playing Series
Playing to Win
Playing to Love
Playing for Keeps

Website:
www.oliviasherwoodbooks.com